I0785118

# a love of my own

WRITTEN BY
KYA L. MONTAGUE

*"A Love of my Own," by Kya L. Montague,*
*Copyright © 2022.*
*Contributing Author, Blazing Entity, for the Poem,*
*"The Last Heaven," © 2022.*

**Cover Design by Kya L. Montague**

All rights reserved. This book or any portion thereof may not be reproduced or used in any manner whatsoever without the express written permission of the author except for the use of brief quotations in a book review. Printed in the United States of America.

Unless otherwise indicated, all the names, characters, businesses, places, events and incidents in this book are either the product of the author's imagination or used in a fictitious manner. Any resemblance to actual persons, living or dead, or actual events is purely coincidental.

*Inquiries:*
*Author.KyaMontague@outlook.com*

WRITTEN BY
KYA L. MONTAGUE

**Also in this series:**
A Love Like This, Part 1
A Love Like This, Part 2
AudioGasmic: A Book of Love Poems

*Dedicated to Poetry.*
*My love for you has stood the*
*test of time.*

## Prologue: Julian

*I didn't know she'd be here, but I guess I should have known she would. Serenity James. She was the last woman I gave my heart to completely, but her heart chose a path that led her to someone else. Despite her husband, R&B singer Wesley Johnson Jr., making it very clear to me to stay away from her; I still couldn't look away.*

*Seeing her back here at Truest Financial Firm for Sharon Jacobs' retirement party reminded me of the first time I saw her three years ago. I was smitten then, and regardless of her now being a married woman, I was smitten now. I would be respectful and keep my distance, but her mere presence made it hard for me to stick to that plan. Her being in the same room with me and not being able to hold her, to kiss her, to do anything other than trying my best not to look at her, was too much for me to handle on a random Friday afternoon. When I couldn't take it anymore, I decided to leave.*

*"Julian—" she called out behind me. Her soft voice caressed every nerve ending in my body when I heard her say my name. She'd left the conference room and caught up with me by the elevators. I turned to look at her, but I didn't speak. "You're leaving? You weren't going to even speak to me?" she asked, her face even prettier up-close.*

*I frowned. "Speak to you? What would your husband have to say about that?"*

*She looked to the floor and sighed. "He wouldn't say anything," she said in a low tone. "I seriously doubt that," I scoffed, tapping on the down arrow for the elevator again.*

*"Wesley and I are separated right now, Julian," she confessed. "Separated?"*

*"Yes. Separated. Why do you think I'm here alone?" she asked, as the elevator dinged and the doors slid open.*

*I stepped inside the elevator and turned to face her. "Well, I hope you two figure things out," I said, pushing the button for the lobby. She stepped inside right before the elevator doors began to close. She stepped towards me and I stepped back until my back was against the wall.*

*"Serenity, what are you doing?"*

*She rubbed her hands up and down my chest and looked up at me with a seductive glare she'd never given me before. "Do you still want me, Julian?" she asked, in a husky voice. Her warm body was pressed against mine and her hands were now resting on my shoulders as I looked down at her; only inches separated my lips from hers.*

*I swallowed hard. "I don't want to play any games, Serenity," I whispered. She moved her hands from my shoulders and gently cupped my face.*

*"I'm not playing," she whispered back, the look in her eyes even bolder than before. She pulled my head down*

*until my lips connected with hers, then, she pulled back. "I'm not playing," she repeated.*

*I could barely think; but one thing I did know was how much I wanted this woman. I wrapped my arms around her waist and kissed her with so much passion, I thought my lips would break her skin. She was moaning, and I'd never heard her moan like this before. The elevator dinged before the doors slid open to the lobby level of the building.*

*I moved my lips away from hers. "Come with me," I said, catching my breath.*

*Then... the sound of my alarm snapped me out of my dream. It was all just a dream.*

# 1

## Julian

"It took you long enough to get here," I said with a smirk, as I opened my front door for Tamika. "Yeah, but don't you think I'm worth the wait?" she asked, stepping into my entryway.

It was a little after 11 o'clock on Saturday night and it had been pouring rain all day. Tamika had run to the door with a hood over her head to protect her hair from the rain. I stepped behind her and closed the door. When I turned to face her, we locked eyes.

I met Tamika at the barbershop last weekend. She had a cute little curly tapered cut, and she was there getting it shaped up. She had a cute face, full lips, reddish brown skin and slightly slanted eyes. Her body was thick, and full of curves I desperately wanted to take on a test drive. Once I saw she was almost done getting her haircut I waited outside for her to leave, almost ready to forfeit my coveted spot in line. I introduced myself, and we chatted for a minute. She told me she had errands to run and for me to hit her up later after we exchanged numbers. It didn't take much convincing for her to agree to come over tonight.

She pulled down her hood and unzipped her hoodie revealing a black lace bra with her breasts pushed up so high, they were almost spilling out. Her thin waist was the perfect prelude to her abundant hips and thighs. I wasted no time pushing her sweater down her arms and onto the floor. She grabbed the back of my neck and pulled me down for a kiss. I began to eagerly return her kiss while my hands found their way to her breasts. I squeezed them as her hands traveled under my shirt and up my back.

I pulled at the waistband of her tiny shorts. "Take this shit off," I grumbled and watched as she slid off her shoes and slipped her shorts down those curvy thighs I'd been fantasizing about all day. She wore itty bitty black lace panties to match her bra. I took her hand and turned her around to get a full view of every inch of her, and I was not disappointed. She stepped towards me and tried to pull my t-shirt over my head. I stepped back and removed my shirt for her. Her chest heaved as she watched me. I saw her eyes travel from my face, down the length of my body and back up. I couldn't tell if the look she gave me was a look of satisfaction or appreciation. It didn't matter though, by the end of the night, she'd be feeling both. I led her down the hall and into the darkness of my bedroom.

*****

**A few weeks later**

"Alright! Alright y'all! Quiet down! We have our last artist coming up to the mic! This man right here, is *a lyrical assassin*! *A professional wordsmith*! *A master of metaphors!* This brotha's pen game stay crazy!" Omar, the host of the open mic at Words and Verses enthusiastically announced as the crowd began to applaud louder. "Every time he comes up here, he never disappoints! We haven't seen him in a while, so I'm excited to hear what he has for us tonight! Y'all make some noise for a crowd favorite here at Words and Verses, Julian Brooks, y'all!"

Hyped up off of adrenaline and the two double shots of Tequila I'd downed awaiting my turn to perform, I was ready. Cassie, a woman I'd invited to sit on my lap a few minutes ago, vacated her seat so I could make my way up to the stage. Cassie was just a friend, but I was working on us having a slightly different, more beneficial, arrangement. I dapped up Omar before adjusting the mic stand in front of me. We had a nice crowd tonight. I'd been missing from the scene for a while so there were a lot of new faces here tonight.

It had been over six months since I came out to a Words and Versus open mic night. Things had changed tremendously in my life compared to the last time I was here. For starters, at that time I was seeing a woman named Nova Shaw. She was a beautiful woman with a lot going for her. She was smart, independent, caring, beautiful and she had an established career as a professor at a local university. She was everything I looked for in a woman, but her timing in my life was off. I've heard people use that as an excuse in the past when they were trying to squirm themselves out of a relationship and I thought it was bull.

But nothing could be closer to the truth when it came to her and I. She wanted a committed relationship. I wanted that too, but at that time, I wanted my freedom more. So, like the jerk I knew I could be sometimes, I strung her along and pacified her with enough sex and attention to avoid the conversation.

Another point of contention I was dealing with back then was accepting the way my feelings had been jolted by Serenity James. Unlike Nova, I wanted to commit to Serenity. I'd only dated her for a few months when I knew she was the one; or at least I thought she was. She was the epitome of class, beauty and grace. I wanted to be her man, and eventually her husband. I spent countless nights dreaming of her and our future together. I truly loved her. Unfortunately, her heart belonged to someone else. And not just *anyone* else, she fell in love with and married Wesley Johnson Jr.; a local celebrity here in Charlotte, and an international R&B singer from the group Xtascy.

The last time I was at Words and Versus, I had an unexpected run-in with Serenity and Wesley. He pulled me to the side and threatened me about staying away from his wife. I can admit now that I'd been playing the friend role with Serenity in hopes that she would somehow see the value in what I could offer her instead of him. However, that didn't go as planned.

That same night, I got into a huge argument with Nova about my confrontation with Wesley and about the lingering feelings I still had for Serenity. Our relationship, or whatever it was we were doing, ended that night. We mutually agreed to go our separate ways. The way she cried tore at my heart, but I knew that decision would be the best for the both of us. After spending some much-needed time alone reflecting, I was trying to get back into doing one of the things I loved most; writing, performing, and being praised by fellow artists for my talent.

It felt good to stand in front of this room full of people again. All eyes were on me. I know some people get nervous in front of crowds, but not me. I thrived off of the attention I received. It made me perform that much better. I looked into the crowd before I spoke.

"Thank y'all for always showing me so much love and support every time I'm here. I appreciate it. I'm sure everyone is ready to go home, so I won't hold y'all long!" I began.

"Take your time! I'm trying to go home with you tonight, anyway!" a random woman's voice yelled from the crowd, causing everyone to laugh.

I wore my Carolina baseball cap low to my eyes like always when I performed, so I couldn't see who the bold woman was, but I quickly replied, "Aww shit! Be careful about what you ask for, baby!" Which caused more laughter from the crowd. I gave everyone a moment to settle down again before saying, "I have something new to share with y'all tonight, it's called *King*." I took a quiet moment before speaking:

*Have your eyes ever seen something as imperious
as me? Royal, ethereal, and a body like a King?*

*I'd bet you'd sail the depths of the seven seas just to
get a peak,*

*I attract the masses to me like wool to a sheep,*

*Seated comfortably on my throne, I sip from my
chalice,*

*While the mistress to your mister begs me to please my
phallus,*

*I may sound callous,*

*But the truth can be hard to eat,*

*I'm adding diamonds to my crown,*

*While your girl is throwing rose petals at my feet.*

*I have a kingdom at my fingertips,*

*And a dynasty within my pen,*

*My monarchy is full of savages,*

*My words, create unknown passages,*

*I was born into magnificence... I don't know what
average is.*

*My kingly rights are inherited and were meant to
ensue, Over every nation, over all people of
every identity, and every hue,*

*If this were a game of chess, my opposers*
*would be pawns, And if this were about the*
*truth, then my doubters would be wrong, I'm*
*right where I belong.*

*I've been called a brother, and I've been called a Son*

*You can call me your highness,*

*But preferably,*

*King's the one…*


Although I heard the positive reactions of people while I performed, nothing prepared me for the eruption I received once I was done. I gave that performance my all. It was the perfect ending to close out the night, and I'd added yet another poem to my archives that was sure to become a classic like so many others I've shared. Tonight was turning out to be a good night and coming here always helped me unwind. Also, with all the new faces I saw here tonight, I was beginning to contemplate whether or not I'd be spending the rest of my night alone. Aside from Cassie, I'd caught the eye of a few women who made it their business to approach me as everyone began to leave the building. That's another thing I liked about coming here; the fact that women usually came to me. Aside from my looks, women seemed to always be attracted to my talent and the confidence I showed behind the mic. And after ending the night the way I'd just done, I wasn't surprised by the offers being thrown my way. However, tonight I felt like flying solo. If I changed my mind, I wasn't at a loss to find companionship. I just wanted to enjoy my night at home in peace.

Eventually, I made it outside where small groups of people had already begun the second part of the night; recapping the nights' events outside with friends.

"Jay! You need your own showcase, man! That piece you did was crazy!" Will said, approaching me as I talked with a few fellas outside.

He was another regular at Words and Verses I'd become cool with over the past couple years I'd been coming to this open mic. He was more of a rapper than a poet, though; but he was nice with the pen as well. "Thank you, thank you! Maybe one day I'll do that," I said, having never really given the idea a thought.

We all began chatting again when a woman's voice said, "Will! Are you ready to go?" We all turned to look at the young woman who had her arms crossed and an irritated look on her face.  My eyes were stuck on her for a moment. I knew Will, and I knew his wife Stephanie, but this was *not* Stephanie. I'd never seen her before. Minus the scowl on her face, she was pretty as hell. Smooth butterscotch brown skin, shoulder length dark brown locs, and big mesmerizing dark brown eyes. She wore skin tight white jeans with a multi-colored turtleneck that hugged her perfect sized breasts. She had on a dark brown motorcycle style leather jacket that hung open and brown ankle length boots; a perfect outfit for this crisp March night. The scent she had on traveled right underneath my nose, prompting me to wonder what exactly that scent was. She smelled so good. She held a phone in her hand and a crossbody purse strap laid across her chest. *Who the hell is this? And why is this the first time I'm seeing her tonight?* I thought. "Damn Layna! Do you have to be so rude?" Will asked.  She rolled her eyes. "I'm ready to go!" she said, now focusing her attention on her phone.

"Y'all, this is my rude ass little sister, Layna. Layna, these are the guys," he introduced. Everyone greeted her at the same time and no doubt admiring every curve she put in those jeans.

She gave us an unimpressed smile and said, "Hey." I tried to keep my perusal of her discreet, but damn! The more I looked at her the more beautiful I saw she was. She had a little bit of an attitude, but she was still one of the finest women I'd seen all night. I played it cool, and I was glad I still had my hat pushed down low, concealing that she was the true target of my stare.

"So did you enjoy the show tonight?" Omar, the host of Words and Versus asked, trying to break through her icy demeanor.

She gave him a slight smile. "I did… I mean it was okay," she replied, with a shrug.

"Cool! Who was your favorite?" Omar questioned, being messy as hell. We all went by the unspoken rule of not naming our favorites; it just kept everything neutral.

She looked around at the group of men in our circle, most of whom had performed tonight, and her eyes stalled on me, and everyone's eyes followed her stare. I smiled. I wasn't surprised though. Several people had already told me I was their favorite of the night and recited some of their favorite lines of my poem back to me. Looking back at Layna, I had to stop myself from licking my lips while I tried my best not to look at her so hard. The only thing prompting me to be on my best behavior was the fact of her being Will's younger sister.

After her eyes met mine, she gave her attention back to Omar. "It definitely wasn't him! *Mr. I'm your King*, over there" she said casually, motioning over to me and returning her eyes back to her phone.


The fellas instantly burst into laughter and I'm sure I was stuck with a confused and shocked expression on my face. *Wait! What?* Did she really just stand here and say that? I didn't know how to react, I mean, was she even serious? "Damn!" I said at her candor, while everyone still laughed around us. Not Will though, he looked extremely irritated by what his sister just said. She looked unbothered, as if she didn't just single me out as her least favorite performer of the night. The fact she didn't follow up her statement with a laugh or an, *'I'm just kidding,'* told me she was serious. I was more shocked than I was offended. I was confident enough to know the piece I performed was fire, I didn't need her validation. But still, damn! "Y'all think that's funny?" I asked, trying to break the tension a bit, and to show everyone my ego wasn't bruised, though admittedly I was bothered.

She looked back over to me. "No offense, but your poem was… mediocre at best. I really don't see why everyone got so excited about it," she added.

"Layna! That's not cool!" Will reprimanded. He then turned to me,

"I'm sorry, Jay. She just—" he sighed, shaking his head. He gave Layna a look that someone other than his sister may have thought was threatening, but she didn't appear to care.

"What? I'm just being honest! It was okay, but it could've been better," she said, doubling down on her assessment.

Will huffed. "Alright, I'll get up with y'all later. Layna let's go," he said.

*Mediocre? Just okay?* I thought, replaying her descriptions in my mind. Now I *knew* she had to be joking.

"Hold up!" I interrupted, finally able to find my voice. "Layna—may I ask, what didn't you like about my poem? I mean, since you have such a strong opinion of it." I asked, staring her down. Of course, I didn't agree with her, but I liked *this* type of confidence in a woman; the type of confidence that will speak up and tell me what they think of me, no matter how I would feel about it. I was much more used to the type of confidence women had to ask me to go home with them, or vice versa. There were a lot of intelligent and talented women who came out every weekend, but more times than not they didn't come alone, and their confidence was usually reserved for what they said once they were behind the microphone. The guys looked to her as if she and I was playing a tennis match, and now the ball was in her court.

"Well, frankly, I think it was too conceited. It *sounded* nice but it was shallow. You had some good wordplay in there but all you did was brag about yourself. It sounded like something you wrote while you were looking in the mirror! Then you ended it with you declaring for people to call you, *King,*" she scoffed. "It was incomplete. You built a whole kingdom around yourself, but there was no mention of a queen? What's a king without a queen, anyway?" she asked, folding her arms in front of her.

I eyed her intently. "He's still a *king*," I replied, matter of fact. I can't remember the last time I debated over a poem like this that didn't address politics or race relations.

"Actually, a king without a queen is merely a man in search of one," she answered boldly.

Who was this girl? And how did she mentally stimulate me within the course of a few sentences?

I nodded, and I became oddly satisfied with the way she spoke to me. I wanted to engage further in this banter, but I saw how much she was stressing her brother out so I conceded.

I heard a few mutterings of, "damn," and "wow," followed by more chuckles from the guys. I returned her glare. "Miss Layna, I can respect your opinion on this *one* poem, but maybe you need to hear more of my work. Maybe I can show you that I have more layers than what's on the surface, and we can have a conversation that's not so… aggressive on your part. But next time you're here, I want to see you up there. I want to hear what you have to say, so maybe, you can show me how it's done," I said, choosing my words carefully. I saw her cheeks redden a little bit. Yeah, she was all bark and no bite.

"So, you're a King, huh? *King Julian,*" a woman behind me commented. I'd seen her around the venue a few times back when I was regularly attending. She boldly approached me, breaking up the tense moment between me and Layna. I gave my attention to this woman who wore a low-cut blouse, and jeans that looked painted on. I rubbed my beard as I turned my whole body towards her. She smiled at me and said, "I'm the one who said I wanted to go home with you tonight," with a seductive look.

"Alright y'all, we're headed out," Will said, causing me to give my attention back to the group of fellas who began to disburse as well. I made eye contact with Layna, who gave me an unreadable stare before looking back down to her phone and walking away with her brother.

"I'll see y'all later," I said, as everyone went their separate ways. I turned back to the woman who was patiently waiting for my attention.

"So, what's your name?" I asked, my voice going a few octaves lower than my regular tone.

"I'm Marcie, but you can call me Peaches," she answered, pulling her bottom lip between her teeth. Although everything about her presence aroused me, I was going to have to pass. I was used to women being this forward with me. I knew I was handsome; I kept my body in shape, I'm always well-groomed, and I never step out looking like I didn't care about my appearance. The way I looked wasn't something I was modest about. I looked good, and women liked what they saw.

However, this particular woman seemed way too eager for my taste. Something about her energy didn't vibe right with me.

"Peaches, huh? Let me get your number, and I'll hit you up some time," I offered.

"That's cool, but I was hoping I'd be able to sit on the *king's throne* tonight."

I raised my eyebrows. Damn, she wasn't wasting any time.

"Word?" I asked, surprised.

"Yeah," she said, running her fingertips down my chest. I cleared my throat and willed myself to think with my big head instead of the little one.

"Not tonight, love," I pulled my phone from my pocket. "Put your number in there," I said, handing her my phone. I could tell she was disappointed, but she played it off and entered her contact information.  Once I locked her in, she looked at me and said, "I'll be waiting for your call," before walking away, as I shamelessly watched every sway of her hips. Before getting to my car, I said goodnight and slapped hands with a few people still hanging around.


During my drive home I thought about my interaction with Will's sister, Layna. I probably should have been more annoyed by her comments, and if it were someone else maybe I would have been.

However, I was intrigued. Even though I didn't like what she said or how she said it, I appreciated how confident she came across with her point of view. Aside from her being beautiful, she was honest, and she didn't care anything about me being a 'crowd favorite,' or how many accolades everyone else gave me. She was not impressed by me at all, and that surprised me.


When she said, '*a king without a queen is simply a man in search of one,*' I felt like she'd hit home with me. I thought about how many times I thought I'd found my queen only to end up alone. When it comes down to it, I'm a relationship guy. I love the idea of being in love; of finding that one person who I can't see my life without— but that has yet to pan out. I'm the type of man who will shower a woman with love, compliments, attention, and affection. However, I've been told that I'm also the type of man who can come off as clingy, overbearing, and having too many expectations too quickly; which can be a turn off. I'll admit that I do have a bad habit of trying to fast track relationships at times, but like I said, I'm a relationship guy. However, once Nova and I officially ended, I decided to put the 'relationship guy' part of me on the back burner. Now, I only cared about getting my needs met in other ways. Ways that didn't require a daily phone call or text, expensive dinners, or buying *just because* gifts. I'd grown tired of putting myself in situations that didn't work.

At 33 years old, I hoped I wouldn't be out here in the streets too much longer. However, the luxury of hooking up and having no strings attached created a much simpler lifestyle. I knew the next woman I would take seriously in a relationship would have to let me know first that's what she wanted.

# 2

## Layna

After spending every weekend at home for the past few months, my brother Will finally convinced me to come out with him to an open mic poetry night. When we arrived, I didn't immediately vibe with the energy in the room. Once the first performer went up to recite her poem, I began to feel much more like this was the type of creativity I needed to be around. I've been an avid writer since I learned how to write, and anything in the creative genre I gravitated to. I wrote poetry too, but writing short stories was my first love. I was thoroughly enjoying myself, and it felt good to out on the weekend for once. My phone had been buzzing from an unfamiliar number most of the night. I ignored it until I couldn't ignore it anymore. I went outside to answer it.

"Hello? Who is this?" I answered, annoyed.

"Layna, sweetheart—Please don't hang up! I miss you, and I need to see you," Derrick said.

I sighed. "Please… don't call me again. You're making this harder than it needs to be. Just stop," I said, before ending the call, and blocking the number he called from. All the joy I'd been feeling being in this creative space slowly fizzled out after hearing his voice.

I went back into the building as the host was announcing the last performer of the night; Julian Brooks.

I'd seen him earlier mingling with several people, mainly women, most of the night. At one point, he had a woman casually sitting on his lap. At the point his name was called, I was just ready to go. Listening to him quickly annoyed me. His overly pretentious poem, and his lack of depth he offered the crowd was not impressive. He acted as if he was in a talent show, and it was him versus him. He seemed arrogant and conceited; as if he expected everyone to love what he'd just said. However, he had the exact opposite effect on me. I was over it and I just wanted to go home.

"I hope you don't think that was cute, Layna!" my brother said, as he drove us home. "I'm cool with Julian, and he's an alright guy. You didn't have to be rude like that to him. Of all the things you could have said, you chose to insult him!" he lectured me.

"I just gave him my opinion, Will. You need to relax," I replied, irritated he was still talking about this.

"He didn't ask your opinion! He didn't ask you anything! But there again, you feel it's your duty to give your opinion where it's not wanted," he said. I shrugged, as he cut his eyes over to me. He blew out a breath. "You need to grow the hell up, Layna! All this, *I'm just speaking my mind* shit, and cute no more! Actually, it never was. Mom and Dad let you get away with that because you were the baby. But you're almost 28 years old, you're not a baby anymore, and that mouth is going to get you in a situation you can't talk your way out of!" he said. I rolled my eyes. "I don't know why I even try to talk to you," he mumbled, before turning up the radio. The rest of our ride home was silent between the two of us as the radio blared.

Monday morning, I found myself barely awake as I listened to a lecture in my English Literature class from Professor Jamal Snyder. He insisted everyone call him Jamal, however, I called him Professor Snyder even though he was just a few years older than me. Being a 27year-old student in a class full of people much younger than me didn't make coming to class any easier. This was my third time attempting to finish my four-year degree.

At this point in my life, I should already have an established career and working towards my doctoral degree or something; not still struggling as an undergrad. The bright side was, with all my credits I was comfortably half way through my junior year. If I stuck with it this time, I'd have my degree in Communication and Creative Writing at the end of Spring semester next year.

I didn't feel as if I needed a degree to be a successful writer in this age of entrepreneurship and boss lady energy. I had the talent, however,

I lacked focus and motivation. I'd freelanced for a few major publications, and my personal beauty blog, *Naturally Pretty*, had regular traffic. The problem was, the money I was making wasn't consistent enough for me to live on my own. Without a degree, I wasn't even a viable candidate for the most entry level positions at major companies.

After having to leave my last apartment because I couldn't keep up with my end of the rent in Raleigh, I went back to go live with my parents. That turned out to be a disaster! On top of my relationship with Derrick beginning to raise suspicions, my parents refused to treat me like an adult. Once things with Derrick came to an explosive ending, I begged my brother to let me stay with him and his wife, Stephanie, for a while in Charlotte. He agreed with his only conditions being that I had to go back to school and get a job. Since he gave me my only reasonable option, I took it. My brother was the academic over achiever between the two of us. He received his degree in audio engineering and music production, and he co-owned a local music studio here with two other guys, called *Dream Studios*. He also had some personal equipment he used to do side work recording artists' demos at the house. His wife, Stephanie, worked the overnight shift as a registered nurse at the hospital.

"Okay class, I'll see everyone this Wednesday, and we have finals next week," Professor Snyder announced, among the crowd of students actively packing up their belongings and heading out the door. I was dragging my feet; I just wasn't a morning person.

"Layna, would you mind staying behind for a minute?" he called out to me, grabbing my attention with the tone he used. He sounded like I'd done something wrong. My brows furrowed in confusion and in irritation. I finished loading my belongings into my oversized tote bag and stood to leave. There were still a few students lingering around.

"Yes, Professor?" I answered, less than enthusiastically as he approached me.

"I wanted to commend you on your last writing assignment. It was well thought out, well written, and gave me a perspective about Toni

Morrison's *'Beloved,'* that I'd never thought of before. You're truly talented," he remarked. His unexpected compliment caused me to give him an unexpected smile.

"Thank you, Professor Snyder. I really appreciate your feedback."

"Please, call me Jamal; and you deserve it," he said walking over to his desk and packing his books into his suitcase. "Have you thought about what you're going to do once you graduate?" he asked. "Ummm… yes and no," I chuckled. "I'm more interested in being an entrepreneur than I am making someone else rich. I just have to figure out how to do it," I replied.

"Hmm.. okay," he said with a smile. His eyes quickly scanned me from head to toe. "Well, if you need me to write you a recommendation, I'd be happy to. Just let me know," he said.

"I'll be sure to do that," I replied, adjusting my bag on my shoulder. "Well, I'll see you Wednesday Professor Snyder," I said, as I began to walk out the door.

"Layna—" he called out, stopping me in my tracks. I turned to him. He looked around the room, I guess to make sure that he and I were alone. "You'll be done with my class soon, and… I was hoping maybe once you're no longer my student, I could take you out to dinner?" he asked, with an unsure smile. I was completely thrown off by his request.

I'd seen him looking at me before, but I didn't think he was interested in me in that way.

"Professor—"

"Jamal—" he interrupted.

"Jamal—I appreciate the offer. I really do, but I'm not interested in dating right now. It has nothing to do with you," I said, as kindly as I could.

"I understand," he replied, and even though I was rejecting him, the smile never left his face. He grabbed his suitcase and gestured for me to walk before him. Once in the hallway, he reached into his pocket and pulled out a business card and extended it to me. I took it, and looked up at him. "Just in case," he said, wearing the same smile. He then walked in the opposite direction.


I had two more classes today before I could go home. I packed in all my classes from Monday through Wednesday, and I worked at a call center Thursday, Friday, and Saturday, afternoons. Sunday was my only day off, and I spent most of the day doing homework and writing. My life was just a monotonous cruel reminder of how much I had yet to accomplish and how far I needed to go. I literally felt like I had no days off to rest and I didn't feel like I was making any real progress in my life.

When I agreed to go with Will to that open mic this past weekend, I was already tired and irritable. That, blended in with how disappointed I was with my life, and hearing Derrick's voice probably contributed to why I was so rude to that Julian guy. Before I realized what I was saying to him, it was already too late. The look of shock spread across his face told me that I'd went too far. His *handsome* face, that is. I couldn't deny how attractive he was when I saw him up close. I quickly understood why so many women were around him all night. He wore a fitted baseball cap that covered his eyes, but there was no hiding them or how handsome he was when we were outside. His smooth caramel skin was only enhanced by his dark eyes, nice smile, and strong masculine facial features. His body looked solid; not bulky, but lean and sturdy. His hands and arms looked strong, and his clothes fit him well. Anyway, I could see why he would be conceited. He was definitely pretty; but about 90 percent of that was erased as soon as he opened his mouth. My phone buzzed, stopping my impromptu daydream of a man

I'd only seen once.

Once I got home that afternoon, Will had a couple guys at the house in his make shift studio he'd pieced together in a small room off to the left of the foyer

"Hey Brother," I greeted Will, who spoke back without lifting his eyes from the small soundboard in front of him. I walked past the group of men who were not as rowdy as ones I'd witnessed before. I guess after his wife fussed at him about needing her sleep during the day after working overnight, he passed the memo on to his guests. He'd soundproofed the room as to not disturb her, so I was surprised when I saw the door opened. I went into the kitchen to heat up some leftovers. "Damn, Will! That's your sister?" I heard one of the men ask as I put my bag down and opened the refrigerator. I was starving. I'd only eaten a breakfast sandwich, and two granola bars from the vending machine all day. It was now almost 5 p.m.

"Yeah. And your old ass better not even think about talking to her," Will responded casually, seeming not to give the guy any real attention.

After I heated up my food, I grabbed my bag and decided to eat in my room. I wasn't interested in watching or listening to whatever Will and his guests had going on in there. Sitting down felt so good, and eating a full meal felt even better.

I showered and changed into some comfortable pj's before going to say goodnight to Will a few hours later. His guests were gone, and Steph had just left for her shift at the hospital. He was working on something on his laptop in the living room.

"How was your day?" I asked, as I plopped down on the couch next to him.

"Busy. The studio was a little slow today so I left early. How was your day?" he asked, still focused on the screen of his laptop.

I sighed. "A lot, as usual," I answered looking at the digital soundboard on his screen. "My professor asked me out on a date today," I spilled. Will closed his laptop and gave his undivided attention to me. "You're a student, he can't do that," Will said, sternly.

"The semester is pretty much over, and I already know I'm passing his class. Besides, he made sure to say he would like to take me out *after* I'm no longer his student," I said. Will looked troubled.

"What's this dude's name, again?" he asked, opening his laptop back up.

"Will—"

"What's his name, Layna?" he demanded.

I sighed. "Jamal Snyder," I answered. A few clicks on his keyboard later, Will had pulled up Jamal's headshot and academic credentials on the school's website.

"I don't know him, but he looks too old for you," he said, switching his screen back to his soundboard.

"I told him no, anyway," I said.

"Then why are you telling me? I thought I needed to do a background on him or something."

"Because, I'm reconsidering his offer. I haven't been out on a date in a while. It might be nice for someone to treat me; even though my life is a mess right now."

"Do you think you're ready to date after what happened with—" Will began. "Please don't say his name; and yes, I think I might be," I answered.

Will nodded. "And what do you mean about your life being a mess?"

"Look at me. I'm 27 with no career, no money, no social life and a pile of student loans. I feel like I'm in a hole I can't get out of. I don't know what my future holds for me, or if I'll ever feel like I'm doing enough," I spilled.

Will closed his laptop and wrapped one arm around me. "Little sister, you're doing okay. Things may seem uncertain right now, but if you keep on pushing forward, you will see things start to change. You had a rough year, but you need to make a plan for your future and start working towards it. Your very smart, resourceful, and you're the best writer I know. You have what it takes to be successful, you just have to light that fire up under you and finish what you start. You have like 20 half written books you need to finish—You have the talent, you just need to follow through," Will said. I found his words to be very encouraging and just what I needed to hear. "And you have to check that mean ass attitude, too! I still can't believe you embarrassed me the way you did the other night. Next time,

I'm not stepping in," he added, removing his arm from around me.

He was referring to what I said to Julian, and it seemed like he wasn't going to let it go. "First of all, I can handle myself. I don't need you stepping in to say anything for me! Second—" I stopped when I noticed the look Will had deadpanned on me. I was proving his point about needing to reel back my attitude. I'd never been afraid to speak my mind, but since my last relationship ended, I did feel like I was being a little mean. I'd never been called mean, and felt like someone actually meant it. It was always more comical, not literal. I had nowhere to filter my anger and my hurt from the way things ended with Derrick, but I knew I had to do better. I sighed. "I see your point. You're right.

I'll be sure to apologize to him," I said.

Will looked at me as if he was seeing me for the first time. "*You're* going to apologize?" he asked, in disbelief.

"Yes. I was rude to your friend and he didn't deserve the way I came at him; even though that poem was trash," I said. Will shook his head. "I said I'll apologize. I didn't say I would lie to him!" I added. "Layna, I don't think you understand how much courage it takes for us to go up on the stage and share our work. A lot goes into that.

You're a writer, but you don't see the faces or hear the reactions of everyone who reads your work. It's okay for you to not like what someone is saying, but it's not okay for you to act the way you did. Julian was only being respectful towards you because you're my sister. I'm sure he wouldn't have been as nice if you weren't. He did make one good suggestion though; next time, you go up there and share something. I would love to see how you receive criticism when the shoe is on the other foot," he said.

I took a moment to think about his words. "I said I'll apologize, but I don't have to prove anything to him," I remarked.

"Well, I guess that's better than nothing. I'm sure he'll appreciate

it."

I hugged him and stood up. "I'm going to bed. I'll see you in the morning," I said through a yawn.

"Goodnight. Oh, before I forget, if you do decide to go out with this Professor guy, I want to meet him first," he said, opening his laptop back up. I didn't feel the need to argue with Will. I knew he was only looking out for me.

"Alright, I can do that."

# 3

## Julian

***The Following Week***

I'd been at Mom's house for over an hour already this morning. I had to not only make sure she ate, but I also needed to make sure she took her insulin. My mother, Sandra Brooks, was a beautiful, vibrant, and social 57-year-old woman. However, she was also stubborn when it came to treating her newly diagnosed Type 2 diabetes.

"Jules, your father told me he's been trying to reach you," she said, as I finished loading her dishwasher.

"I've been busy," I said, as I moved over to the trash can, and pulled the almost full bag out and tied it. I felt my mom's eyes watching me as she sat at the kitchen table.

"Jules, you could at least talk to him. Our marriage ended a long time ago, and I'm okay with it now. You can't hold on to the past forever," she said, gently. I didn't answer. I opened her back door and threw the bag of trash into her large trash can. I then moved over to the sink to wash my hands.

"Is there anything else you need before I get going, Momma?" I asked, ignoring anything she had to say about my father. "Sit down," she said.

"Mom, I gotta—"

"Sit down, Julian," she repeated, sternly. I knew anytime she called me *Julian* instead of *Jules*, I was better off not protesting. I sat down and looked over to her. "I know you're still mad at your father for how he treated us in the past. But he's not the same man he was back then. He's trying to have a relationship with you now, and I think you should give him a chance."

I shook my head. "Momma, how do you expect me to get along with this man after all he did? He cheated on you, he lied to you, and even after you two were divorced he didn't even try to be a good father; it's bad enough he wasn't a good husband. He's never shown me anything about being a man besides me not wanting to be like him! If his guilty conscious has caught up with him in his older age, then that's on him. I'm a grown man now, I don't need him," I said, trying my best to keep my tone respectful.

"You do, Julian. You do need him. Can't you see he's trying? He gave you a house last year on top of paying for the… how many is it? Three degrees you went to school for. He's constantly calling me asking me how you're doing, and he seems hurt that you won't speak to him. You're his only son. What else do you want him to do?" she asked.

"Nothing. He owed me that house. He owed *us*. Just because I accepted it doesn't mean the past is erased," I said, my knee now shaking under the table.

"All I'm asking is for you to have a conversation with him. That's all. Can you do that for me, Jules?" she asked, reaching over and placing her hands on top of mine. I inhaled and exhaled deeply.

"Alright. I'll talk to him."

"Thank you. That's all I ask."


After going back home and changing, I did my best to put the conversation I had with my mom to the back of my mind. Just thinking about my father and all the shit he did to my mother upset me. I would keep my word and talk to him, but it wasn't going to be today.


The crowd tonight at Words and Versus was light. After spending the majority of my day thinking about how much easier my life could have been if my father chose to be a part of it before I cut him out, I definitely needed a distraction. I was in a rare mood where I didn't want to share, I just wanted to listen. I socialized with a few familiar faces before finding a seat near the back of the room with a cold Heineken.

"Is this seat taken?" a woman's voice asked. I looked up to see Peaches, the same woman who'd given me her number last week but I'd yet to hit her up. She began to sit down before I had a chance to answer.

I'll admit, she was cute and her body was sitting up in all the right places, but she wasn't really my type. I liked a more natural look and she was way too made up for me. That ass was my type though. She had so much ass in them jeans that I didn't really care if it was natural or not; it was nice.

She looked at me. "I thought you would have hit me up by now," she said flirtatiously, as she leaned over giving me a better view of her breasts.

I took a swig of my beer and eyed her. "I've been a little busy," I offered.

"Well, will you be busy tonight? What are you doing after this?" she asked, with a seductive grin. There was no way Peaches knew she was offering me exactly what I wanted tonight; a release without any strings attached. However, as sexy as she was, her eagerness turned me off. I mean, there were plenty of men here for her to choose from—many of which I know wouldn't turn her down, but she was here with me. I couldn't help but to wonder why.

"I'm just gonna kick it by myself tonight, love," I answered, as I finished the last of my beer. She raised her eyebrows, and gave me a confused look. She ran her tongue over her top row of teeth. She was getting ready to speak when her alerting phone caught her attention.

"I'll be back. Keep my seat warm," she said with a wink, and sashayed her way away from my table.

After another ten minutes had passed, I was ready to go home. As hard as I tried, I just wasn't feeling it tonight.

"Hi Julian, do you mind if I sit here?" Layna asked, hesitantly. I didn't expect to see her tonight, but her face was a welcome intrusion into my thoughts. And I loved the way my name sounded coming from her lips.

"Go ahead," I answered, a little too eagerly. She sat down and her fragrance intoxicated me. I needed to know what scent she wore, if it was the last thing I did. We looked at one another, and I couldn't stop myself from staring at her. Her locs were pulled up into a bun, showcasing her delicate features and she had multiple ear piercings that

I hadn't seen last time because her hair was down. Her beauty was effortless, and dangerous, because I felt how easily I could lose myself in her eyes.

"You're not going up there tonight?" she asked, with a slight smile.

I was surprised by her question. "You mean you actually want to hear more of what I have to say?" I asked. She looked embarrassed but she didn't answer. All I could notice was how pretty she was. "You look nice. I like your hair like that," I complimented, causing her head to jerk back a little.

"Thank you," she responded. She looked a little flustered. *Was I getting under her skin?* I wondered. "Um, I didn't want to take up too much of your time, I just want to say I'm—"

"Sorry I took so long to get back!" Peaches interrupted, giving me a grin. She looked over to Layna and back to me. "I asked you to keep my seat warm, but that's okay. I can sit right here," she said, and took it upon herself to sit across my lap. Layna gave us a disapproving look, and she stood abruptly.

"I'm sorry. I didn't know this seat was taken. Y'all have a good night," she said and quickly walked away, leaving her scent behind. I watched her walk away until I could no longer see her. Peaches sat on my lap so fast and so unexpectedly that I didn't even have time to react or respond. Also, I didn't know what Layna was getting ready to say before she was so rudely interrupted.

Once I got Peaches off my lap, and kindly asked her not to ever do that shit again without an invitation, I decided to go home. I looked around for Layna, but I didn't see her. The good thing about her not being able to finish whatever it was she was trying to tell me, was that it gave me a reason to see her again.

*****

A week later, Will invited me and a few guys over to his house to watch college basketball. I walked up the stairs of Will's house with a couple of six packs I'd bought over. Right behind me was Omar, and a couple other guys, Joe and Tony, I was cool with from Words and Versus. I came dressed in my Carolina blue hoodie and matching fitted baseball cap and black jeans. It was nearing the end of March, but it was a mild and sunny day. I was glad to be hanging out with the guys today; just laughs, wings, and beer. A perfect Sunday afternoon; that is, until *she* answered the door.

Layna opened the door for the four men on the other side who were eager to come in and get comfortable. I was surprised. I didn't know she lived here; or maybe she was just here visiting. I don't know, it had been a while since I'd been over Will's house. Either way, I didn't expect to see her, but I wasn't mad she was here. She was barefoot wearing black leggings and a black hoodie. Her locs were pulled back into a low ponytail, and in this light, she was prettier than before. My eyes briefly met hers before I said, "Hi." Because of how our conversation was cut off last week, I wasn't sure of her vibe. She had a neutral look on her face; not happy, not sad, just present.

"Hi," she answered. Then, she looked around me to see the other guys on the porch. She stepped to the side and opened the door wider. "Will's in the kitchen, you guys can come in," she offered. We all piled in single file and headed into the kitchen where Will was filling a couple of bowls with chips and pretzels.

"Hey y'all!" Will said. We all returned his greeting at the same time while putting down the food and drinks we'd brought over on the counter. "You got on that blue like you play for Carolina!" he added, grinning at me. Everyone laughed.

"All day, every day!" I returned, and we all began to get a little rowdy.

"Y'all need any help in here?" Layna's small voice asked, causing Will to look up at her among the laughter and side conversation between Omar and Tony.

"Naw, we're good Layna," he said, as he picked up a bowl of chips and a platter of spice rubbed wings and left the kitchen. Joe picked up the other bowl of chips and a six pack, following him out. Omar grabbed the small bowl of dip from the counter, and left the kitchen with Tony, as they were still talking trash to one another. Layna and I stood in the kitchen and looked at one another for a brief moment again.

I don't know what it was about this girl, but I felt like my words came out a second too late anytime I wanted to speak to her.

"Well, I'll just put this other six pack in the fridge," I said, grabbing for the beer "I got it," she offered, jumping in front of me.

"Okay," I responded, offering her a smile. She didn't smile back; she just gave me an anxious look. We began to speak at the same time.

"You go first," I said, assuming she wanted to pick up where she'd left off last week.

She nervously chewed her bottom lip. "Umm," she said, fiddling with her fingers. "How have you been?" she asked, out of nowhere.

"I've been good. You?" I asked, engaging in her awkward small talk. Her behavior was light years away from the confident woman I deemed her to be. She seemed so unsure of herself.

"Hey Layna. Hey Julian," Will's wife, Stephanie said, strolling into the kitchen.

"Hey Stephanie," I greeted her with a one-armed hug. "I guess you're off tonight?" I asked.

"Yes," she sighed. "I was off last night and I'm off for the next two nights, so I'm on a semi-normal sleeping schedule," she laughed. She then looked between me and Layna who still had an unreadable look spread across her beautiful face. This girl was so pretty, it was hard for me *not* to look at her.

"Am I interrupting something?" Stephanie asked, with a knowing grin on her face.

"No! I was just helping put the drinks away," Layna said, before turning to the sink and grabbing a dishrag. Stephanie looked at me, and I shrugged. *I make her nervous?* I thought Layna's behavior was actually cute, but I stopped my thoughts right there. Aside from her being Will's younger sister, I knew pursuing my interest in her wouldn't be a good idea right now. Will and I were cool, and all I was willing to offer women these days were casual hookups anyway.

Stephanie turned to me. "So, I hope you guys don't mind if I crash your get together? Layna, do you want to join us?" she asked, as Will came back into the kitchen. He wrapped his arms around Stephanie's waist, kissed her on the neck and nipped her ear with his teeth. She smiled, and I began to think that maybe Will should have scheduled this gathering for another day, because it didn't look like they wanted to watch anything but one another.

"You two," Layna said playfully, shaking her head at their open affection for one another. "Nah, I gotta finish studying for my finals next week." *So, she's in school?* I wondered what she was studying.

Will let go of Stephanie's waist and grabbed a roll of paper towels.

"The game is about to start.  Y'all ready?" Will asked. I looked over to Layna who looked like she still wanted to say something, and then glanced back to Will and Stephanie. "Yeah, I'm ready," I answered, walking into the living room.

After the game, we all began talking and laughing in the living room. It was still early in the evening, only 5 o'clock, and Layna hadn't come out to join us at all. I was curious about her, but again, I needed to remind myself to check my curiosity. As if I'd conjured her up, Layna came into the living room with a plate of fruit and squeezed herself between Will and Omar on the couch. She'd taken her hair out of the ponytail, and her locs framed her face perfectly. I quickly turned my eyes to my phone. I didn't want to get caught staring at her because I definitely was staring, and without my hat shielding my eyes, everyone would have noticed. Joe and Tony's eyes made no secret that they liked what they saw as well.

"What are y'all in here talking about?" Layna asked, looking around the room.

"Sex," Stephanie said, casually. Will cut his eyes at her. We weren't specifically talking about sex, we were talking about relationships, but I could understand Will not wanting to engage in certain topics with his sister. "Will, your sister is grown…" Stephanie said, catching Will's vibe. Will exhaled deeply and shook his head.

"Thank you, sister-in-law! I am grown! I'm grown enough to know that all men between the ages of 15 and 35 are either hoes, or liars, or both!" she said, as she popped a grape into her mouth, causing the room to erupt in laughter and protests. Will had a slight smile at her comment as well. It looked like he was forcing himself to loosen up.

"Hold on now! Hold up! I'm 31 and I'm not a hoe! I'm actually looking for a nice woman that I can settle down with," Tony said, breaking through the laughter. His eyes were stuck on Layna as if he was making more of an offer than a statement. Will looked at Tony as if he wanted to interject, but I saw Stephanie lightly tap his thigh, stopping him from speaking. Layna didn't acknowledge Tony's comment with words, she just nodded at him.

"Not all men are like that! Some of us actually want to be in a relationship," I said, putting my bid into the conversation.

Layna gave me a challenging look. "Even you?" she asked, skeptically.

"Yeah. Even me. Why? Is that so hard to believe?" I replied.

"I don't know. I've seen you two times and both times a different woman was on your lap. That doesn't seem like a man who wants to be in a relationship to me. It looks like a man who's for the streets! But that's just my humble opinion!" she said, with the cutest look on her face. Everyone laughed in agreement. She may have thought she was insulting me, but really, she was stimulating me more than I cared to admit.

"They were just friends. And sweetheart, if you want to sit on my lap just say that!" I joked, but it wasn't really a joke. She had an open invitation to sit on my lap. I just couldn't say it. Layna and Stephanie's mouths dropped open. Will gave me an unamused look, and I held up my hands in surrender. Admittedly, me saying that to his sister was a little over the line.

"Speaking of which!" Omar said, interrupting excitedly, "what happened with you and that girl from the spot? Her name was

Peaches, right?" he asked. He had to be the biggest instigator I knew! But he was my boy though, and he never took things too far. "Nothing happened," I said, shrugging. I saw Layna's eyes on me.

"The way she was all up on you that night, and nothing happened?" Joe asked, doubtfully.

"I took her number and I went home," I answered.

"Alone?" Omar asked.

"Yeah. Why is it so hard for y'all to believe that I sleep alone?" I asked, amused.

Trying to be respectful of the two women in the room, Omar said,

"It just seemed like something you wouldn't turn down. I know I wouldn't have!" Everyone began laughing again.

"See! That's what I'm talking about!" Layna said, with a victorious smile. "All y'all need is a fat ass and an opportunity!" she said.

"That's only partly true! You can find a pretty face anywhere! But I know for me, I need a woman who can stimulate my mind, too," I said, and I couldn't help but to make eye contact with her.

Layna scoffed, "Really?" she asked with her brows furrowed. The conversation then quickly shifted from me when Omar added in his thoughts. The more I stole glances at her, and listened to her perspective on different topics, the more I found myself being attracted to her. I couldn't help it.

"Y'all want some pizza? It's my treat," Layna offered. Omar and Joe declined, stating they had to get home. Tony and I offered to stay. After we all pitched in and helped clean up the mess in the living room, we found something else to watch while waiting for the pizza to arrive. My phone buzzed in my pocket. I pulled it out to see it was my father calling me.

I stood. "I need to take this," I said, answering the call as I walked out the front door for a little privacy.

# 4

## Layna

I needed a study break. Besides, listening to everyone laughing and shouting uncontrollably for the past few hours was a bit distracting. After I couldn't focus anymore, I joined the crowd in the living room.

I'd completely embarrassed myself in front of Julian earlier as well when we were alone in the kitchen. I told Will I'd apologize to him, but the words didn't come to me as easily as I thought they would have. The way his eyes peered into mine didn't help either. I couldn't deny the obvious physical attraction he and I had to one another, but that's all it was. I didn't know anything about this man besides the way my stomach warmed every time I looked at him. But again, that's just physical and it has nothing to do with compatibility.

Will's other friend, Tony, made no secret he was interested in me. He didn't seem to care about all of the warning looks my brother gave him, either. Thankfully, Steph was there to keep my brother in check. I knew he only wanted to protect me, but he needed to understand I could protect myself.

Once Julian went outside to take a personal phone call, I took that opportunity to tidy up the kitchen. Steph joined me as Tony and Will remained chatting in the living room. Steph looked over her shoulder to make sure no one was listening. "So, what's up with you and Julian?" she asked, in a hushed tone.

"Nothing's up," I answered, trying to play it off. I knew she'd already sensed the attraction between the two of us. She gave me a look that said, *'girl, please.'* "He's an attractive guy, and he seems to like you," she said.

I shook my head. "Yeah, but… I don't know. I told Will I'd apologize to him for what I said about his poem when I met him the other week. When you walked in on us earlier, I was trying to do that, but I froze," I explained.

"Apologize? What did you say to him?" she asked, as she began wiping down the counter. After I told her the whole situation that had taken place at Words and Versus, and what I said to Julian, she shook her head at me. "Layna, now you know your little mean ass went too far! I agree with your brother on this one, you need to apologize to that man. I'm surprised he's being as nice to you as he is. I've known Julian to not bite his tongue, sort of like you—so he must really like you if he's being cool," she said, causing me to chuckle.

"You really think he likes me?" I asked. Steph turned around again to make sure we were still alone.

"Yes, he *likes you*. Everyone would have to be deaf and blind not to see the chemistry between you two. You should give him a chance. I think you two would get along," she said, with a hopeful smile.

I picked up a hand towel and began to dry my hands. "Well, I don't think he's interested in me like that. He's out here in these streets too heavy for my taste. Steph, you should have seen the way this girl came up to him and sat on his lap like it was nothing while I was having a conversation with him. He is cute, but he loves attention too much for me to deal with him. Besides, I already have someone else on my radar.

I didn't get a chance to tell you, but my English professor, Jamal, asked me to have dinner with him. I told him no, but after thinking about it, I may take him up on it."

Steph's eyes examined me. "Julian is a young and single man, and he's only doing what young and single men do! They act a fool until they find someone worth *acting right* over," she said, holding up her hand to show me the 4-karat diamond ring my brother slid on her finger. "So, he's not going to turn down a woman sitting on his lap! However, I do think Julian's a really sweet guy on the inside," she laughed. "You're young and single, too. It's okay to have a couple options on your plate. This is the time you should be having the most fun. But, I will say this, if you don't look at this Jamal guy the same way you've been trying to hide the way you've been looking at Julian, then you may be wasting your time," she said before going back into the living room. I leaned against the counter and let her words sit with me for a moment.

When I joined everyone back in the living room. Julian was still outside on his phone call. Tony's face lit up when I came back into the room and he scooted over to make room for me to sit down. I felt Will's tension from the other couch as he watched us. I checked my phone.

"The pizza should be here in less than five minutes," I said, abruptly standing back up. "I can get it for you," Tony offered, with a sweet smile.

"No, it's alright. I need the fresh air for a minute. Thank you though," I said. Tony nodded and turned his attention back to the TV, while Will and Steph were doing their best not to grope one another on the couch adjacent to him.

I went to the door and slipped on my slides I kept by the door. I wasn't thinking when I stepped outside on the porch without a jacket. It had been a mild day, but the night time was a cold reminder of Spring not being here just yet. When I closed the door behind me, Julian turned around and looked at me.

"Alright, I'll see you then," he said, to the person on the other side of the phone before he ended his call.

"I'm sorry. I didn't mean to interrupt your call. The pizza is a few minutes out and I wanted to wait for it," I offered. His mood had shifted. He seemed irritated by whomever he was talking to.

"It's alright. I was just finishing up." He looked me over. "You look cold," he chuckled.

"You can go inside and I'll wait," he offered.

"No, I'm good," I said, and we both knew that was a damn lie. My feet were already freezing and the gentle breeze felt like ice moving across my face. I lifted my hood over my head.

Julian chuckled. "I see you're stubborn, too."

"Too?"

"Yes," he answered, moving closer to me. He opened his arms as if he was offering me a hug. "Come here. I'll keep you warm since you're too stubborn to go back in the house," he said, with a charming smile. I hesitated, but then I reluctantly stepped into his arms. The side of my face leaned against his chest and he wrapped his arms around me. He was so warm, and he had a fresh, clean, masculine scent. He rubbed my arms and back, trying to generate some heat, but I was already getting hot in places his hands weren't touching. "Is this better?" he asked, in a low voice that sent shockwaves through me. I nodded. I was too much in a trance to offer him any words. He didn't understand how good this simple gesture felt, and I couldn't believe I was letting him touch me like this.

"Julian—" I began, I moved my head and tilted it up to look at him. He looked down at me. I don't know what lay behind his eyes, but every time I looked into them, something inside of me shifted. He didn't respond verbally, but his eyes spoke a thousand words. "I—I want to apologize for the way I acted the other night. When I said that stuff about your poem." He jerked his head back in surprise, but he didn't speak. "I was rude, and I shouldn't have said what I said. I'm sorry," I offered, and I felt a weight lift off my shoulders. His hands began to rub my arms again. I wondered if this felt as good to him as it did to me.

"So, you *did* like my poem?" he asked, studying my eyes.

"No! I didn't like it. I'm just sorry for how I said it!" He chuckled. "You're too pretty to be so damn mean," he said, sweetly.

"I'm not mean! I'm honest," I defended, and my heart raced at his compliment. "Well, you're too talented to write stuff so superficial. So, I guess we're even," I quipped back.

He gave me a slight grin. "And you like to challenge me," he said, but it was more like he was saying it to himself. "So, you think I'm talented?" he asked.

"Well, yeah. I know a good writer when I hear one. That's how I know you could do better."

"That was just one poem. I have notebooks full of stuff that no one would probably ever hear. But in all seriousness, Layna, your honesty is refreshing. Rude, but refreshing," he chuckled, causing me to blush. Our eyes were pinned to one another as the silence of the moon swallowed our breaths. Our gaze was broken by who I believed to be

the pizza delivery guy driving down the quiet street. I began to step out of Julian's arms, although I didn't want to. Feeling my resistance, he held me tighter to his body. I looked up at him.

"Layna, I want to kiss you. Is that okay?" he whispered softly as he leaned in closer to me. My words escaped me from the boldness of his question. Before I knew what was happening, his soft lips pressed against mine. He pulled back and looked at me, and the intensity behind his stare silenced me even further. He leaned in again to give me another kiss, and I willingly submitted to his offering. This time he ran his tongue across my bottom lip and gently sucked on it. His hands cradled my back and I planted my hands at his waist. He deepened our kiss; tilting his head to the side and making a welcomed invasion with his tongue in my mouth. My knees weakened by the taste of him. I felt parts of my body begin to tingle that I hadn't felt tingling in months.

The care he took in kissing me made me feel like I'd been starving for this type of consideration. I heard myself moan as he pulled away from our kiss. The look in his eyes said more than what I could translate in this moment. Just then, he abruptly let me go. He took a few steps back just as the pizza delivery person parked in front of the house. He had an uncomfortable expression when he looked at me, but I didn't know why.

Before I could speak, he said, "Can you tell everyone that I had to leave? I have to go," and quickly jogged down the stairs towards his car. He got in his car and started the engine.

By the time the pizza made it to my hands, I had a flurry of emotions coursing through me; confusion, anxiety, lust—I didn't know what was going on. I do know that his kiss ran circles through me and turned up my internal temperature a few notches. Once I felt the cold seeping back into my bones from Julian's absence, I went back into the house.

"I was just getting ready to check on you," Tony said, meeting me at the door and grabbing the boxes of pizza from my hands.

"Thank you. I'm good," I said. He looked outside just as Julian was pulling off. "Julian said he had to go. Something came up," I offered. "Oh. Okay," Tony said, with a smile. Tony was cute, but he and I didn't have any chemistry. My five minutes alone on the porch with Julian gave me more of a spark than anything Tony had given me all day.

Later on, when I walked Tony to the door, he'd built up the courage to ask me for my number. I was upfront and told him that I was only interested in being friends, and he seemed cool with that. Back inside the living room, I walked in on my brother and Steph whispering to one another and sharing kisses on the couch. I knew that was my cue to go into my room. They had always been an affectionate couple which was weird for me to see my brother behaving that way but they had been trying for a baby, so their affection was on one hundred. I was just glad my bedroom was on the first floor, and theirs was on the second floor on the other side of the house.

"Alright you two, I'm heading to bed." They both looked at me.

"Okay," Will said. I'm quite sure my head could have been on fire at the moment, and he wouldn't have cared. I could tell he wanted some alone time with his wife.

"Honey, go get in the shower. I'll be up to join you in a few minutes," Steph said, to which my brother quickly got up and headed towards the stairs. He barely acknowledged me when he walked past. She motioned for me to sit down.

"So, what happened with Julian out on the porch?" she asked.

"What makes you think something happened?"

"From the way he never came back after his phone call, and from the silly expression written all over your face when you came back in the house. So, what happened?" she pressed.

I rubbed my forehead and felt uncomfortable for some reason.

"He offered to keep me warm and I let him wrap his arms around me," I said.

Steph's eyes grew wide. "Yes girl! Yes! What else?" she asked.

"Um… I apologized to him… and we kissed. More like he kissed me. And it was soooo good!" I swooned, getting goosebumps just thinking about how he'd taken my breath away.

"What?! I thought you were going to say y'all exchanged numbers or something! Not kissed!" Stephanie said excitedly.

"Steph, he was looking good, smelling good, and looking at me with those beautiful eyes of his, and I let it happen. It felt nice. But then he pulled back from me and practically ran to his car. It was like he remembered something and he had to go. It was strange," I said.

"That *is* strange. Well, what are you going to do?" she asked.

"About what? I mean, what can I do? He ran away from me. We didn't really say much."

"Do you like him?"

"I don't *know* him. I just know what I've seen."

"Do you *want* to know him?" I took a long moment to think about it. I couldn't deny my attraction to him, and I thought it was mutual before he left the way he did. Besides, not even an hour ago I was telling Steph how Julian was not the type of guy who I thought took dating seriously. I didn't want to get married tomorrow, but I did not want to be one of his options either. "Maybe," I finally answered.

"Well, from what I know about Julian, he's a decent guy," Steph shrugged. "We'll talk about this some more later. If I don't get upstairs soon, your brother will come down here and drag me upstairs with him!" she chuckled.

"TMI, Steph. T.M.I." I said, shaking my head.


Once I got settled in bed, my thoughts of Julian wouldn't go away. I couldn't believe he kissed me like that and left. I wondered if I did too much by letting him kiss me. I then wondered if that was something he did often; kissed women he didn't know to give them a preview of how well he used his mouth, cause *whew*! And what about that Peaches chick? I wondered what type of situation they had going on too, and if I was just someone he wanted to add to his roster of bed buddies. I couldn't believe I was obsessing over a man I knew nothing about. I tossed and turned for a while before I sat up, turned on my bedside lamp, and grabbed a notebook and a pen. I felt so inspired to write about how I was feeling. My thoughts spilled on to the pages that turned into a poem I titled,

*Unbutterflied*, to describe how I was feeling. Once I closed my notebook, I fell to sleep instantly.

# 5

## Julian

When my father called me last night, I decided to take the call to expedite the one conversation I agreed to have with him. I'm certain he'd spoken with my mom and he couldn't wait for me to reach out to him first. We agreed he would meet me at my house after work this

Wednesday to talk. I don't know what he needed to talk about, but he seemed very eager to see me.

My phone call with him was thankfully cut short when Layna came out onto the porch. I noticed how Tony was trying his best to impress her, but the interest she showed in him wasn't mutual. She and I had been stealing looks at one another and debating topics all night, and I was praying no one noticed our silent conversations we held with our eyes. The connection I felt when I held her in my arms was one of comfort and familiarity. She felt like she'd always been there. When I kissed her, it felt right. The sensations I felt from that kiss had my mind racing with no finish line in sight. When I realized what I was doing, I had to leave. I had to start managing my impulses better. That was a big part of my problem, I always hit the fast forward button too soon. Layna wasn't the type of woman I could be casual with. She was the type of woman I would date and want to get to know better. I hadn't felt like that about any woman in at least a year.

I'm sure she probably thought I was crazy by the way I left, but I didn't care. I found myself caught between a rock and a hard place. On the one hand, I loved my freedom and the countless options afforded to me. On the other hand, I wanted to eventually be with a woman who I could give all of my love and passion to who appreciated it. Was I even ready to stop having casual hookups? Was I ready to put my heart into a relationship again when there was the possibility of it being crushed?

Not just with Layna, but with *any* woman. Was I ready? I didn't know. What I did know was there was something about *her* that pushed all of these thoughts to the forefront.

Seeing the love Will and Stephanie shared last night reminded me of how far away I was from having a love like theirs. I am a single man with no kids, a regular ass job, and no real goals outside of saving money. I realized I had to step up my game if I truly wanted different for my future.

It was a typical Monday morning at work, and my mind had been distracted all day with my thoughts of what I was doing with my life. Mostly, I was stressing about this pending conversation I was going to have with my father later this week. Thankfully, my job didn't require me to be super focused. Although I held two bachelor's degrees and a master's degree in the communications field, I worked as a security guard at Truest Financial Firm by choice. My job was to check people in for their appointments, and provide an escort when needed. Even though I didn't work in one of the big offices upstairs, or wear a suit and tie to work, I completely maximized my time there.

I'd been working in a building with some of the top financial advisors in Charlotte for the past three years, and it didn't take me long to start siphoning some of their financial knowledge. Remembering their names, birthdays, and important milestones allowed me to casually get a ton of financial advice without having to pay. I learned how to set up brokerage accounts, how to read spec sheets for different stocks, and the best ways to save money for retirement. Since my father gifted me with a house last year, and my car was paid off, I was able to save a ton of money on my modest $46,000 annual salary. I was smart with my money, and I had a nice nest egg saved up outside of my investments. I took care of a few of my mom's bills, too, but they were minimal.

*Wednesday*

I'd become so anxious about this conversation with my father, that I barely slept the night before. I asked Mom if she knew what my father wanted to talk to me about and she told me she didn't know. The last time he was so adamant to speak with me, he handed me the keys to a house that he spent the last 20 years paying off. The house was old, but he'd upgraded quite a few things before he gave it to me. I think he felt his generous gift would somehow turn us into the father-son duo he'd probably hoped for, but it didn't. I appreciated the gesture, but just like I'd told my mom, he *owed* me that house; and a relationship with me wasn't for sale. I wanted to know what he wanted this time, but mostly, I wanted to get this over with. I'd given up on the idea of us having a real relationship or the hope that he would come to me one day and take accountability for his poor example as a man and as a father when I was growing up. Truthfully, I didn't know if I'd be able to accept those things if he did want them.

He said he'd arrive at 7 p.m. and he rang my doorbell at 6:59. I opened the door to see a man with my bone structure, my build, and my eyes staring back at me. I hadn't seen my father, Julius

Brooks, in a year, but this was the first time I noticed how much I looked like him.

"Come in," I offered, extending the door wider. He stepped in and took a look around at the minimal decorating I'd done with the space thus far. My house was fully furnished, and I'd hung a few pictures, but there was no real personality within these walls. "Have a seat," I offered, following him into the living room. He sat down on the loveseat and I sat on the couch adjacent to him. "The place looks good," he said, still looking around.

"Thanks," I replied, and I stared at him. I wasn't in the mood for small talk, I just wanted to know what he wanted.

"So, how have you been?" he asked.

"Fine," I answered, impatiently.

"That's good," he said, clearing his throat. "There are a couple things I wanted to talk to you about. First, I got a call from my sister Anita down in Georgia, and my father is very sick. He's not doing well and he's only expected to live for the next three or four weeks. I'm driving down to see him this weekend. I know it's short notice, but I wanted to know if you would like to come with me," he began, with a look of regret on his face.

I didn't know how to respond. I'd hadn't seen my grandfather in 20 years. I didn't really know him anymore. All I knew was he and my dad weren't close, and because of that, I never had an opportunity to really know him as I grew older.

I sat back and sighed. "I'm sorry Granddad is sick, but I'm not sure if me going to see him is a good idea. I barely know him now," I said honestly.

"I know, and that's my fault. He and I spent all of these years barely talking to one another, and now I'll only have a few weeks with him before he's no longer here," he said, somberly. I saw the look of torment on his face, and I felt the irony behind his words. "That's the other reason I wanted to talk to you. Julian, I know you're not too fond of me because of how things were when you were growing up. I was young, stupid and immature. I know I didn't treat your mother right, and I've apologized to her several times over the years. However, I've never apologized to you. I know I wasn't there for you the way you needed me to be. I know I wasn't the best example for you," he began. I felt my chest beginning to tighten. I took a few deep breaths to help calm my nerves before looking back over to him. He looked as if he was being genuine. He continued, "I'm sorry for not being the man you needed me to be as your father. I'm sorry I exposed you to the worst way you could ever treat a woman. I know I can't change the past, but I'm asking you to allow me to be a father to you now. You're my only son. You're the only thing I've ever done right in this world and I want to be a part of your life."

I felt tears welling in my eyes. I quickly swiped them away and gained my composure. How could he be saying the words I'd only dreamed he'd say. I was overwhelmed.

"What do you want me to say to that?" I asked, clearing my throat. "I want you to say whatever you feel. I can take it," he answered. I took a few long moments of silence before I began to speak.

"So, the only reason you're here now is because Granddad is sick, and you now realize how shitty our relationship is?" I asked, shaking my head. "Do you know how it feels to see your mother hurting and not being able to do anything about it? And the man who is supposed to love her, who is supposed to protect her, is the one causing the pain?!" I asked, spearing the words at him.

He dropped his head. "I'm not proud of the way I behaved back then, but I'm a different man now. And I'm here because you're my son, and I mean what I'm saying," he said.

"Well, I'm a different man now, too. I'm not the same kid who would cry himself to sleep at night because he felt like his own father didn't want him! You were never there for me! Never. If you weren't working, you were too busy running the streets. I spent a lot of years trying to figure out what was so important out there that you couldn't be at home with us! I wanted to believe you were going to change, but after that night, I knew I would never look at you the same way," I said, trying to control my emotions. I felt my anger rising, and I knew I needed to try and stay calm.

"That was a mistake! And I've regretted it every day since!" he said.

I stood. "You left my mother crying and in pain on the floor! She said you didn't touch her, but how do I know she's not just covering up for you?! That fall, on top of the stress you caused her, is the reason why she lost that baby. You did that!" I yelled.

"And I live with that regret! I'm the one who has to answer for that! I wasn't trying to hurt your mother—or you! My head was in a different space back then. I was selfish and I had a bad temper and running away was the only way I knew how to deal with my problems," he explained, as he stood in front of me. "Son, I'm not perfect, and I've made a lot of mistakes. I'm trying to make things right. Let me be a part of your life. I—I love you, Son."

I was not prepared to handle all the emotions I felt. I can't remember the last time I'd heard my father tell me he loved me. I was even more overwhelmed now. I didn't realize tears had begun to fall until I noticed my vision was blurry.

"You need to go, man."

"Julian, let's just talk," he begged.

"I can't do this today. I need some time. Just go," I repeated, not able to look at him. By now, my hands were shaking from all of the emotions running through my body.

"Son, I'm sorry," he said. I tried to tell him to leave again, but my voice wasn't there. He attempted to wrap his arms around me, but I stepped back.

"Just leave, man!" I said, finally finding my voice. He tried to hug me again, but this time I pushed his arms away before he could reach me. My father is bigger than me and I know without a doubt he's stronger than me, but when he saw the look of rage and hurt in my eyes he chose to retreat.

*****

"I didn't think you were ever going to hit me up," Peaches said, as she strolled through my door just after 10 o' clock. After talking to my father, I needed to release my frustration in the worst way. I didn't intend on hitting up Peaches when she gave me her number, but I thought she'd be able to give me just what I needed tonight. I think the half bottle of vodka I downed contributed to my decision, but I just needed something besides a drink to help numb the emotions running through my mind.

Peaches looked up at me with a sexy grin. "What do you want to do?" she asked, in a husky voice. I didn't answer her. Although Peaches wasn't my usual type, her sex appeal was on *a hundred.*

My eye lids felt heavy as I watched her hands rub up and down my chest and eventually moved to the growing bulge behind my sweatpants. "Mmm…" she moaned. She backed me on to the couch and got on her knees in front of me. I continued to watch as she took her time rubbing her hands up and down my thighs and eventually freeing me from my pants. She raised her eyebrows and looked up at me. "This is *big king* energy right here. You deserve the royal treatment," she mumbled, before wrapping her lips around me. She took me into her mouth as deeply as she could before she began working me over like a pro. Already drowsy from the liquor, I allowed my head to fall back on the couch and I relished in the feel of her lips and tongue giving me her all. The more I groaned the harder she worked; and the harder she worked, the better I felt. I

allowed Peaches to give me more of the *royal treatment,* as she called it, for the better part of the night before she went home. This was exactly what I needed tonight. A release. Afterwards, I was finally able to have a good night of sleep.

# 6

## Layna

Finals were finally over and I had a three-week break before the start of

Spring semester. My job at the call center wasn't able to offer me fulltime hours during my break, but they did give me a couple extra days to work. After finishing my semester, I had a renewed energy that seemed to come out of nowhere. I sat down and wrote out my personal and professional goals, like Will had suggested. Then, I began to plan out each goal into attainable milestones. I knew creative writing is what I wanted to do, and I knew I wanted to work for myself, but I realized that getting a nine to five to help fund my entrepreneurial ambitions was the best way to go.

I'd already freelanced for a few recognizable publications, and I had my beauty blog, but that wasn't enough. Now that I had a plan in place, one of the first things on my agenda to complete was to update my writing portfolio. I wanted to polish up my writing samples, and ensure I had stellar examples of my work for potential employers. I knew I needed help with this, so I hit up Jamal via text to see if he'd help me get things together. He eagerly agreed. Although we were able to complete everything virtually, he insisted for us to meet in person. I was on the fence about an in-person meeting, and ever since I'd felt chemistry with Julian, I decided to keep things between Jamal and I completely platonic. I needed to figure out the feelings I was having for Julian or if it was something worth exploring. However, when I closed my eyes, I could still feel Julian's arms around me and smell his scent; and anytime I thought about that kiss, I melted. I assumed he wasn't seeing anyone seriously, but I didn't know for certain, and there was no way I was going to ask my brother.

"So, I think once you add this in, your portfolio will be complete. Your samples are very strong, and I believe you'll be a stand-out candidate for any job you apply for," Jamal said, with a warm smile.  I'd met him at the local library to put the final touches on my portfolio, and although I knew he was attracted to me, he kept things very professional. Jamal was cute in a studious kind of way. He always looked neat; nice clothes, fresh haircut, trimmed nails—and although he wore glasses, they fit his face well. He was a little on the thin side, but he didn't look frail or weak. He was really a nice guy from what I could tell.

"Good!" I sighed. This was one task I was glad to check off of my list. I closed my laptop and began to load my belongings into my bag. "Thank you so much again for helping me, Jamal. This really means a lot to me."

"It was no problem. And remember, if you need a recommendation, let me know," he said as he began to gather his items as well.

"I definitely will. Well, I need to get home. I have a few more things I need to finish up tonight," I said, as I stood.

"Okay. Can I walk you to your car?" he asked. My first instinct was to say no, but I was working on not being so standoffish. Besides, he did just volunteer his time to help me over the past couple weeks.

"Sure," I answered, as I picked up my purse. Once we got to my car, an older model Honda Accord that still looked good, Jamal opened the door for me. He stopped me before I got in.

"Layna, I'm getting ready to grab something to eat. If you're hungry, maybe you would like to join me?" he offered, with a smile that showed off his dimples. I would bet money that he'd gotten his cheeks pinched all the time when he was a child. My first instinct was to say no, but again, I was trying to be more approachable these days.

"Like a date?" I asked, returning his smile.

"Ahh… You told me you're not interested in dating. This is more like, friends hanging out."

"So, we're friends?"

"If you would like to be," he answered.

I looked at the time and felt the rumble in my stomach. "Okay, that's fine. Where'd you have in mind?" I asked.

"I know a spot not too far from here. You can follow me, or I can drive you and bring you back," he said.

"Umm… I can ride with you, I guess," I said. The smile on his face extended.

"I'm parked right up here," he said, gesturing in front of us." I was surprised to see that Jamal drove a BMW. Not that I thought he couldn't afford one, he just seemed like he'd have a more economically friendly car. He opened the passenger side door for me and a spicy masculine scent hit my nose. The inside of his car was pristine, almost like new. Once we were headed to our destination, Jamal and I talked about his academic background and a little bit about his upbringing.


After we ate, Jamal drove me back to my car at the library and we talked for a few minutes more. I was having a nice time with him, and having no pressure about forming more than a mutual friendship made our time together that much more enjoyable.

I looked at my watch. "Well, I gotta get going. It was really nice hanging out with you today. You're good company."

"You are too," he said, unbuckling his seatbelt. "Let me grab the door for you," he offered, before quickly getting out the car. He was already on his way over to me before I could tell him that it wasn't necessary. He helped me out of his car and walked me a few steps over to my car. I unlocked the door and he opened it for me.

"Thank you again, Jamal," I said, turning to him. I gave him a quick hug.

"You're welcome. Text me when you get home," he said. I nodded before he closed the door. I drove off and I saw him get into his car through my rearview mirror.

Once home, I was ready to relax in my room after spending a few minutes catching up with Will. After I showered and changed into some comfy loungewear, I checked my phone only to notice Jamal had texted me:

*Jamal: Hey, are you home? You never text me to let me know you made it there safely*

*Me: Sorry about that. I'm home safe and sound. I was talking to my brother and forgot to text you*

*Jamal: No problem*

*Me: Thanks again for helping me with my portfolio*

*Jamal: You're welcome. You're an amazing writer, and you'll have no problem finding the job of your dreams!*

*Me: I hope you're right!*

*Jamal: I am. Just be sure to thank me when you make it big!*

*Me: One can only dream…*

*Jamal: You already have what it takes. I know you'll do great things*

*Me: Thank you*

*Jamal: You're welcome*

*Me: I'm headed to bed. Goodnight*
*Jamal: Goodnight.*


After I settled in bed, I read over the poem I'd written the other night when my mind was in a flurry over Julian and our kiss. I wondered if I would have the courage to read it at the open mic next weekend.

# 7

## Julian

It had been over a week since I had that conversation with my father, and it still bothered me. I didn't know how to feel about what he said, or if he was only saying it because my grandfather was sick. I used to dream about him coming to me and telling me he wanted to be a real part of my life, but those dreams stopped years ago. I wanted a relationship with him, but I didn't know where to start. And what if he discovered he didn't really want to be a part of my life? Those thoughts burdened me, and my sleep suffered greatly over the last week and a half as I mulled this over. When my insomnia was really bad, I hit up Peaches to come through a few nights to help me get my mind off things. I even missed a couple days at work because I was so tired.

I also skipped a few days seeing my mom to catch up on some rest, but I did text her to make sure she was okay. I didn't tell her the specifics of me and Dad's conversation, but since I was seeing her today, I knew I wouldn't be able to escape it. I was helping Mom get rid of some junk she'd been holding on to for some years. Most of it was trash, but some things I was going to take to the Goodwill for her. We sat down on the couch together to take a break.

"So, who's the new girl?" Mom asked.

"New girl?"

She raised her eyebrows at me. "Jules, I've known you since before *you've* known you," she answered, with a radiant smile. My mind instantly went to Layna. It had been about a month since we shared our kiss on the porch that night, and I hadn't seen her or talked to her since. I thought about her often; her pretty face, her sweet scent, her soft lips, and her intellect — which was honestly the sexiest thing about her. I didn't know if she was feeling me like that, though. Yeah, I kissed her, but that didn't mean she thought about me as much as I thought about her. Kissing her was probably a mistake and it was typical of me to always *put the carriage before the horse.* Besides, the way I had been carrying on with Peaches this past week confirmed I'm not ready to get to know any woman on a deeper level. And now that I had this stuff going on with my dad, I definitely wasn't in a good headspace to invite someone new into my life. On top of all of that, I doubted Will would easily approve of me dating his sister. Not that I *needed* his approval, though.

"I did meet someone, but I think it's better that she and I remain like we are. We're friendly, but we're not really friends," I answered.

"Why is that?"

"Because getting too close to her can end up bad for the both of us," I answered.

Mom nodded. "Or are you just afraid that you'll give your heart to the wrong woman again?" she countered. "That too," I answered honestly.

"Jules, I've told you this before, and maybe this time you'll listen; friendships lead to the best relationships. I know it's easy to see a woman you like and immediately want more from her, but forming a genuine friendship with a woman first can lead you to a love like you've never known. Becoming friends with this woman first is a step in the right direction," Mom said.

"I'm supposed to sit back and be a friend while I'm interested in her? So, I can sit back and possibly watch her date other people? Nah, I'm good on that!" I chuckled.

"Well, you don't have to listen to me. But I'm telling you what I know. You love hard, Jules. You have a big heart, and you *love hard.*

Don't you think you owe it to yourself to slow down and allow someone to know you before you take it to a romantic level?" she asked. Then my mind went to Peaches. Peaches was definitely someone who I would never consider an arrangement with outside of the one we had; and I'd already made up my mind to cut that off. Hearing my mom say I owed myself more was sobering, and quite frankly I didn't want to continue talking about it. She must have sensed my energy because she swiftly changed the subject.

"So, what did your father have to say? Do you want to talk about it?" she asked.

I shrugged. "I don't really have much to say about it, Mom," I answered, as I went through a box of old pictures and keepsakes.

"Jules, your father told me how upset you were when he came to see you last week. What happened?" she asked.

"You two sure seem to be talking a lot these days. Are you sure he didn't already tell you what happened?" I asked, sarcastically.

"You can lose that attitude with me! I'm not your father! You better fix your tone before you open your mouth and speak to me again!

And no, your father didn't tell me what was said. He only told me you were upset," she repeated.

I shook my head and fixed my tone before I looked over to her. "I'm sorry, Mom. I didn't mean to snap at you. But honestly, have *you* forgiven him?" I asked, bluntly. She was quiet for a long moment. I assume she didn't expect me to ask her that question.

She sighed. "It took a long time, but yes, I have forgiven your father."

"How? After everything he did to you—to us—how can you forgive him?"

"It wasn't easy, but it was necessary. Your father did a lot of things back then that hurt us; and I stayed with him as long as I did because I loved him. But he was damaged. He and his father had a strained relationship, and I thought I could love his broken pieces until he was whole. But loving a broken man is an impossible task. I realized I had to love myself, and I couldn't do that if I carried the burden of what he'd done to us. I had to free myself from all of that so I could be a better mom to you, and a better person for myself. It took years, but I let it go. And once I let it go, things in my life started to change for the better," she explained.

"I don't know if I can forgive him, Mom. I want to, but I don't know how," I said, with a sigh.

"You have to be open to forgiveness. Right now, you're still so mad about the past that you're ignoring the present. Look at what's in front of you," she said.

Mom was right. I was stuck on the past when it came to my father, and I had no idea exactly what issues he had with *his* father. I thought I knew a lot about the man who helped create me, but I guess there was a lot I needed to learn. I decided I would give us having a conversation another try. At least this time I knew what to expect.

# 8

## Layna

I decided tonight would be the night I went up and shared my poem for the open mic night at Words and Verses. I was nervous as hell. Will couldn't believe I was actually going to do it, but I'd given Julian such a hard time about his poem, that I couldn't be all talk and no action. Even Steph came out tonight. She switched shifts with a co-worker whose babysitter fell through at the last moment earlier in the week, so she was off tonight.

When we arrived, there were about the same amount of people and chatter that had been there the first time I came. We greeted Omar at the door, and we casually spoke to people Will knew. I discreetly looked around for Julian. I wasn't sure if he'd be here tonight, but I had a hard time getting him off my mind since he kissed me a few weeks ago. Will, Steph and I found a good table in the middle of the open space before the open mic started. Right now, the DJ was getting in his set of 90's hip-hop and R & B. Once seated, I couldn't stop myself from looking around, hoping to see Julian.

"Are you sure you want to go up there? Is not as easy as it looks," Will said, with a childish grin. Steph playfully slapped him on the hand.

"Layna's got this!" she said, turning her eyes to me.

"Thank you Steph! I'm glad *someone* is here to support me!" I replied, giving my brother the evil eye.

Will chuckled. "You'll be fine, *Zion*," he said, with a smirk. "I know I will, *Zechariah*," I answered back.

Will shrugged. "You can call me Zechariah. I like my name!" he said. Will knew I hated when he called me Zion. Most people outside my family didn't know that my first name was Zion, and Will's first name was Zechariah. My parents wanted us to both have names from the bible, but I went by my middle name, Alayna or Layna as everyone called me, because I liked it better. Will went by his middle name because he claimed it was just easier for people to say.

"You two are hilarious," Steph said, not really paying us much mind.

After looking around again, I took in a deep breath and asked, "Do you think Julian will be here tonight?"

Steph gave me a surprised expression. She knew just as well as I did how protective Will could get when it came to me because of my last relationship. Thankfully, Will didn't look too deeply into my question when he answered, "He should be. He told me he was coming. Why? Are you scared he's going to tell you your poem is trash like you did to him?" Will asked, with a grin.

"Whatever. I just want him to see how it should be done!" I answered.

"You got a lot of courage for a first timer! Julian has been doing this for years, and I know he'll tell you the truth after the way you did him! Thicken up that skin now!" he said. I rolled my eyes. I felt relieved knowing that I'd see Julian again, but now my anxiety transformed into butterflies going crazy in my stomach. I worried about how Julian would feel about my poem, and if he would be able to tell it was about him. I'd never done anything like this before and I hoped I didn't end up regretting it.

About 20 minutes later Omar went up to the mic to begin the show, and there was still no sign of Julian. Just as I began to think he wasn't coming, he appeared at our table and slapped hands with Will. He greeted Steph with a small hug, and when he looked at me, he nodded and said, "Hi Layna, it's nice to see you again," before he pulled up a chair and sat right next to me. My heart was racing out of control and that cologne he wore made me wish I was in his arms the same way I'd been on the porch that night. I looked over to Steph and she raised her eyebrows in approval. Julian and I didn't look like we were a couple, but having him this close to me made me feel warm. I made sure to wear an outfit that hugged me in all the right places, and I wore my locs side parted and loosely flowing around my head; a simple style that always looked good.

I looked down when I felt Julian tapping his fingertip on the notebook I held in my lap. When I looked in his eyes, I felt that shift again.

He leaned over to my ear, "So are you going to go up there and teach me something new?" he whispered. His deep voice ran right through me. When he leaned back, our eyes met again and he smiled. "Just wait and see," I answered, returning his smile. When I gave my attention back to the person performing, I noticed Will giving Julian and I a questionable stare. I just ignored him. Men were allowed to talk to me whether he liked it or not.

I then leaned over to Julian's ear. "Where's your notebook?" I asked.

"I'm not going up there tonight. I'm just here to listen and now I'm excited because I get to hear you," he replied. That statement made me both nervous and flustered. I could see more of Will's disapproving looks as Julian and I continued to have our private conversation.

Thirty minutes later, Omar was up at the mic ready to announce the next act. When he made eye contact with me, I knew he was going to call my name. My heart dropped into my stomach, but I remained cool. Julian had left his seat ten minutes prior to go socialize, but he assured me that he wasn't leaving until he heard my poem.

"Next up, we have a virgin to the mic, y'all! So, I need y'all to show her some love! Words and Verses, please welcome Miss Layna to the mic!" Omar announced. The crowd clapped and Steph and Will gave me huge grins as I stood up and walked over to Omar. When I got over to the mic, Omar gave me a quick hug and discreetly whispered, "Take your time," in my ear. He adjusted the mic stand to my height before leaving me there. Looking at all of the people from this angle immediately intimidated me. *Shit! Will was right! It's not as easy as it looks!*

I cleared my throat and said, "Um. Like Omar said, my name is

Layna and I'm going to share a poem I wrote inspired by —" I began, as my eyes found Julian's eyes fixated on me. I lost my train of thought for a moment and quickly turned my eyes to my notebook before anyone noticed who I was looking at. "This poem is called, *Unbutterflied*," I said, and I was sure not to look out into the crowd again as I began to read:

*I once found myself bonded to the common theory of unsaid*

*words hoping someone would hear me,*

*Of mutual attractions attracting somewhere near me,*
*Of being afraid of myself but hoping no one would*
*fear me, I am now unbutterflied.*

*So, when I looked at him, my eyes knew what I liked before*
*I did, So, I conversed with myself as I closed my eyelids.*
*Unavailable and unaware,*

*Taken aback, but didn't care.*

*Intrigued by all surrounding him…*

*I absorbed his pheromones willingly through my skin tone,*

*Past my soul, traveling to the middle of my bones…*
*Speaking a language that to most is unknown.*

*I am now unbutterflied.*

*I speak to him in visual illusions,*

*And I let him draw his own conclusions,*

*He likes that I speak to him that way, so I'll keep it that way.*

*I am his wish,*

*I knew as soon as he felt the softness of my lips,*

*There was no way he could ever resist…*
*this. I am now unbutterflied.*

*I crave to bathe him in rose petal saturated liquid hot heaven,*

*I'll drown with him after his prayer and my*
*blessing, I'll kneel down in servitude to you, this is*
*my confession, Tell me yours.*

*Tell me with your eyes.*
*Release your soul into*

*me, I am now*
*unbutterflied.*


My brother and Steph stood and was clapping like they were proud parents. I was happy with the response I received, but there was one person's opinion I couldn't wait to hear. The night went on for another hour or so before we all began to pile outside. Will, Steph, Omar, and me were talking and recapping the night. I now felt like I was a part of the crew. Julian strolled up to us and joined the conversation. He stood right next to me, and bumped me with his shoulder.

"So how did I do?" I asked him, causing the background conversations to quiet down a little bit.

He wore a smirk on his face that appeared to be holding back a full smile. He nodded. "You did aight!" he replied, causing everyone to laugh.

"Come on Jay! You have to admit that she killed it for her first time!" Omar said.

Julian reluctantly nodded, and looked at me, "You did really good. For real," he said.

I nodded. "Thank you for not being salty," I joked.

"Salty?" he asked.

"Yeah. Salty because I showed you how it's done!" I joked, bumping his shoulder back. I noticed Steph studying me and Julian's flirtatious behavior while Will tried to hold back a scowl.

"While everyone is here," Steph said, "I want to remind you to come to our house next weekend for the party. We're having a movie night outside since the weather is getting nicer. Just text me or Will and we'll let you know what to bring if you want to bring something," she said. Everyone began to chatter about it. I looked up at Julian, he wore a fitted baseball cap, it was different from the other ones I'd seen him wear, and his eyes were shielded from everyone but me when he looked down at me; I melted a little bit. He was *so* fine; I couldn't deny it.

"Are you going to come to the party?" I asked, smiling up at him.

He smiled back and began to speak when a woman's voice interrupted him.

"A movie night?" the voice eagerly asked, approaching us. We all turned to look at who was intruding in on our conversation. It was that

Peaches girl…again. Julian told us he didn't mess around with her, so I guess she wasn't interested in giving up so easily. Her thirst level at this point was bordering desperation. Unless, there was something going on between her and Julian. She rudely squeezed herself between Julian and I, causing me to take a few steps back. She threaded her arm between

Julian's and looked at the crowd of people now watching her. Everyone became quiet.

"Julian, would you like to introduce us to your friend?" Steph asked. I'm sure she was only being nice, because I peeped the *what the hell* look on her face.

He sighed. "Y'all, this is Peaches," he introduced, sounding like all his energy had deflated by her presence. Everyone greeted her, except me. She was rude and obnoxious, and girls like her either got cursed out or ignored by me. In the spirit of not being *mean*, I chose the latter. The fact was, I had no claim on Julian anyway.

"So, there's a movie night next weekend? Is Julian allowed to bring a plus one?" she asked. Everyone looked at her as if she was an alien.

"Actually—" Steph began.

"Actually, yes!" Will interrupted. "Julian, be sure to bring your friend with you next week," he said. Steph gave him an evil look.

"I'm not sure if I'll be able to make it," Julian finally said. He sounded completely irritated.

"Well, I hope you two can," Will said, smiling. Then an awkward silence fell between all of us.

"Honey, I'm ready to go. Layna, are you ready?" Steph asked, before walking away. She didn't even give me or Will a chance to respond.

"Goodnight y'all," I said to the group.

"Layna, right?" Peaches called out to me.

"Yeah?" I answered, wondering what the hell this girl had to say to me.

"That was a cute little poem you did. *Real cute*," she said with a fake smile, still holding on to Julian's arm. My eyes moved to Julian's and he looked like he was doing his best to bite his tongue.

"Thanks," I said plainly, then I began to walk away to catch up with Steph.

"Am I coming back to your place again tonight?" I heard Peaches ask Julian while I was still in earshot. I'm sure she wanted me to hear her, though. I cringed. If that was the type of woman

Julian got down with, there was no way in hell he and I would ever be together.

"Why the hell did you invite that rude ass woman to our house?" Steph snapped, once we were 30 seconds down the road. Will sat behind the driver's seat and seemed completely unbothered by his wife's attitude.

"We invited Julian, and if he wants the woman he's seeing to come with him, I don't see the problem with that," he answered. Steph shook her head. She knew she couldn't say she wanted Julian and I to get to know one another better, because that was a can of worms neither one of us wanted to open.

"Next time, don't cut me off when I'm speaking. And don't invite rude ass people we don't know to our house," Steph said. Will sighed, but he knew saying anything more would probably cause a firestorm he didn't want to put out. The rest of our ride back to the house was quiet.

Once I was in the privacy of my bedroom, I allowed my true feelings to crown. I dropped my notebook to the floor. I was crushed and I felt like an idiot. I put myself out there with that poem because I thought Julian and I had a connection. Also, he said he didn't mess around with that girl; which he obviously did. Honestly, I wasn't too bothered that he was messing around with her, I was more bothered that he lied about it and he kissed me. The sweet kiss we shared began to turn my stomach as I thought how I didn't know where his lips had been. That was probably why he ran off the way he did that night. He felt guilty. Will's intuition was right. He hadn't said it, but I knew he would've had a problem with me seeing Julian. Now, he didn't have to worry about that. I didn't deal with liars.

I laid down in bed and began my mental detox of Julian Brooks.

I'm glad I found out who he was before I really put myself all the way out there. Before I let my thoughts travel too far, I grabbed my phone to see if there was a video or something I could watch to help take my mind off things. I saw that Jamal had emailed me a few job postings 30 minutes ago. I looked at the time and saw it was just past midnight and I wondered what he was doing up. I hit reply on the email and typed,

"Thank you. I'll check these out in the morning," before hitting send. A minute later I got a text.

*Jamal: You're a night owl like me lol*

*Me: Not really, I'm trying to sleep now*

*Jamal: Ok, I didn't mean to disturb you*

*Me: You're not disturbing me*

*Jamal: Ok, good. Are you ready for Spring break to be over? You have one more week.*

*Me: No! Lol! I could use another week! Are you ready to go back?*

*Jamal: Of course. I love teaching*

I laid on my back and pondered my next question for a minute or two.

*Me: Are you free next Saturday? We're having an outdoor movie night here at my brother's house and I can invite a friend.*

I saw bubbles appear instantly.

*Jamal: Sure. That sounds fun. Send me the address and tell me what to bring. Me: Will do*

# 9

## Julian

When I sat next to Layna, I kept cool and tried not to appear too eager until the scent she was wearing began to entice me. Once that happened, I got up to socialize with other people to get away from her. When she stood up to recite her poem, I was thanking the person who made that stretchy jean material and V-neck shirts. She'd decorated her locs with little beads and a few colorful ribbons. Her skin looked soft, and her lips made me want to kiss her again in front of everyone. She had an effortless beauty about her. She was easily the most beautiful woman in the room.

It took a few lines of her poem for me to realize she was talking about me. I had to do my best not to come out of my skin when I came to that revelation. No one had ever written a poem about me, and it was so… romantic. I don't think any woman has ever turned me on the way she had done with her words. I was turned on physically, mentally, and creatively. I quickly learned that a woman expressing her feelings towards me through poetry was my love language, and I'd never been spoken to that way before. Ever. It's what I'd been missing. I had every intention of taking my mother's advice and trying to become friends with her first, but I didn't know how I could do that now. I wasn't sure if I could just be a friend to a woman who I was this attracted to.

Peaches on the other hand was completely out of line, and out of control. Her bombarding her way into our conversation, and inviting herself to Will's house infuriated me. I hadn't even had the opportunity to ask Layna about the origins of her poem, or to enjoy her presence a little more before we were interrupted. And that little dig Peaches took at Layna instantly confirmed our situation had run its course. I had to restrain myself from not embarrassing her ass in front of everyone. In the past, I wouldn't have cared about getting her straight in front of people, but I was trying to turn over a new leaf. I saw the way Layna looked at me and Peaches. She looked confused and I could tell she was bothered. With all I had on my mind this past week with my father, I didn't have the strength to confront anyone with my usual snapbacks, but I was ending this shit with Peaches tonight.

Peaches trailed me to my car after I'd said my goodbyes to the few remaining people outside at the venue. I turned and looked at her.

"Peaches, you're cool and everything, but this ain't working out," I said.

"What does *that* mean?" she asked, folding her arms.

"It means our little arrangement is over. I won't be texting you to come through anymore. I won't be texting you at all," I said.

"Oh! Is it because of your little girlfriend who wrote you that third grade poem?" she asked, raising her eyebrows.

I scoffed at her insult, and shook my head. "No, this is because you crossed the line. You're taking too many liberties with me. You invited yourself to my friends' house! You and I are not together and that's not what this is. We're not dating!" I snapped, but still trying my best to be respectful.

She cocked her head back, "So is that how it is? You must really think you're special! Your sex is not that good for you to be acting like this!" she said, looking me up and down.

I raised my eyebrows. "Shit, now you know that's a lie! Two seconds ago, you were ready to get some of this *it ain't that good* sex. Now who's acting up?" I asked, glaring at her.

"Whatever Julian! They told me this is how you were anyway! A pretty face, a nice body, and enough inches to have me speaking another language! And they were right! But they also told me how quick you are to switch up as soon as you see another pretty face! They were right about that, too!" she said.

I shook my head. I didn't know who *'they'* were, but I'm glad *they* at least had most of their opinions about me correct. This petty ass conversation is exactly why I needed to get away from casual flings. I don't know why she was testing my patience like this, but I knew it was time for me to go before I said something to really hurt this girls' feelings, and then she'd have her brother, father or her play cousins looking for me.

I scoffed at her and exhibited an amount of self-control I didn't know I possessed when I said, "Lose my number," through gritted teeth. I opened the door to get into my car and got in. I was doing my best not to assault this woman with my words. She meant nothing to me. She was just something to do, and she served her purpose. If she wanted to talk about who had bad sex, she was going to go home with her feelings hurt if she took another shot at me.

"Gladly!" she said, folding her arms with a scowled expression. I closed my car door. Peaches stomped away in the opposite direction just as I started the engine and drove off.

I was hoping I would feel better by going to the open mic tonight. Mission failed.

*One Week Later…*

It had been two and a half weeks since my conversation with my father and he was still in Georgia with my granddad. I reached out to him to let him know I wanted to talk again once he got back to Charlotte, and I could hear how happy he was about it. I'd talked on the phone to my granddad, too. I knew he was sick, but he didn't sound as weak as I expected him to. On a whim, I decided I would go to Georgia to see him. I had plenty of vacation time to take, and once I explained the situation to my manager, my time off was approved. It was Saturday, and I would be leaving early Monday morning.

Today was also the Saturday of Will and Stephanie's movie night, and I was on the fence about going. Layna, her poem, and her smile had been running marathons in my mind over the past week. I was impressed by her bravery. Hearing her words about me made me feel *different.* I was already attracted to her physically, but now, I was attracted to her mind. And that attraction felt indescribable. I wanted to have deep conversations with her. I wanted to know what made her, *her*. I was so intrigued that I Googled her and found she had a beauty blog called *Naturally Pretty* that focused on her favorite natural beauty products for Black skin and hair. She was a talented writer and she had a unique voice that separated her from the masses. I hoped the situation with Peaches last week didn't deter her from wanting to know me more.

After visiting with Mom this morning, and packing for my trip this afternoon, I decided I would go to the movie night at Will's house. They asked everyone to arrive at 6:30 p.m., so we had time to eat and socialize before it was dark enough to watch the movie outdoors. Also, I made up in my mind that I would be letting Will know that I was interested in his sister. I wasn't sure what I would say to Layna, but I wasn't going to stress about it.

I arrived at the house at a quarter to seven and saw several cars parked on the street and in Will's driveway. There were more people here than I thought would be. I picked up paper plates, plastic cups, napkins, and a couple bottles of Vodka as my contribution to the gathering. As I was walking up to the front door, I heard music and laughter coming from the backyard, so I decided to head that way. Will and Stephanie had their backyard set up like a mini-drive-in theater. They had a huge projection screen set up with a few rows of comfortable looking outdoor furniture. I saw there were some people who'd brought their own chairs, too. I looked around even more and saw women who I'd never seen before standing around talking and laughing. I assumed they must have been some of Stephanie's nurse friends. The smell of meat on the grill led me to where Will and a some of the guys were gathered. As rowdy as they were, they must have already been sipping.

I walked up to the guys holding up the items I'd brought with me.

"The party can start now!" I announced.

"Jay!" They all seemed to greet in unison. I put my bags down on a nearby table.

"We gotta get you caught up!" Omar said, holding up a red cup that was full of—hell, I don't know what it was full of, but I knew it wasn't apple juice. "I'm good for now," I said.

"You didn't bring your date?" Will asked, looking around the yard and then back to me, along with everyone else.

"She's not my girl. I don't mess with her like that," I answered.

"Well don't worry, man! Steph invited a few of her single friends from work and I'm sure you'll find something you like," Will said, with a grin. I could tell Will was one and a half drinks away from being noticeably intoxicated. I just hoped he didn't burn the meat! I nodded. "We'll see," I answered.

Just as the thought of her entered my mind, Layna came out into the backyard carrying empty aluminum pans. My heart skipped a beat at the sight of her. Her skin looked as if she was glowing, and her locs were in two large braids with the ends dusting her shoulders. She smelled like she was ready to be devoured and I wondered if she smelled like that all over. She wore white leggings, white sneakers and a long-sleeved white top that barely hid her ass. If I was going to get through this night without kissing her again, I had to stop looking at her. She walked over to Will.

"Will, Steph wants to know if you need anything else before we get the movie started," she said. "Nah, I'm good. I'll be done in about 10 minutes," he answered. She put the empty pans down and turned in my direction. She looked surprised to see me. Just surprised, not happy. She didn't have the same warm energy towards me that she had last week, and she didn't look like she was going to speak first. So, I spoke.

"Hi Layna, how are you doing today?" I asked.

"Good. You?" she asked curtly.

"I'm alright," I answered. Will looked between the two of us and remained silent, then he began to put food into the empty pans Layna had brought out.

"Layna, I think your friend is here," Will said, gesturing to the side of us. I turned to see a clean cut, casually dressed man carrying a grocery bag, with a big smile on his face. I looked back to Layna and her expression was unreadable. Who the hell was this, *friend?* I thought. He beelined his way over to where me, Will, Omar and Layna were standing.

"Jamal! You made it! I didn't think you were coming!" she said, throwing her arms around him. He looked surprised by the gesture, but he gladly returned her hug. She pulled back from him.

"I told you I would, and I'm a man of my word," he said, smiling at her. The look he gave her clearly indicated he was not interested in being just her *friend.*

"Everybody, this is my friend Jamal. Jamal this is my brother, Will, and his friends, Omar and Julian," she introduced. We all shook his hand, and sized him up as he stood there with the woman I came here to see.

"It's good to meet you, Jamal. Layna's told me a lot about you," Will said. "Same," he replied. *She's been talking about this guy?*

Jamal then pulled what looked to be an expensive bottle of liquor out of his bag. "Layna told me you liked Whiskey. I hope this bottle is okay," he said, extending the bottle to Will.

Will's eyes stretched open. "Thank you, man! You didn't have to bring this! I appreciate it!" Will said, admiring the bottle.

I felt my jaw tighten. When did all of this have an opportunity to take place? Just a week ago, she was spilling out her feelings about me in front of everyone. And now, she had a whole other dude here with her? I was ready to leave right then, but I remained cool. I decided I would just slip out when the movie started. There was no way I was going to hang around and watch this play out.

# 10

## Layna

*Earlier in the day...*

Me, Will and Steph were moving at a hectic pace getting the house ready for our party. We'd done the outdoor set up last night, and prepped the food. We now had to make sure the house was clean and we had everything we needed. We were finally able to sit down and eat something at 3 o'clock. We hadn't even had breakfast this morning. We were all seated at the table eating lunch. "So, your friend Jamal said he's coming tonight?" Will asked. "Yeah," I answered, flatly. Steph looked between the two of us, before turning her attention back to her phone and her plate of food. "Good. He seems like he would be a nice guy," he said. I rolled my eyes. I was tired of dancing around the elephant in the room. I knew him well enough to know what he was hinting at.

I sighed. "What's that supposed to mean?"

"It means what I said. He seems like he would be a nice dude," he repeated, as he eyed me. I eyed him back.

"Nicer than Julian?" I asked, because I was ready to mash this out. Although I decided I wasn't going to pursue anything with Julian anyway, I could no longer endure Will being so overbearing about the subject of me dating. Steph put her phone down and her eyes shifted between us. Will took another bite of his sandwich, completely unphased by my question.

"Yes. Nicer than Julian," he finally responded, after taking his time chewing his food.

"You get on my nerves, Will! You know you're not my father, right?" I barked at him. Still, he seemed unmoved.

"You don't know Julian the way I do. He's a cool guy, but the way he handles women is not anything I want you dealing with," he said, as he wiped his mouth with a napkin. Steph's eyes widened, but she remained a spectator.

"I am grown. I can make my own decisions, Will."

"Like you did back in Raleigh?" he asked, as his stare penetrated through me.

Steph finally spoke up, "Honey, don't do that," she said, grabbing his hand. "No Steph! Let him! Say what you have to say! I'm a big girl," I baited.

"Okay," he said, turning his body towards me. "You're not a good judge of character when it comes to men. You're too trusting. That's why you were in a six-month relationship with a man you didn't know was married! You believed whatever lies he told you! And I know it's messed up for me to say this because I'm a man, but that's what men do! We will say whatever we need to, to get what we want!" he said. Steph dropped her head and sighed, but she didn't say anything else.

"I made a huge mistake, and I learned from it. That doesn't mean that you have to police every man who shows interest in me," I replied, on the verge of tears. Recalling my relationship with Derrick was still a painful memory for me.

"Julian tried to stop a woman from getting married the night before her wedding a couple years back, and he kissed that same woman after she was married. Did you know that?" he asked. I was silent, because I didn't expect him to divulge that type of information. "He had commitment issues with the last woman he dated, and she got tired of him and broke things off. And you saw the type of woman he's dealing with now. That Peaches girl—He's all over the place when it comes to women, and you're too good for that," Will said, and held his stare on me.

"You didn't have to go there, Will," Steph said. She looked shocked by the information as well. She couldn't have known about everything Will said or she wouldn't have pegged Julian to be a *decent guy*.

Will looked over to Steph. "Yes, I did have to go there, because this is the only way Layna will understand this shit!" he snapped. He took a breath and placed his hand over Steph's, "I'm sorry, baby. I didn't mean to yell." He then turned his attention back to me, "Layna, I love you, and I don't want to see anyone hurt you again the way that Derrick guy did. He's lucky I didn't break his neck! I'm only looking out for you," he said, in a much softer voice.

I remained silent while tears ran down my face. I didn't like being reminded of Derrick and how I had to move from Raleigh to get away from the backlash that situation caused. "Okay," I croaked out.

Will stood. "Come here little *Zion*," he said, which gave me a small smile. I stood, and he pulled me into his arms and rubbed my back. "I know you can make decisions for yourself. I just don't want to see you hurt again. Just think about what I'm saying," he said, in a soothing voice, "you'll be okay."


***Back to the party…***

"Alright everyone! The movie is starting in about five minutes! So, grab a plate, grab your date and get comfortable!" Steph announced walking into the backyard. She walked up to where me, Will, Jamal, Julian, and Omar stood.

"And who do we have here?" Steph asked, looking between me and Jamal.

"Steph, this is my friend Jamal. Jamal, this is my brother's wife, Stephanie," I introduced. "Nice to meet you," Steph said, with a guilty grin.

"Thank you for having me. Your home is beautiful and your set up back here is really nice! What movie are we going to watch?" Jamal asked. As much as I tried not to look, my eyes kept making their way over to Julian; and he looked so scrumptious. He wore a light gray polo style shirt that was nicely contoured to his broad chest and hugged the lean muscles of his arms. He had on black cargo shorts along with gray and black sneakers; a silver watch and small diamond studs in both ears completing his simple look. Like all the other times I've seen him, he didn't have a hair out of place. His line-up was sharp, leading into a head of thick jet-black waves. He'd thinned out his beard a little bit more than when I'd last seen him, but it still looked good. The feeling of his mustache tickling my lips swarmed over me. I internally kicked myself for discreetly admiring the landscape of this man; but I couldn't help it. I didn't think he would be here tonight, but I was at least glad he didn't bring that girl with him.

"Thank you! Well, I lost a bet so we're watching *American Gangster* with Denzel. If everyone is up to it, we'll watch *Love Jones* afterwards," Steph said, answering Jamal.

"Both are very good choices, but *American Gangster* is one of my favorite movies!" Jamal said.

"Good! Layna, help your friend make a plate and find a seat," Steph said. I grabbed Jamal by the wrist and led him away from the group. I heard her talking to the guys as we walked away.

I'd forgotten how violent this movie was in some parts. I cringed at the screen, which made Jamal chuckle. We were seated comfortably next to one another enjoying the movie.

He leaned in close to my ear, "I'm having a nice time. Thank you for inviting me," he said. When he pulled back, I turned to him and I saw his eyes travel to my lips.

I turned away. "Jamal, I'm going inside to use the bathroom and to grab a blanket, I'll be right back."

"Okay," he said with a smile that showed me his dimples. This alcohol was starting to run through me, and when I stood up, I began to feel it. I let Will make my first drink, which was strong as hell, and Jamal made my second. I had a couple shots after that, and now I was nursing my third one half way through the movie. I was having trouble staying awake. I didn't normally drink this much, but between being reminded of Derrick and finding out Julian was the complete opposite of who I thought he was, I needed something. Since I was already home, I figured drinking a little more than usual would be okay.

My legs were a little wobbly when I stood, causing Jamal to grab my hand. "I'm good, I'm good," I assured him. He sat back and began to watch the movie again along with everyone else. I wobbled into the house and over to the guest bathroom. The way my bladder felt once I emptied it made me feel like I had a new lease on life! I washed my hands and swished some of the courtesy mouthwash around in my mouth to get the taste of alcohol out. I looked in the mirror. There was no way I was going to make it through the second movie, I was barely making it through the first! I chuckled at my reflection. I looked ridiculous getting drunk at this party. I opened the door and the sight of Julian waiting there sobered me up for a quick moment.

# 11
## Julian

I had every intention of leaving the party once the movie started, but I couldn't go out like that. If Layna meant everything she said over the mic last week, then I needed to at least talk to her. I'd made small talk with a few of the women there to pass the time, but my eyes found Layna every chance I got. I shamelessly watched how she interacted with her *friend.* Everywhere she went, he happily trailed after her and held his hand at the small of her back which irritated the hell out of me.

I saw how he'd tried to kiss her, and I was relieved when she moved her head away from him. Seeing her with another man, a man who seemed to catch the eye of many of the other women at the party, was humbling. It reminded me that there was always someone waiting in the wings to shoot their shot with a woman like Layna, and I may not even have a chance. I didn't like this feeling. Competition wasn't anything new to me, but this time I felt like I had so much at stake to lose.

I saw her wobble her way back into the house, and I figured it was the perfect time to talk to her alone. I waited for her to open the bathroom door.

"Excuse me," Layna said, ready to walk by me.

"Layna, can we talk?" I asked.

She shook her head. "Nah. I have to get back to Jamal." I sighed. "I just wanna—" I began.

"Why did you lie?" she blurted, and the fresh smell of minty mouthwash accosted me. "Lie about what?" I asked.

"About you and that genetically modified girl, Peaches?! You said you weren't messing with her, but I heard her ask you about going back to your place," she said with a slight slur, leaning against the wall for support.

I smirked. "I didn't lie. I didn't start messing with her until after that night on the porch."

"Yeah, whatever," she said, pushing herself off the wall. She stumbled and I caught her.

Holding her up, I asked, "Is that why you invited your friend here tonight? Because you thought she was my girl?"

"Let me go!" she said, trying to get out of my hold. I don't think she realized I was the only thing keeping her upright.

"Layna, I like you and I know you like me… and I want us to be… friends. And although you're a little twisted, I know you understand what I'm saying. That poem you wrote—" I began.

"Wasn't about you!" she croaked out.

I chuckled. "Yes, it was," I said with a grin, and I knew I sounded conceited. "I haven't stopped thinking about you. I'm not dealing with that girl anymore…that was a mistake. I want to know you, Layna." She began to look queasy. "Layna, I think you need to lay down. You've had too much to drink." I began to almost carry her towards the living room. "I'm going to sit you down, and I'll go get your brother," I said.

"No!" she objected.

"Yes, Layna. You're a mess right now," I was amused by her behavior.

She stopped moving her feet as we made our way down the hall.

"My brother will be mad if he sees us together," she whined. *Mad? Why would he be mad?* I wondered. I was going to ask her what she meant, but then she said, "But the way you kissed me. I've never been kissed like that, Julian. You have the best lips," she whined, her eyelids starting to go low. "Did you like kissing me?" she asked with a grin.  I couldn't help but smile. "Yes, I did. I liked it very much," I answered, trying to get her feet moving again. She was light enough for me to carry, but I thought that would be overboard. "Come on, Layna. Let me get you to the couch," I insisted.

"Kiss me like that again, Julian," she whined.

"You're drunk. You don't mean that," I said, but shit! I did want to kiss her again.

"I do mean it! I've dreamt about it. Please Julian, do it again," she begged, with a drowsy smile. I looked down the hall to ensure we were alone. I leaned over and gave her a quick peck on her lips. Then I gave her an even longer kiss, tasting her lips. Then, I pulled back. Her lips were so soft; I could kiss on her for days. "Mmm…" she groaned, with a wide smile.

"Okay, now come on," I said, trying to hold back my excitement from being able to put my lips on her again; even if she was drunk. She began moving her feet again, and we made it into the living room. As we began to approach the couch, I heard someone come in from outside. It was Layna's friend, Jamal. He looked at us with a confused expression.

"She's drunk, I'm just trying to get her to the couch. Can you go grab Will or Stephanie?" I asked.

He nodded. "Yeah, no problem," he said, and quickly went back outside. I sat her on the couch and kneeled in front of her. She leaned forward and grabbed me around my neck. Her head fell onto my shoulder hard as hell. All of her weight was on me.

I cringed. "Are you okay?" I asked. Then, she began crying. *What the hell?* I thought.

I rubbed her back, because I didn't know what else to do. Will,

Stephanie, and Jamal came running into the house like they'd just been notified that she'd been shot or something. Will gave me a questionable look before pulling Layna off of me. Stephanie followed and Jamal just watched.

"Layna, how much did you drink, honey?" Stephanie asked, going into nurse mode as she felt Layna's face, while Layna just cried. Will backed up and I stood next to him, while Stephanie assessed her. She turned to look at us. "She's just drunk," go grab a bottle of aspirin and a couple bottles of Gatorade. She'll have to sleep this off," she said to Will. He looked relieved and hurried himself to the kitchen. "Layna, we're going to get you in bed, so you can rest," Stephanie said. "Julian, can you help me get her up?" she asked. I stepped closer and began to pull her up from the couch.

"Jamaaaallll! I'm such a bad host!" she cried out to him. We all wanted to laugh, but didn't. This was turning comical now.

"It's okay Layna," he said, with that same goofy ass smile he'd been giving her all day. Will came back into the living room with the Gatorade in his hand.

He quickly eyed me holding up Layna and he didn't look pleased. "Where's the aspirin?" Will asked.

"Oh, it's upstairs in our bathroom. Go grab it, and we'll get her laid down," Stephanie said. Will headed for the stairs and Jamal walked over to me, Stephanie and Layna.

"Get some rest. I'll call you tomorrow, sweetheart," he said, and then kissed her on the forehead. I could have punched this dude in the face!

"You have the cutest little dimples! Do you know that? With your cute chocolate self! I like chocolate!" Layna said, as she lifted her hand to rub his cheek, and began chuckling. This girl was a whole comedian.

"Thank you, Jamal. We'll take care of her," Stephanie said, as she led us in the direction of Layna's room. Stephanie opened the door to Layna's bedroom and it smelled like her. I wanted to look around, but Layna was starting to feel heavy and I had to get her in the bed. I sat her on the bed and she slumped forward. I kneeled to take off her shoes while Stephanie got a cold rag to put on Layna's forehead.

She began to cry again. "I'm not an awful person, I just made a mistake! I didn't know!"

"I believe you," I said, as I slipped off her socks, having no idea as to what she was talking about. I know this was the wrong time to look at her like this, but damn! Her feet were so pretty.

I heard Stephanie come back in the room, just as Layna said, "Julian, I don't feel so good!"

"I got the aspirin," I heard Will say, following right behind her.

Still kneeling in front of Layna, I turned to look at them when I heard Layna whine, "Oh my God!" then I heard a puking sound, followed by an unpleasant sensation of thick, warm liquid hitting the side of my face and sliding down onto my shirt.

"Shit!" I yelled. Stephanie's eyes got big and she put her hands over her mouth, and Will just looked shocked. Layna began crying even harder as I was stuck kneeling in front of her covered in her vomit. This shit smelled vile. It made me nauseous. I slowly turned my head to look at her. I breathed as best I could. I placed my hands on the bed on the sides of her to give myself leverage to stand.

"I'm so soorryyyyy!" Layna cried. She held on to my neck and leaned her head on me again, stopping me from standing.

"I know. I know. Let me go!" I said, beginning to panic. I didn't know if she had to throw up again, and I didn't want to be in her way. I was starting to get sick. Will came over to assist me.

"Layna, let him go," he whispered, grabbing her arms, and I swear I think he wanted to laugh. Once he got her hands off me, I quickly stood up and looked from Will to Stephanie. Stephanie handed me the rag she was holding in her hand that never made it to Layna's forehead. I wiped my face and had to stop myself from gagging. Will laid Layna down.

"Honey, please go get Julian a change of clothes and show him where the shower is. I'll get her cleaned up," Stephanie said, calmly. I'm sure both Will and I was glad Stephanie was a nurse, because I know neither one of us wanted to clean this up.

*****

This was weird. I never thought I'd be taking a shower at Will's house in the middle of a party. I'm glad I didn't have to ask to use the shower because there was no way I'd be able to drive home in the condition I was in. I had to scrub my beard at least three times to ensure there were no… remains left. Will provided me with a fresh set of clothes, and an unopened pack of brand-new underwear. He told me to just keep the pack; I understood. Once I was showered, I went outside to find Will. I was ready to go home. I no longer had the desire to be here after being thrown up on by the most beautiful woman I'd seen in recent memory. When I found Will outside, *Love Jones* was playing and it was nearing the end. I asked him to come inside so I could talk to him before I left.

Once inside, we had a seat on the couch. I asked him how Layna was doing.

"She's knocked out! She's a lightweight! I don't know why she drank that much! But she'll be alright," Will said.

"Good," I answered. I gave him a condensed version of what was going on with my grandfather and told him I'd be going out of town. Not wanting to keep him away from his other guests for too long, I decided to get to the point. I wanted him to know I was interested in Layna, and now I also needed to know what she meant when she said that Will would be mad if he saw us together. I was going to shrug it off, but when I saw the disapproving look he gave me earlier, I assumed she was telling the truth. "Listen, I wanna be straight up with you about something," I began.

"Okay."

"It's about Layna," I said, and Will's face remained neutral.

"What about her?"

"I like her, and I want to get to know her better," I said plainly. "I ain't on no foul shit. I just want to see if we can be friends first, and see what happens from there. I didn't want to come at her without you knowing my intentions," I said.

Will sat back on the couch and shook his head. "I appreciate you coming to me, but my sister is not the right type of woman for you," he said, and I was surprised.

"What type is that?" I asked.

"The type you can play games with. Julian, you my boy and everything, but I know you're out here real heavy in the streets right now. Come on, man, you had that whole issue with Serenity Johnson and her husband. Plus, the foul way you kept Nova hanging on by a string. And now this Peaches girl? Let's be serious, man. If the roles were reversed, would you be cool with me dating *your* sister?" he asked.

I understood why he said what he said. I even understood him wanting to protect his sister, but honestly, I wasn't asking his permission. I was merely letting him know my intentions.

I nodded, and thought about his words for a moment. "Did you tell her all those things about me?" I asked.

"More or less," he answered without hesitating. "I already knew y'all had a little vibe going, and I thought it was innocent, so I fell back. But when I heard that poem she wrote — it was easy for me to read between the lines," he shook his head. "Listen, Jay, she's my sister and she's been through a lot. I want what's best for her, and I don't want her to be hurt again. I know I can't make decisions for her and I can't protect her from everything and everyone. But I'll tell you this; make sure you know what you're doing before you come at her. She deserves someone who knows what they want and that will treat her right. We cool, but I go hard for my family," he said.

I nodded again. I was irritated at the fact that he told my personal business to Layna, but he didn't do anything I wouldn't have done to protect someone I loved. Also, Will did have a point. I hadn't handled the unpredictable cycles of relationships well in the past, so I understood where he was coming from. In that moment, I decided that I did need to back off with pursuing Layna for the time being. I needed to be sure within myself with 100 percent certainty that I would come at her correct. "Okay. I respect that. I'll fall back. We good?" I asked.

He smiled, "I guess after my sister threw up on you, I would be wrong to have beef! We good," he laughed.

"I knew yo' ass thought that was funny!" I said, and we both began to laugh. "Listen, I'm heading out. Do you mind if I peak my head in and say bye to Layna?" I asked.

"Yeah, go ahead. I'm sure she's still knocked out! I wish I would have recorded her acting a fool! I would be able to blackmail her until she had grandkids!" Will laughed, shaking his head.

"But that's my little Zion," he said.

"Zion?" I asked.

"Oh, yeah. Her first name is Zion; Zion Alayna Pierce, but she hates it. So don't call her that," he said as he stood from the couch. He patted me on my shoulder. "I'm going back to the party. Good luck with your granddad and everything. Let me know if you need anything," he said, before leaving.

"Thanks," I said. *Zion, that's a dope ass name,* I thought.

I walked over to Layna's door and knocked softly; the door was already slightly opened. I listened to hear movement, but I heard nothing. "Layna," I called out in a low voice. Still nothing. I pushed her door open a little and stuck my head in. She was bundled up under so many blankets, that I barely saw the top of her head. "I just wanted to let you know that I was leaving, and I hope you feel better. Goodnight," I whispered. Before I closed the door,

I heard her groan. I opened the door a little wider. "Are you okay? Do you need something?" I asked. She pulled her arm from under the blanket and held it out towards me. I still couldn't see her face though. I pushed the door wide open, because I certainly didn't want to be in here with the door closed after my talk with Will. I walked over to her bed. I grabbed her hand and she opened one eye to look at me. "I'm sorry," she mumbled.

"It's okay. Just feel better. Do you need me to get Stephanie for you?" I asked. She shook her head. "Okay. Well, I'm leaving," I said. She tugged at my hand and I leaned closer to her. I moved her hair out of her face with my free hand, I just couldn't help myself. *So pretty,* I thought. She let go of my hand and closed her eyes. Then I heard light snoring. I chuckled and stared at her for another minute or so. I leaned over and I stole a kiss on her forehead, and then on her cheek before standing. I know I just told Will less than five minutes ago that I would back off, but I was still so drawn to her. Even while she lay there drunk and passed out, I knew I wanted her. When I turned to leave, I saw Stephanie standing by the door watching me.

"Is she okay?" she asked. I nodded, and walked towards her. We stepped outside of Layna's bedroom and closed the door behind us.

"I'm going home. Thank you for having me, Steph," I said, and started my way down the hall.

"Julian—" she called out. I turned to her. "I know Layna really likes you, and I also know you have a past, but everybody deserves a second chance," she said, with a small smile. "Where's your phone?" she asked. I pulled my phone out my pocket, unlocked it and handed it to her. "I'm putting Layna's number in here for you.

If you tell my husband I did this, I'll deny it!" she said, with a smile. "When you're ready, use the number," she said.

"Thank you." I gave her a one-armed hug and headed towards the front door.

# 12

## Layna

### *Sunday, the following day*

I woke up with the most terrible hangover I'd ever had. I felt dizzy and completely dehydrated. On top of that, I don't completely remember when I got in the bed. The last thing I clearly remember is Julian waiting for me outside the bathroom last night. Everything else is a blur. I felt around for my phone to see the time was nearing noon. I had a text message waiting for me from Jamal:

*Jamal: Hey, I hope you're feeling better this morning. Call me if you need anything (9:06 a.m.)*

I rolled over and groaned. I didn't want to talk to anyone. I didn't even want to see the sun that was now blinding me. I looked on my nightstand and saw Gatorade and aspirin. I pulled myself up into a sitting position so I could guzzle down a few aspirin. I laid my head back against the headboard and tried to remember which part of last night was real and which parts weren't.

Twenty minutes later I heard a knock on my door.

"Come in," I answered. Steph walked in with a cup of coffee in one hand and a plastic bag in the other hand. She sat on my bed and offered me the cup and placed the bag on the floor.

"I figured you could use this after last night," she chuckled.

"I don't even want to know what happened," I drawled out.

"Oh, yes! You do want to know what happened!" she said, smiling. "Please don't tell me I embarrassed myself," I said, sipping into the cup of fresh coffee.

"I won't tell you that, but I will tell you that you cried and threw up on Julian, then you cried again!" she said, holding back her laughter. I put my cup of coffee down and covered my face with my hands.

"Ahhhh… I remember that now that you're saying it. Oh my gosh!" I groaned.

"Well don't feel too bad about it. After he got cleaned up, he came in here to tell you goodnight. He didn't know I was standing at the door when I watched him kiss you and stare down at you like you were his dream," she said.

"What? I don't remember that. Are you sure?"

"Yes. I know your brother is only looking out for you, and I agree that you should be cautious, but you have to make your own decisions.

Julian cares about you. It's written all over his face. Any man that will come back and kiss the woman who threw up on him is worth getting to know!" she said. She then leaned over and picked up the plastic bag she'd placed on the floor and sat it next to me.

"What's this?" I asked, looking in the bag.

"It's Julian's clothes he left here last night. I washed them. I think you should bring these to him. It will give you a chance to talk to him with no one breathing down your neck. And you may want to apologize for last night. That beautiful poem you wrote… I know it was about him," she said.

I looked at her strangely. *Did everyone know that poem was about him?* I wondered. "Do you really think he'd want to see me after last night?"

"I do. I don't think he wanted to leave your side at all."

"But Steph, he lied about messing with that Peaches chick. He told us he wasn't messing with her, but I heard her ask him about going *back* over to his place the other night. It's not my business who he chooses to lay down with, my problem is he lied about it. I don't do liars."

"I get it, but maybe he wasn't messing with her then. Besides, that girl could have been talking out the side of her neck just to have something to say! You never know with girls like her! If I didn't think

Julian cared about you, I wouldn't be in here vouching for him. He's had a few bad situations, but who hasn't?"

I sighed heavily and picked my cup of coffee back up and began to sip it, absorbing her perspective.

"Where's Will?" I asked.

"He had to go into the studio for a morning session."

"On a Sunday? I know he wasn't happy about that."

"He wasn't, but the client offered him double his rate."

I nodded. "So do you have to work tonight?"

"Uhhh… yeah, but—" Stephanie hesitated. I waited in suspense for her to finish her sentence. She sighed. "I took a test this morning… I'm pregnant," she said.

"What?!" I put my coffee down and grabbed her into a tight hug.

"Congratulations! I'm so excited! I'm going to be an Auntie!" I gasped,

"And my brother is going to be a dad! And you're going to be a mom!" I said, excitedly, rubbing her non-existent baby bump. I saw tears forming the Steph's eyes. They had been trying to get pregnant for the last year from what she'd told me. I was happy her dreams of becoming a mom were finally coming true.

"I have to see the doctor to confirm, but I think I'm about six weeks along. I haven't told your brother yet, so please don't tell him I told you first," she said, wiping her eyes.

"I'm the first to know?!" She nodded and I hugged her again.


Steph and I sat for about an hour talking about babies, the events from last night, and gossiping about who hooked up with who. From what I could remember, it was a good party. I was glad my brother found someone like Steph; she was always such a kind-spirited person to me and our family. She and my brother had been married for four years, and they dated for a year and a half before that. In the five months I'd been living with them, I saw just how much Stephanie changed my brother. When they'd met, he was a 29-year-old bachelor hopping from one woman to the next. It seemed like he went cold turkey when Steph came into his life. She made him work hard for her affection, and from what he says, she *put him through the ringer.* In the end, I know he made the right choice by marrying her. Before she left my room, she gave me Julian's address and told me the rest was up to me.


I took my time getting out of bed and eating a small breakfast that was more like an early lunch. I was starting classes for Spring semester tomorrow, and my life would go right back into grind mode. I would have my degree by this time next year if I stuck to my plan. I can admit in the past I'd been lazy and inconsistent in trying to secure down a career. Seeing how hard Steph and Will worked, and admiring all they had accomplished motivated me to get my own life on track. I had to take my gift of writing seriously, or no one else would.

I called Jamal before I took a shower and got dressed for the day. I wanted him to know that I was okay and thank him for coming yesterday. Steph told me how much of a fool I acted in front of him while I was drunk, but I wasn't going to bring that up if he didn't. He was having brunch with his mom when I called, so he told me he'd call me later. I was hesitant to go to Julian's house uninvited and with no warning. I had to really think about everything Will told me Julian had done in the past with other women. I knew firsthand how complicated relationships could be, but I also knew there's always another side to the story.

I grabbed the bag of Julian's clothes, and the biggest pair of sunglasses I could find to shield my eyes from the sun that made my hangover headache worse; by now, my headache was almost gone though. I put Julian's address into my GPS, put my car in drive and took a leap; hoping I wouldn't regret it.

# 13

## Julian

I'd been writing all morning. Once I sat down with my notebook and pen, my thoughts spilled onto the paper like never before. My talk with Will last night opened my eyes. I never thought about how my erratic behavior with women appeared from the outside looking in. I understood from his eyes how I didn't appear to be a suitable match for his sister. And although I agreed to fall back from Layna, I still couldn't ignore how she'd spoken to me through her poem and how I became hypnotized anytime I looked in her eyes. I didn't understand what all of my feelings for her meant, but I assumed things would become clearer with time. My priority right now was me going to see my father and grandfather. I had so many unanswered questions about who they were, and in the process, I would be sure to learn more about where I came from.

I didn't know how long I'd be in Georgia. I had approval to be off for two weeks from work, but I didn't think I'd use it all. I secured a hotel room for my stay in Macon, Georgia, and I was hitting the road first thing tomorrow morning. I'd finished packing my bags and went outside to load them into the car when a black Honda sedan parked in front of my house. I stood in the driveway with my luggage trying to figure out who was showing up to my house unannounced on a Sunday afternoon. When I saw Layna get out of the driver's side of the car carrying a bag, I nearly lost my breath by the sight of her. She had on a gray sweatsuit, oversized sunglasses, and her locs pulled up into a ponytail. I watched her slowly make her way over to me as I leaned against the back of my truck with my arms folded in front of me. Once she was a few steps away from me, she stopped walking.

"Hey," she greeted.

"Hey."

She cleared her throat. "I wanted to return your clothes you left at the house last night," she said timidly, raising the bag. She walked closer to hand it to me.

"Thank you," I said, grabbing the bag. She stepped back.

"And I also wanted to apologize for… last night. For throwing up on you, and acting like a complete fool. I've never done that before," she said, and I could tell she was embarrassed. I held back my grin. I wanted to forget her getting sick on me; because I could get sick if I thought about it too hard. However, her talking about the way I kissed her, and the way she asked me to do it again was fresh in my mind.

"It's okay. I'm just glad you're alright," I said. She nodded, and the quiet street filled in the quieter spells of silence between us.

"So, you're going on a trip?" she asked, motioning to my luggage. I looked down, suddenly remembering why I'd come outside in the first place.

"Yeah. I'm going to Georgia. My grandfather is sick, so I'm going to go see him for a few days—maybe a week. I'm not sure yet," I answered, before popping the trunk and placing my bags inside. "Oh. I'm sorry to hear that," she said.

"Thank you. I appreciate you saying that," I responded. Then silence.

"Um, well… I just wanted to drop your things off to you and apologize for last night. I'm going to go home," she said. Instantly I had an internal war; should I invite her inside or should I just let her leave? I'd let my next words decide for me.

"Okay, well thank you for coming by," I said, immediately regretting it. She looked around and over to my house.

"Actually, do you have a minute to talk? I won't stay long," she said. I sighed internally and I was glad that she made the choice instead of me.

"Yeah, you can come inside," I offered, leading the way to the front door.


Once inside, I saw Layna's eyes roam all around my open space. I was a neat guy, but I was glad I took the time to deep clean my house earlier in preparation of my trip. I lead her into the living room and invited her to have a seat.

"Would you like something to drink?" I offered. We both looked at one another and laughed, thinking about how a *drink* got her into the position she was in last night. "I'm good," she chuckled.

I sat down with the space of one couch cushion between us. "So, what's up?" I asked. Even after all that happened last night, I was still drawn to her. She had an energy that was magnetic. She removed her sunglasses and put them on her lap.

She looked over to me. "I had a talk with my brother about you yesterday, and he told me he thought it would be best if I kept a little space from you," she began. Since I knew what Will told her, I appreciated how she was very considerate and thoughtful with her words. I also noticed her non-accusatory tone. She continued, "However, I make my own decisions. It's no secret that you and I are attracted to one another, and that's something I want to explore with you," she said. She then inhaled and exhaled deeply. I could tell those words were not easy for her to say. She was in good company, because the response I knew I had to give her wasn't easy for me to say either.

"Layna, I am attracted to you. Even though the first time I met you, you were being a hater!" I joked, causing her to playfully reach over and slap my hand. I held on to her hand. "I really like you; a lot. And I do want to know more about you, but I can only do that as your friend," I said, going against every instinct in my body. I wanted to grab her and kiss her, then rub my hands all over her soft body while telling her how beautiful she was to me. I saw disappointment in her eyes, and I felt like

I was losing a battle I didn't know I was in. She tugged her hand, but I wasn't ready to let her hand go. I held on tighter.

"Is it because you're seeing that girl from the other night? The rude one? Did you lie when you said you weren't messing with her?" she asked, scrunching up her face.

"No. I don't lie. I didn't start anything with her until after that night

I kissed you on the porch. This has nothing to do with her, and I'm not seeing her anymore. I told you this last night; you really don't remember?" I asked. I then saw what I believed to be recognition of what I said last night coming back to her. I sighed, "Layna, on the stage that night — your courage to put yourself out there like that was very special to me. And I've been trying to sort through your words ever since. I have a lot of things I need to figure out before I can give you, or anybody, the type of attention and commitment I want to give. So right now, I hope you can accept my friendship," I said. I think diving off a bridge into freezing waters would have felt better than what I just said.

She nodded, and she looked disappointed. I kissed her hand. "Come here, let me hold you," I offered. She shook her head and pulled her hand from mine.

"No, that's okay. I'm good," she said, dropping her head. But she wasn't good. She was hurt. She poured her emotions out to me and I rejected her. I knew all too well how that felt. I moved over on the couch next to her and pulled her into my arms. She resisted slightly, but then she began to melt onto my chest. I held her close and stroked her arm and we sat in silence for several minutes.

"Layna, I'm not saying I don't want to explore what I'm feeling with you, I'm saying I need time. Can you please give me that?" I asked, in a low tone. She nodded, which gave me a sigh of relief. I grabbed a throw blanket that was on the arm of the couch and covered her with it as she laid against me. I didn't know how long she'd stay, and once she left, I didn't know when the next time I would be able to have her like this, so I enjoyed it.

"I'm glad you liked my poem, but I only did that because no one knew I was talking about you," she whispered, as her head laid against my chest. A kiss on top of her fragrant, neatly groomed locs was my response. After ten minutes, she was sleep. I stole a few pictures of her while she slept. Having her in my arms like this confirmed that I was ready to do what I needed to in order to have her like this all the time.

An hour so later, Layna was awakened by the sound of her phone ringing. I'd moved her head to a pillow on my lap as I watched TV on a low volume. I glanced at her phone before she answered it, and saw it was her *friend* Jamal calling. I really hoped

I didn't have to worry about this guy. She rejected the call and typed out a message to him. She slowly sat up.

"You let me sleep?" she asked, covering her mouth and yawning.

"Yeah. Obviously, you needed it," I chuckled. "I need to get going. Can I use your bathroom, please?" she asked. I pointed her in the direction of the bathroom down the hall and stood to stretch my legs. I folded up the blanket on the couch and grabbed my shoes. I decided I was going to go see my mother since I would be gone for the next week or so.

Layna came back into the living room and began to put her shoes on as well. She grabbed her purse and sunglasses.

"You're going out?" she asked.

"Yeah, I'm going to go see my mom for a few," I answered. "Oh, okay."

It was still relatively early in the afternoon, only 5 o'clock, and it was a nice warm Spring day. I walked her to her car. "Thank you, Julian. I hope you have a safe trip."

"You're welcome. It should be interesting," I replied, smiling at her. I was doing my best to take her all in. I wanted to commit every curve of her face to my memory.

"Will you… let me know when you've made it there safely? I'll give you my number," she said, grabbing for her phone.

"Stephanie gave me your number last night," I smiled. "I'll be sure to let you know once I'm there tomorrow."

She shook her head. "Steph is determined! I can definitely say that!" she laughed.

Then I hugged her, and she squeezed me tight. She looked up at me and our eyes locked. *I can't kiss her. I just can't*, I said to myself. But my thoughts went in vain when she lifted to her toes and laid a soft kiss against my lips. I stayed as still as a statue. She pulled back, and stared into my eyes.

"Layna, we shouldn't—" I began, but she kissed me again, and this time I returned her efforts. I placed my hands on the sides of her face and deepened our kiss. Her arms were planted around my waist. I felt my body beginning to react to our exchange and I knew if she didn't get in the car and leave right now, I was going to hoist her over my shoulder and bring her back into my house. I used all my strength and a silent prayer to break our kiss. Her lips looked so good after I'd just tasted them, and her eyes hushed any words I thought I could say.

We slowly let go of one another and I backed away. Without words, she opened her car door and got in. I stood back even further and watched her drive down to the end of my street. I knew I had to get my shit together.

# 14

# Julian

*Macon, Georgia*

My four-and-a-half-hour drive from Charlotte to Macon ended up being more like six hours. Between stopping for gas and food, and the unexpected traffic, I thought I would never arrive. I drove through the quiet city trying to jog my memory of anything that looked familiar. The last time I was here was 20 years ago, so the things I would have remembered where probably gone.

Pulling up to my grandfather's house, Ishmael Ervin Brooks, was the first recognizable thing I'd seen since arriving. He lived in a huge dark blue colonial style house, with a wraparound porch and bright white shudders. The house was surrounded by several acres of lush green land. Memories I didn't know I had of me playing in the backyard with my cousins rushed over me. I saw two older men sitting on the porch watching the sky. Once I got out of my car, my father emerged from the house and came down the stairs to greet me.

"Julian, I'm so glad you decided to come. Your grandfather will be happy to see you," he said, giving me a big smile. He saw my body language indicated I did not want to hug him, so he patted me on my back instead.

"I'm glad I came, too," I said. He led me on the porch and past the two older men who were sitting there and into the grand entrance of the house. When I was younger, I believed my grandfather lived in a mansion, and looking around now, I still felt the same way. Once my father closed the door behind us, I turned to him and asked, "Who are those guys on the porch? Are they family?"

"They're my cousins. They don't talk much, but I'll introduce you to them later," he said.

Following my father, he led me down a couple familiar hallways with soft gray painted walls and mahogany hardwood floors. I stopped in front of a picture that I don't ever remember seeing. In the picture, I recognized my father, and my granddad, but the child he held in his arms was me. I had to be two or three in this picture. I was looking at the camera showing all my teeth, and both my father and grandfather were looking at me with a look of pride in their eyes. Noticing I wasn't right behind him, my father joined me in front of the photo. I don't ever remember my father looking as proud of me as he did in this photo.

"I've never seen this picture," I said, still in awe of the image.

"Yeah. This was taken right outside. You didn't like taking pictures when you were a kid for some reason. So, in this picture, I'd just told you that I would give you a scoop of ice cream if you smiled for the camera. And this was the result," he chuckled.  I nodded, wishing I could remember those days that were so long ago. "Come on, let's go see the old man," he said.

My father walked into the room ahead of me and sat down in a chair that looked like he'd made himself comfortable in over time next to Granddad's bed. There was another chair on the opposite side he gestured for me to sit in. I expected to see him hooked up to machines and monitors, but he just laid in the bed with his eyes closed. He was so still; I was afraid he had died, but I didn't want to say anything. At 83 years old, he looked like he was still in his 60's with the exception of his gray hair and barely noticeable wrinkles. His face did look a little thinner, but nothing too alarming. My grandfather is so light skinned, I remember thinking he was a white man when I was a kid.

"Pop," my father called out, causing my grandfather to shift a little. "Pop—" my father called out a little louder. His eyes opened slowly and he turned his head in the direction of my fathers' voice.

"*Brooks*, what did I tell you about doing all that hollering in my face! I'm not dead, dammit! I'm just sleep!" he huffed. I'd forgotten my grandfather called my dad Brooks instead of his first name, but I didn't forget how him and my dad always seemed to have tension between them. My grandfather had always been nothing but loving towards me anytime I saw him, though.

My father ignored granddad's outburst, and said, "Pop, Julian is here to see you," nodding his head in my direction. He turned to look at me and I already had a smile on my face.

"Hey Granddad," I said, putting my hand on his shoulder. His eyes softened and a smile cracked through the scowl on his face.

"Baby boy… I can't believe you're here. You a full-grown man now," he said.

"Yes sir. I am," I answered proudly.

"You look just like *Brooks*. It's like I'm looking into the past," he said, reaching for my hand.

I grabbed it. "It's good to see you, too, Granddad," I said, beginning to feel a little emotional. "Mmm hmm," he groaned.

"You bring any great-grandbabies with you?" he asked, which confused me. I glanced over to my dad who watched the interaction.

"I don't have any babies, Granddad," I answered.

"Well, why not?! You're young, you're a good-looking young man, you're smart—what's holding you back? Unless you don't fool with women! I know you new age kids fool with everybody and everythang! I seen that Maury Povich show! These women out here don't even know who their baby should be calling daddy! Men out here just making babies everywhere!" he said. I glanced up at my father again who was now smirking.

"I like women Granddad, I just don't have any babies yet," I answered amused, still holding his hand. Looking down at our joined hands connected the history of my family with the future of our family.

"Then you betta' get on it! Find you a nice young lady to settle down with. But make sure she clean! That's important! She has to be clean! And then have you some babies. They make your life so much better," he said, before loosening his grip on my hand. He turned is head to my father, "Brooks, I wanna go sit out on the porch with my grandson. Go grab my wheelchair," he commanded. My father stood up immediately to retrieve his wheelchair on the other side of the room.


I hadn't asked my father what the source of Granddad's illness was, but from what I could see right now, he seemed perfectly healthy for a man his age. There were no bottles of medicine, no nurse, no anything that would indicate that he was in his final days. That was until he pulled back his blanket to help him into his wheelchair. His body looked so frail from the strong man I once knew. The sight of him made me gasp and instantly tears welled in my eyes.

Granddad saw the look on my face, "Baby boy," he groaned. "I know I don't look like much, but I'm still strong up here," he said, tapping his finger against his temple.

I got out of the way while my father sat Granddad comfortably in his wheelchair and I followed them out to the now vacant front porch.

On the porch, I sat in a chair next to my grandfather, and watched him look at the sky. My father went back in the house to make granddad a small snack. I began to feel saddened by how much time I missed with him over the years. Seeing him like this was sobering. He was right, his mind was still sharp, but his body seemed to be failing him. I didn't know what to say to him as we sat there. I didn't know what topic would be appropriate to bring up.

"What's on your mind, Son? I feel you over there fiddlin', like your nerves are ready to jump out ya' body," he said. *Damn, his intuition is on 10!*

"I'm just thinking about the last time I was here. That's all," I said, wanting to give him some type of answer.

"Are you sure that's all?" he asked, turning his head to look at me. "I've done all I could in my lifetime, and my days are running short. So, if there's anything you want to know ask me now; tomorrow may be too late." Now I *definitely* didn't know what to say. My father came out on to the porch with a small plate that had pudding, and sliced fruit on it.

He tried to get granddad to eat some of it, but he'd only accepted a few bites. I saw the frustration on my father's face at his refusal of food.

The three of us sat on the porch for what seemed like hours without more than two words between us. I began to feel tired and hungry from my commute, and I figured it was time for me to get something to eat and go to my hotel. My father wheeled granddad back in his room and got him ready for bed. I sat with him for a few more minutes before telling him I'd see him in the morning. Before I left the room, Granddad told my father that he needed to see Charlie before the end of the night.

I didn't know who Charlie was, but he was very adamant about not going to sleep until Charlie came.

My father walked me to the front door. "Julian, you know you can stay here. There's plenty of space, and I have a room all made up for you," he said. He saw the hesitation on my face. "Listen, the night nurse will be here in a few hours to take care of Pop, so you and I can have a chance to talk. Go shower, rest, and when you come back down, we can eat," he offered.

I couldn't find a reason to turn down his offer other than me being stubborn. Besides, being here *did* feel like home.
"Okay, I can do that," I said. He smiled.

"It's upstairs and to the right. You'll find everything else you need in the bathroom," he said.

"Alright, let me go get my bags and cancel my hotel reservation."

Once I was showered and settled into my room, I laid down. I was more exhausted than I thought I was. I found my phone and texted my mother to let her know I'd made it safely and everything was going okay so far. I opened the pictures I'd taken of Layna sleeping, and just stared at them. I texted her too. I've never felt a connection with any woman the way I felt with her, and there was still so much we didn't know about one another. Hitting the brakes with her yesterday by telling her I could only be her friend right now was tough, but I knew moving too fast could be disastrous.

In the past, I would dive into a situation head first ignoring all protocol and being blind to any red flags. I did that because I wanted to *love*, and I believed any issues could be resolved if we truly loved one another. This theory had been proven wrong time and time again. Now, I've finally accepted that loving someone simply isn't enough to maintain a healthy and fulfilling relationship especially if it's one sided.

Pushing those thoughts to the back of my mind, I began to think about the two men downstairs; my father and my granddad. I was surprised by how comfortable I felt since being here. I set my alarm to take a short nap, and I'd be sure to join them back downstairs after I got some rest.

*****

Three hours later, I was waking up to my alarm that I'd hit the snooze button on at least five times already. I was in such a deep sleep that I almost forgot where I was when I woke up. I went to the bathroom, rinsed out my mouth and went back downstairs. I followed my father's voice to the kitchen where he was stirring something on the stove that smelled good as hell. The rumble in my stomach reminded me of how many hours it had been since I'd eaten. A fair-skinned woman with long wavy gray and black streaked hair sat at the table talking to my father. They seemed to be having a lively conversation.

I crept my way into the room. "Hey," I said, bringing their conversation to a holt. They both turned to look at me. The woman stood up and approached me. It was my Aunt Anita. She almost looked the same way I remembered her.

"Oh my goodness! Look at little Ju-Ju!" she greeted, wrapping her arms around me. I smiled and took the childhood nickname in stride.

"You look just like your daddy! It's amazing!" she said, inspecting my face and looking me over. "It's good to see you Aunt Nita," I greeted back.

"You too! I'm so happy you're here! Your cousins will be so excited to see you!"

"They're here?" I asked, excited to see my four cousins; Eric, Marcus, David, and Taryn.

"No, they'll be over tomorrow. They're just as grown as you! They have their own lives and their own families now," she said. *Families? I really had missed a lot.* "Well, I can't wait to see them," I said.

"Julian, if you have a seat, I'll make you a bowl of this Jambalaya with white rice," my father offered.

"That would be great. I'm starving," I said. I sat down at the table with my aunt and she drilled me with so many questions that I felt like she was part of the CIA or something. I understood though, she hadn't seen me in so long, and she wanted to catch up.

My father made us bowls of some of the best-looking Jambalaya over white rice that I'd ever seen. And when I tasted it, I couldn't believe that it was made from scratch. I didn't know my dad could cook like this. After we finished our meals, Aunt Nita went to go sit with Granddad and his night nurse giving me and my father a chance to talk.

It was a perfect night to sit out on the porch, and it was quickly becoming my favorite part of the house. I sat next to my father under the bright light of the moon. It felt so calming.

"Your grandfather is so excited to see you, Julian. He's really happy you're here," he said.

"And what about you? Are you glad I'm here, too?"

He turned to me. "Of course I am. I would like to see you all the time if I could," he answered.

I nodded. "So, what's wrong with Granddad? He doesn't look—" I began, trying to find the right words.

"Like he's dying?" he asked, filling in the blanks.

"Yeah."

"Cancer. He was diagnosed four months ago. We had to beg him to get treatment, and after a few weeks on it, he said he didn't want it anymore. He said he would rather go peacefully instead of being on medicine that made him feel worse. He's a stubborn old man, so once he made up his mind that was it," he explained.

"Wow," I said.

"Hmph. What you see now is a man determined to die the way he chooses to. His appetite is starting to go, he's losing more weight, he's getting weaker and he's sleeping more—so, it probably won't be too much longer now," he added.

"How do you feel about all of this?"

"I'm making my peace with it. Me and Pop, have always had a tough relationship, but I always believed he loved me. You know your grandmother died before you were born. When she was alive, everything was good, everybody was happy. Pop was always hard on me, but Mom always made sure I always felt extra loved to balance out Pop's harshness. She umm… she died the day of my high school graduation. She had been running herself ragged trying to plan the perfect graduation party for me, and the morning of my graduation she was sick in the bed. She tried to get up, but I remember she looked so weak and tired laying there. Pop didn't want to leave her, but she insisted that he went to my graduation to be there for me. I was the first one to graduate, so the whole family was there. He asked our neighbor to check on Mom while we were gone, and when we got back there was an ambulance in the driveway. Long story short, she had a heart attack in her sleep. I believe that's when Pop started to resent me. He's never said it, but I know he felt like she wouldn't have died if he were there with her instead of at my graduation. Maybe he's right. I don't know. But our relationship changed from just being tough, to being more and more distant. Then after a while, it was just easier to stop trying to force things," he explained.

I was in shock. I knew my grandmother died of a heart attack, but I didn't know the story behind it. I saw how torn my father was telling the story, and I felt empathy towards him. I began to understand why him and his dad never seemed to truly get along. I was beginning to understand *him.*

"Is that why you left Georgia? To get away from all of this?" I asked.

He nodded. "I enlisted into the Army and ended up stationed in Fort Bragg after my fourth-year in. That's where I met your mom. I came down here a few times over the years to visit him and Nita, but I could never stay too long," he explained. "When you were born, I tried harder to mend our relationship, but by that time, it was too far gone. But Son, I want to fix *our* relationship. We still have time. And I know I didn't tell you enough while you were growing up, but I love you, Son. And I am so sorry for everything," he said, looking back at me with the same eyes I saw when I looked in the mirror.

I believed his words. I believed he was genuinely sorry and he did want to be a part of my life. I knew we had more work to do beyond this conversation, but this was a necessary starting point.

"I love you too, Dad," I said. He closed his eyes and exhaled. I stopped calling him 'Dad' years ago, I simply didn't address him by any title. He stood and I stood with him and we hugged for several minutes.

Being embraced this way by my father was something I didn't know I needed.

# 15

## Layna

It had been three days since I took the leap to tell Julian how I felt about him. We'd been texting a little bit since he'd been in Georgia, but we hadn't talked. Although he said he only wanted to be friends, the way he kissed me said different. I knew he felt just as strongly I did, but I couldn't blame him for wanting to take his time. I needed to take my time, too, considering what I'd been through in the past. Since Sunday, I'd started my new semester of classes, and Steph told Will she was pregnant. I'd never seen my brother so happy in my life! I knew they would be great parents.

After finishing up a homework assignment, I began to read over one of my half-written novels hoping I'd be inspired to finish it. A call from an unknown number interrupted my reading. It was 7 p.m., so it was too late for me to get a call for any jobs I'd applied for. I hesitated, but I answered.

"Hello?" The person on the other end didn't respond. "Hello?" I said again.

"Layna—" a familiar man's voice said.

"Who is this?"

"I wanted to let you know I filed for divorce," he said.

"Derrick? Why are you doing this?"

"I miss you Layna. I need to see you, baby. I'm in Baltimore right now; just say the word and I'll fly you out tonight. I'll be sure to make this up to you once you're here," he said, ignoring my question. The thought of allowing Derrick entrance into my body again turned my stomach.

"Derrick, Let me make this clear; I don't want you calling me! I don't want to see you! I don't even want to know you exist! Leave me alone!" I said through a strained voice. I ended the call, and blocked his number as quickly as I could before he could call me back. I wasn't afraid of Derrick, I just didn't expect to hear him on the other end of my phone. I began to feel sick to my stomach thinking about all the lies he told me, and all the tears I shed over him. "Bastard!" I said into my empty room. At that moment, I almost had the right mind to call him back just so I could let him know how I really felt about him. But I knew giving him that much of my energy wasn't a good idea.

### *18 Months Earlier. Raleigh, NC*

When I first met Derrick Bennett, it definitely wasn't love at first sight. In fact, I didn't even like him. I was twenty-five, going to school fulltime for the second time, and trying to make a little money by working at a coffee shop on campus. I was good at talking with the customers, but I was horrible with making the drinks. My manager liked me, so I was tasked with taking the orders and getting them to the right customers. If it wasn't busy, I would help out and make the simple drinks I knew how to make.

Derrick came in one day wearing a dark blue suit and a light gray tie. He had earbuds in his ears, having a conversation with someone. I hadn't seen him before but I immediately noticed how handsome and well put together he was. He was tall with bronzed skin, strong looking hands, and chiseled features. I could tell he was older than me, but he was a welcome dose of eye-candy for sure. I didn't know if he was faculty or just visiting the campus on business. He came up to the counter, still holding a conversation with the person on the other end which was one of my biggest pet peeves: if you're still having another conversation, then wait to place your order. He specifically asked me for a large coffee with two French vanilla creamers and four packets of sugar. Since it wasn't busy, I took his order and made his drink. All the while, he was still on the phone having what didn't seem to be a very important conversation, from what I could tell. I handed him his coffee, he nodded and walked away.

Five minutes later he came back up to the counter and placed the cup down on the counter and just stared at me. "Can I help you?" I asked.

To which he replied, "I asked for Hazelnut. I don't know what this is," he said, pushing the cup in my direction.

"Sir, you asked for French vanilla, and that's what I gave you," I responded.

"I know what I asked for, and it wasn't this," he said, with a little too much bass in his voice for my liking. I took a deep breath to stop myself from snapping back at him. The job didn't pay much, but it was my only source of income at the time. Also, I'd had classes that morning, schoolwork to do that night, and another 45 minutes in my shift. I was too tired to deal with his mess.

"Okay. I'll make you a new one," I said, and busied myself making him a new cup while he scrolled on his phone. I didn't hide the fact that I was irritated with him either. I placed the coffee in front of him and didn't offer him any words.

He looked at me, picked up the coffee and smelled it. "Yeah, this is what I asked for the first time," he said with a smirk, and he began to walk away. His words were like a key that unlocked my mouth.

"I believe the words you're looking for are thank you!" I said nicely, but with a sarcastic undertone. "Excuse me?" he said, with furrowed eyebrows.

"It's called having manners. Just because I'm on this side of the counter doesn't mean you get to be rude, or inconsiderate. I fixed *your* mistake; a mistake *you* made because you were too busy paying attention to your phone call instead of placing your order." I was so thankful my manager was in the office during my little outburst. He looked shocked and amused at the same time. He looked somewhat important, so I'm sure he wasn't used to people talking to him the way I did. I didn't care though.

He tapped a few buttons on his phone to place a call, put the call on speaker, and placed the phone down on the counter. "Derrick? Did you forget something?" a man's voice answered.

"No, I didn't. Quick question John, a few minutes ago did you hear me order my coffee?" he asked.

"Uhhh… yeah. Why what's up?" the man asked.

"Can you tell me exactly what I ordered? I'm just trying to clear something up," he said, looking up at me. I was focused on the phone, cause now I was questioning whether or not I'd heard him right.

"Okay," the man chuckled. "You ordered a large coffee with two French vanilla creamers and four sugars," he said. Derrick looked at the phone as if he wanted it to disappear. "Alright thanks. I'll talk to you soon," Derrick said, before ending the call. He put his phone in his pocket and we just stared at one another. I assumed from his embarrassment I wasn't going to get an apology, but I was more than content just being right.

"You have a goodnight, Sir," I said, before walking away. He cleared his throat, and without a word, he left.


The next day he came back. He wasn't on his phone this time, and he greeted me by name by looking at my name tag. He ordered his drink, and this time one of my co-workers made it for him. I told him to have a goodnight, but he had a seat and lingered around. He had his laptop open, so I assumed he was working. When I was leaving to go home, he caught up with me once I got outside. He gave me a sincere apology for being rude the day before and coupled it with a smile I couldn't refuse. We exchanged numbers and began to communicate almost daily. Even though he was ten years older than me, he didn't make me feel like I was too young for him. He worked as a marketing consultant and lived about forty minutes outside of Raleigh. He traveled a lot for his work, and he would always call me anytime he went out of town.


After about two months of talking and video chatting he told me he loved me. At that point, I wasn't in love with him but I was definitely falling quickly. He flew me out to Cleveland for the weekend where he was attending a seminar. I was a little shy about sleeping with him, because I knew things would change once I did. I learned very quickly just how much sexual maturity increases pleasure in the bedroom. He made me feel things I'd never experienced dealing with men my age, and cemented his sentiments of love. He completely owned my body that weekend, and I was drunk on lust for him. Our communication and meet-ups increased whenever he was in town. At the time, I was living with my parents, and I knew they would have objected to me seeing someone so much older than me, so I didn't tell them much about him. We had a mutual agreement that we were in an exclusive relationship.

Things were good, but I always felt like something was missing.

I'd only been to his place a few times when he was in town, he had a small one-bedroom condo that barely looked lived in, but I attributed that to him being out of town so much. We mostly spent our time laying up in expensive hotels out of town and ordering room service which his clients paid for. With my busy school and work schedule, and his traveling, things seemed okay on the surface. Looking back on it, I could see how my inexperience allowed me to believe whatever excuse he gave me to keep me from learning too much about his personal life. He answered almost every time I called or text, so it was hard for me to believe he was hiding anything.

One day after we'd spent the day in an expensive suite having what I still labeled the best sex I'd ever had; he went to shower. He'd mistakenly left his phone out on the nightstand, which he'd never done. He had a lock on his phone, but I saw that he had an appointment in an hour at a restaurant with someone named Shelby on his locked screen. He had a lot of business meetings for his job, so I didn't find it strange. However, my gut told me I needed to see who Shelby was. I took note of the name of the restaurant and I remained neutral once he emerged from the bathroom to get dressed. He told me he had to get going, but he would call me later. I was still naked under the sheets when he looked at the time and asked me to lay back and spread my legs for him. He spent the next ten minutes ensuring the only person I'd ever want to put their lips on me was him. After he washed his face and brushed his teeth again, he got dressed in a hurry to leave.

I'm sure he hadn't made it to his car before I was in the shower. I was dressed in record time and I drove to the restaurant even faster. The whole ride over, I had to convince myself that he wasn't hiding anything from me and I was just being paranoid. I was sure to park far away from his car. I assumed he was already inside until I saw a woman walk up to his driver's side door. He got out, hugged her, and kissed her with the same amount of passion he'd been kissing me with for the last six months. I felt like my breathing stopped. My heart dropped down to my stomach and I didn't make a sound because my body couldn't decide between screaming and crying. At this point I loved this man, and he'd been playing me. I watched as they walked hand in hand into the restaurant. That's when my tears started to flow. After about ten minutes, my tears turned to rage. I didn't want to be one of those crazed women I laughed at online, but now I certainly was able to rationalize what I once considered irrational behavior. I went into the restaurant and into the bathroom undetected. I called Derrick, and of course he didn't answer. So, then I texted him:

*Me: I know you're at Brixton's. I need to see you now. I'm five minutes away.*

Two minutes later, I peeked out the restroom and saw him walking outside. I looked down to see him calling me. I ignored him. I took that moment to walk over to the table where the woman was still seated.

I pretended as if I was walking by, and said, "Excuse me, the gentleman that was just here—he does marketing? His name is Derrick, right?" I asked with a smile I hoped looked innocent enough.

She looked at me cautiously, but then she smiled. "Yes, Derrick Bennett. My husband," she said, still holding on to that same smile. I did my best to hold on to my fake smile when I noticed the diamond ring on her finger. I swallowed hard.

"I thought that was him. I'm actually on my way out, but tell him that Layna says hi," I said, as sweetly as I could while I felt my heart melt into my stomach.

"I will," she said, before eyeing me with a suspicious look.

"Have a goodnight," I said, and nearly sprinted towards the exit. I saw Derrick outside looking panicked. I hadn't thought about how I was going to leave without him seeing me, but I said screw it. He and I were done anyway. I quickly brushed by him, trying to make it to my car. "Layna! What the hell are you doing here?" he asked.

"I just met your wife! Really nice lady," I said, and stared at him. His eyes stretched open and he didn't say a word. "That's what I thought," I said, and continued to walk to my car.

"Layna! Layna! Stop! Please let me explain!" he called out to my back, but I kept walking. He reached me as soon as I got to my car, and stopped me from opening the door. "Move!" I yelled.

"Layna, I was going to tell you when the time was right. I'm only here to let her know I want a divorce! I love you! You know that! And I want to be with you!" he said. Now, I was enraged. Without thinking twice, I slapped him across his face so hard that my hand was burning. He grabbed me by my arms and held me still.

"Are you crazy?! Calm yourself down!" he yelled at me.

"Let me go!" I yelled, as I squirmed; but he was too strong and I couldn't get free. "Derrick!" his wife's voice called from across the parking lot as she approached us.

"Shit!" he said, as he let me go and began to walk towards her. I took that opportunity to get in my car and leave.

From what I could figure, he'd told his wife that I was a crazed college student he'd met that had become obsessed with him. He said I was stalking him, that's how I knew where he was. And she believed him—I mean, he was a professional liar after all. Anyway, she did her best to make my life a living hell. She tried to have me arrested, fired from my job and even tried to get me kicked out of school with her claims. Everyone knew about it, and I was labeled a woman who sleeps with married men. When the pressure got too much for me to handle, I had to tell my parents what was going on which happened to be the same weekend Will and Steph were visiting. That's when I begged them to let me come and live with them after the semester was over. My family was so upset with me, but Steph was the only one who showed me any type of empathy.

Derrick called me a few times when he was out of town, but after the third time of me asking him to stop, I blocked him. I decided to get a new number altogether. I had a lot of sleepless, tear-filled nights over Derrick. But one thing I knew for sure was he would never see me again if I could help it.

***Now...***

My phone rang again, and my anger soared through the roof. Assuming it was Derrick calling me again from a different number, I barely looked at the screen before answering it. This time I was ready to tell him exactly what I thought about him and his lying, cheating ass.

"Hello?!" I yelled into the phone.

There was silence for a moment then I heard an unsure voice say, "Layna?" It's Julian. Did I call at a bad time?" he asked cautiously.

I blew out a breath and relaxed my nerves before speaking. "You're fine. I just—I just thought you were someone else. I'm sorry," I said. I was slightly embarrassed. This was the first time Julian called me, and this was the second time I made a less than friendly first impression on him.

"Well, I'm glad I'm not whoever you thought I was! I thought I had the wrong number!" he chuckled. "It's all good though. Are you okay?" he asked.

"Yeah. I'm just finishing up some homework, then I'm going to get something to eat. How's your granddad doing?" I asked, to move the conversation away from my bothersome thoughts about Derrick.

He sighed heavily. "He's a fighter for sure. His mind is so sharp.

I've been sitting with him for hours and talking to him whenever he's awake; but he's getting weaker, so my family called for Hospice care today. I can't believe I wasted so much time not seeing him because of family drama. It wasn't worth it. That's part of the reason I'm calling you," he said, taking another heavy sigh.

"Okay—" I responded.

"When I get back to Charlotte, I wanted to know if you would like to hang out? We can do whatever you want. I just want to be around you. I know I said I needed time, and I do, but I don't want to waste any time either. Being here is showing me just how precious time is," he said.

"Yeah. I would like to hang out with you," I said, and I'm certain he heard my smile through my voice.

"Alright, good," he replied.


My whole face warmed listening to his words. I didn't expect for him to have a change of heart so quickly, but I was glad he did. Instead of spending the rest of my night thinking about Derrick, I was able to spend part of my night talking to Julian. We talked about school, our shared love for writing, and whatever other random conversation came up. I was surprised to find out that Julian had three college degrees in communications, but chose to work as a security guard for an investment company. He didn't expand on why he chose not to build a career in writing and communications, and that was very odd to me. I was also surprised to learn that not only did he not owe any student loans for his education because his father paid for his schooling, but he also owned the house he lived in. I told him that I hoped he knew how fortunate he was to have a father that would take care of him that way, but he didn't reply. I told him more about my upbringing and how being the 'baby' of the family worked for me and against me as I've gotten older. Neither one of us decided to bring up past relationships, which I was thankful for. I didn't want to talk about anyone from my past, and I got the feeling that he didn't either.

*****

The next night, Will, Steph and I had a rare moment during the week when we were all home together. Steph made a crockpot chicken and mushroom dish for dinner, and I made the sides. We were all enjoying the meal at the dining room table, while catching up.

"So how have you been feeling working overnight now that you're pregnant?" I asked Steph.

She smiled and rubbed her stomach. Will smiled too. "So far it's fine. I do get a little more tired around two or three in the morning, but I'm okay."

I nodded. "I just know you're going to have a girl! I can feel it!" I said, causing Will to roll his eyes. I knew more than anything he wanted a son, especially after being in this house with two women who sometimes gave him a hard time. He wanted to even out the playing field.

"How's school and work going? Any callbacks for the jobs you applied for?" Will asked.

"School is alright. I'm on target to graduate next Spring semester—and I've gotten some correspondence for a few jobs. I'm definitely working on it," I answered, taking a large forkful of my food.

"That's good. It's like I told you, make a plan and start knocking down your goals one by one," he said with a smile. I nodded, just as my phone buzzed on the table next to my plate. I looked down to see it was

Julian who'd just text me:

*Julian: I hope your day is going well. I'm just sitting here with my dad and my grandfather. Can I call you later tonight?*

I didn't know I was smiling until Steph said, "Who's got you over there smiling like that?"

I looked over to Will whose expression wasn't as light anymore, then I looked back to Stephanie.

"It's… Julian. We've been talking a little bit since he's been in Georgia. I've been checking in on how his grandfather's been doing," I said. Both Steph and I looked to Will who continued eating as if he didn't have a care in the world. "So, how's his grandfather doing?" Steph asked.

"Not well. They called Hospice yesterday," I said. Still no words from Will.

"Well tell him that our thoughts and prayers are with him and his family," Steph said.

Will picked up a napkin and wiped his mouth, still offering nothing to the conversation. Will's presence reminded me so much of my father at times; his presence said so much without saying a word. "Will?" I said.

He turned to me. "What do you want me to say, Layna? I already told you how I feel about you dealing with him, and he knows how I feel about it, too. As long as he doesn't do anything stupid with you, me and him are cool," he said, casually.

"Okay," was all I offered, because I didn't want to get into another argument with him about it.

"I do have a question though, what's going on with you and your friend Jamal? I like him. He seems stable. He has a good career going for him, he seems polite, and I can tell he really likes you," Will said.  Stephanie rubbed her forehead and continued to eat. She could gauge when it was okay to step in between me and Will and when to leave our sibling relationship to us.

"There's nothing going on with us. We're just friends. Nothing more," I answered.

"All I'm saying is maybe you shouldn't be so quick to put him in the friend zone. Sometimes it's the dudes you ignore that end up having the most to offer. Just think about it," he said. I nodded in response, but to me there was nothing to think about. Jamal didn't make me feel like Julian did.

# 16

## Julian

*Macon, Georgia*

I woke up early Friday morning to the smell of bacon and fresh coffee.

My dad had been cooking every meal for me since I'd arrived on Monday, and he had no complaints from me. I made sure to call and check in on Mom a couple times a day, too. She told me not to worry about her, and to spend more time with my family. It did feel good to be surrounded by so much family and to feel so much love within

Granddad's house. My reunion with my cousins was much better than I had hoped for. Seeing them, meeting their children and their spouses gave me a type of joy that was foreign to me. I was so happy their lives were going well. I was spending every night talking for hours with my dad once the night nurse came, and if I had energy, I would call Layna too.


This particular night felt different. The air around us felt more calm than usual and the moon shone brighter than it had previous nights. Dad read a book while he and I sat in the room with Granddad, and now, he did have a couple monitors hooked up to him. He had been sleeping the majority of the day, and when he was awake, he didn't speak much. I had a feeling he would not wake come morning. I watched intently as his chest rose and fell. I knew there was nothing anyone could do for him at this point, but I couldn't stop watching him. I held is hand. My dad remained quiet, he seemed very accepting of the man who had raised him being at peace.

Breaking the silence, Dad asked, "Who's the young lady you stay up talking to all hours of the night?" I looked over to him and he had a half of a smile. Dad and I had been getting along so well, that I didn't feel any resistance answering his question.

"Her name is Layna and I met her at one of the poetry nights I go to. She's a sister of one of my friends," I answered.

"So, she's a creative person like you? How's that been going?" he asked.

"We're just starting to talk, and she agreed to hang out with me when I get back home."

"Okay," he said, nodding his head proudly. "What do you like about her? I mean, what makes her special?" he asked.

"Everything," I chuckled. "The first time I saw her, I felt an immediate connection. But… I don't know. I'm just not good at relationships and I don't want to mess things up with her," I replied.

"Why do you feel you would mess things up?"

"I just… either move too fast or I move too slow. I want to move at the right pace this time. Before I came here, I told her I needed time to handle a few things in my life before I could pursue anything with her. Now being here, and seeing first-hand how precious time is, I don't want to waste any time I could be spending getting to know her," I answered.

"Julian, the only way you will know if things will go right with this woman is if you actually allow yourself to be with her.

And if you're afraid you're going to mess things up, then don't mess things up. Everything you do is a choice, and it sounds like you made enough wrong choices to know the right ones to make now," he said.

"Thanks, Dad." I didn't have anything more to add after his advice. This was the first time I'd allowed him to offer me any guidance as an adult, and what he said was actually helpful. I thought back to my mom telling me that I *did* need my father in my life. Seeing him in this light; vulnerable, open, and taking care of his ailing father, made me see now how right she was.

Another hour later, we were still sitting with Granddad while the nurse sat in the corner and checked his vitals like clockwork. I was still holding tight to his hand. When I went to remove my hand from his because I needed to go to the restroom, he squeezed my hand tightly.

"Granddad, are you okay?" I asked, prompting my father to stand, and the nurse to come over to him. He was still holding tight to my hand.

"I'm going to get Nita," Dad announced and hurried out of the room. My Aunt Anita was asleep in the living room. She'd come over once she was informed of Granddad's worsening condition. The nurse held on to his wrist checking his pulse. She looked over to me and shook her head, and I knew what that meant. He managed to open his eyes a little, and I was directly in front of him. Tears I didn't know I had begun falling. I wiped my face and gently leaned over onto his chest. I heard my dad and Aunt Anita hurry back into the room.

"I love you Granddad," I whispered in his ear.

"Never stop loving," his voice strained in my ear. His grip on my hand began to loosen and I stepped back so his two children could spend his final moments with him. My Aunt Anita was crying almost inconsolably, while my dad comforted her. My dad remained stoic, only flicking a few tears from his eyes. I stood back and watched my grandfather die peacefully with his two children by his side. It had to be the most gut wrenching, and emotional experience I'd ever had. It was also liberating in a way to know he was no longer suffering, and he left the way he wanted to.


By the time we were all able to get to bed, it was close to 3 a.m. The house felt so empty without Granddad no longer here. As tired as I was, I couldn't sleep, and I'm sure my father and my aunt where still awake too. For the first time in hours, I checked my phone. I saw Layna had texted me, checking up on my Granddad, but that was hours ago. I texted her back:

*Me: He died peacefully a few hours ago*

A minute later my phone rang; it was Layna.
"Hey. I didn't mean to wake you," I
answered.

"It's okay. I was having trouble sleeping. I'm sorry about your grandfather. How are you feeling?" she asked, and she sounded so tired.

"I'm okay, right now. I just…uh," I began to answer and felt a lump in my throat. A mental picture of me as a kid with my Granddad, followed by the image of him being wheeled out in a black body bag an hour ago flashed in my mind. My voice began to shake, and tears blurred my eyes. I inhaled and exhaled deeply. "I'm sorry. I just wish I had more time with him," I continued, clearing my throat. Layna was quiet for several moments. I'm sure she didn't know what to say, and I didn't want my emotions to betray me again, so I remained quiet too.

"I understand. You don't have to apologize. When is his service?" she asked, quietly breaking through the silence.

"It's tomorrow. Sunday afternoon. My dad spent the last couple hours making calls to ensure everything is in place. Granddad had everything pre-arranged. He said Granddad wanted to be buried as quickly as possible," I answered.

"I can come to the funeral if you want. I can drive down this afternoon and be there," she offered. I didn't know how to respond. Her generous offer caught me off guard, and caused even more tears to form in my eyes. Of course I wanted to see her, but I couldn't believe she'd be willing to drive down here just to support me and my family.

"I really appreciate that, but you don't have to do that Layna. I'll be alright. It's a long drive, and—"

"I want to do it. Send me the address and I'll be there," she interrupted. I didn't know what I was feeling, but I agreed to send her the address and we ended our call shortly after.

The next morning was full of friends and family swarming the house giving their condolences and sharing their fond memories about Granddad. If felt so bittersweet. My aunt seemed to be in a better space, and my dad remained all business as he still was making the final arrangements for the service tomorrow. Since I'd been here, I hadn't gone further than the grocery store or the pharmacy to pick up a few personal items. My dad hadn't really left the house in weeks. Once everyone had gone home, I suggested to Dad that we take a ride, just for a change of scenery. He agreed. He drove me to a lake about 15 minutes from the house. It didn't look familiar at first, but then I remembered this was where Granddad had taken me a few times to go fishing with him. We got out and walked silently to the edge of the water before sitting on the ground. We didn't talk, we just sat.

"You'll never understand how truly sorry I am for not being a part of your life for all these years, Julian. I'm so happy you're here now," Dad said, almost at a whisper.

"Me too, Dad."


Back at the house, my father went to lay down to rest. I wasn't sure he'd even slept since last night. I was holding up okay. I had a few moments where I needed to allow my tears to flow, but I was good. I told Dad that Layna was coming down to the funeral, and she would be arriving sometime tonight. That seemed to be the only thing that made him look a little content all day. The last time I checked in with her, she was less than an hour away. She booked a hotel, but I told her she could stay at the house if she wanted to. I didn't want to put too much pressure on her though; it was enough that she was driving all this way to begin with. I was nervous and excited to see her.


It was a little after 4 p.m. when Layna's car pulled into the driveway. I was sitting on the porch with my cousin Taryn, catching up with her. My heartbeat instantly accelerated. I honestly couldn't believe she was here. I stood.

"So that's your girl?" Taryn asked, as Layna seemed to be gathering her things in the car. "She's my friend," I answered.

"Friend? If she drove all this way to be with you, she's your girl!" Taryn said, with a smile. I left the porch to meet Layna at her car. It was so good to see her face. I opened the car door for her and helped her out. I hugged her and kissed her on the cheek. She had on sunglasses, dark blue sweatpants, and a white short sleeved cropped shirt that gave me a glimpse of her toned stomach, Her hair was pulled back into a ponytail, and even after all the hours she'd just spent in her car, she still smelled good.

"Thank you for coming," I said, smiling down at her. I could never get used to how good she felt in my arms.

"You're welcome. How are you feeling?" she asked, still holding her arms around my waist.

"Better," I answered, at the risk of sounding corny. I didn't care. Her being here *did* make me feel better.

"Good! Now, I need to use your bathroom!" she said, like she was embarrassed.

I chuckled, "Come on. I'll show you."


"This house is beautiful!" Layna said, as I showed her around downstairs. I kept my eyes on her. I still couldn't believe she came all this way for me.

"I thought this house was a mansion when I was a kid," I chuckled.

She saw the picture of me, Dad, and Granddad that I'd seen on my first day here.

"Which one is your Granddad?" she asked, examining the photo.

"That's him here, that's my dad, and that's me," I said, pointing everyone out.

She leaned in closer, "That's you?! You were so cute! And your father and your grandfather are very handsome, too. I see where you get your looks from," she said, grinning at me. I felt my cheeks warm, and I quickly became embarrassed when I realized I was blushing.

"Thanks," I said, before leading her into the living room. "You can have a seat. I'm sure you're tired from that drive.

Just as we sat down, Taryn came back into the house from the porch. "I'm going to go pick up Granddaddy's programs for the service tomorrow, and bring them over to the church," she said.

Layna stood. "I'm Layna. I'm sorry I didn't get a chance to introduce myself earlier, my bladder was getting ready to explode!" she chuckled.

"That's okay, girl. I understand. I'm Taryn, Ju-Ju's younger cousin," she introduced. I grimaced at the nickname she refused to let go.

"Ju-Ju?" Layna repeated, looking as if she wanted to laugh as she turned to look at me.

I shook my head. "Don't even think about calling me that. She's barely getting away with it," I said, giving Taryn a salty look. Both Taryn and Layna laughed.

"Well. I gotta get going. After I leave the church, I need to make sure my husband has the right clothes picked out for tomorrow. I'll be back over tonight with Momma and my brothers," Taryn said.

"Nice to meet you," Layna said. Taryn nodded and left. Layna sat back down on the couch next to me.

"I need to let Will and Steph know I made it here," she said, pulling her phone from her pocket. She made a strange face when she looked at her phone, but quickly changed her expression. "You good?" I asked.

"Yeah, it's just an unknown number called me. No big deal," she said. She seemed uncomfortable by whatever it was she saw on her phone, but I thought better of asking any more questions.

"Are you hungry? Do you need anything?" I asked, while I tried my best not to grab her and cradle her in my arms. Her being here with me only intensified my attraction to her.

"I just want to rest for a second," she answered, through a sigh. "Okay," I got up and grabbed a blanket for her so she could get more comfortable, and turned on the TV. Ten minutes later, she was sleep. I looked at her and only wished I could fall asleep as quickly as she seems to.


I decided to get up and check on Dad, and to find something to snack on. My family and Granddad's friends would be bringing food over later tonight for the repast. I knocked on the door to check on my father. He didn't answer and when I looked in on him, he was knocked

out. I didn't want to wake him, because I'm sure he needed all his rest for tomorrow.

# 17

## Layna

After talking to Julian early this morning and hearing how sad he sounded, I wanted to be there for him. Although we still didn't know one another well, I didn't think twice about offering to drive down to support him. When I told Will and Steph I was going, they were both surprised, but they told me to be safe and to give Julian and his family their condolences. Their reaction made me think maybe I was doing too much. Maybe me offering to take this five-hour drive to a town I'd never been in, to attend a funeral for a man I didn't know made me look desperate for his attention. Or maybe it made me look too clingy.

Once I was in hour three of my drive, I began to wonder what the hell I was doing. I began to get anxious, and I wanted to turn around and go back home, but it was too late for me to turn back. I only hoped my initial intentions of wanting to support him is what came through to him and his family.

I woke up on the couch to the sound of laughter, music, and the smell of something delicious cooking. I also heard the faint sounds of kids playing outside. My stomach rumbled. I looked at the time to see it

was close to 7 o'clock. I couldn't believe I'd slept like that. I also saw I had two more missed calls from an unknown number to accompany the one I ignored earlier. This time there was a voicemail. I knew it was Derrick calling me, but I would just have to ignore it for now.

I got up and went to the bathroom to freshen up. I didn't want to meet anyone in Julian's family looking like I'd just woken up. I slowly walked into the kitchen where all of the chatter came to a holt; everyone's eyes were on me.

"Hi," I said, nervously. I immediately recognized Julian's dad at the stove, because they looked almost like twins. Everyone else was either sitting at the island or around the huge kitchen table. Julian stood up and walked over to me.

"Everybody, this is my friend Layna. She came down for

Granddad's funeral. Layna, this is my Aunt Anita, my cousins, Eric, David and Mark; their wives; my dad Julius, his cousins Pete and Elvin, and you met Taryn earlier," he introduced.

"Nice to meet everyone," I said, feeling nervous as hell. I'm not shy, but I didn't know what to say. I wasn't sure what he'd already told everyone about me. Everyone spoke back.

"Okay Nephew! Okay! It looks like you got yourself a fine little hen in the hen house! You can make *Brooks* some real pretty grandbabies with her!" his second cousin, Pete remarked.

"Ain't she pretty?" his Aunt Anita added

"I told you, Momma," Taryn said. I was thoroughly embarrassed and didn't say a word. I just smiled.

"Come sit down," Julian said, shaking his head and leading me to the stool he'd just vacated. He stood by my side. Everyone returned to their own separate conversations.

"We really appreciate you coming down for my father's funeral. As you can see, he had a lot of people who loved him," Julian's dad, Mr. Brooks, said. He looked at me with those same eyes Julian has. There was no question in my mind that Mr. Brooks had his pick of women back in the day. Hell, I'm sure he still had his pick right now! He could definitely be a member of the *Silver Fox* crew online. Julian and his father were just too attractive to ignore. His aunt and his cousin Taryn were beautiful, and the other men who occupied the room were easy on the eyes, too.

"Thank you, Mr. Brooks. I appreciate you having me," I said.

Although Mr. Brooks was talking, I felt Julian's eyes on me. His father smirked and turned his attention back to the stove.

"Are you hungry?" Julian asked.

I nodded. "I can eat before I head over to the hotel," I said.

"I told you you're welcome to stay here. There's plenty of space. You can have your own room. No one will bother you," he said. I looked around the noisy room skeptically.

"Everyone's going home tonight. It will just be me, you, and my dad here," he said.

"Okay. If it's not too much trouble," I said.

"It's not," he replied, looking down at me so intently, I thought I could get pregnant from that look alone.

"Son, why don't you get her bags and make the room up for her. By the time you're done, dinner will be ready," Mr. Brooks said, with a huge smile. It was obvious that he'd been watching me and Julian's interaction. Being here with Julian and his family felt nice and seeing him in this light was refreshing. He wasn't as arrogant as I initially thought he was. He was kind and caring, and I liked it.

"Good idea," Julian answered. "Layna, where's your car keys?" he asked. "They're in my purse on the couch. I'll get them," I said, and began to get up.

"No, I got it. If you don't mind me looking in your bag," he said.

"No, it's cool. There's nothing in there anyway."

"Okay, I'll be back in a few," he said, disappearing from the kitchen.


After dinner Julian's family began to leave one by one. They were such a loving bunch and his cousins' children were adorable, a little rowdy, but adorable. I'd spent time with Julian and his father in the living room, while he told embarrassing stories of little Julian. I nearly passed out from laughing when he told me the story of how Julian took his bottle of cologne to school and poured half of it on himself to impress a girl when he was in the first grade. After a while, Mr. Brooks called it a night leaving me and Julian alone in the living room. I'd had an eventful day, and even though I had a power nap, I was ready to call it a night, too. The funeral was tomorrow at 10 a.m., and I was going back home first thing Monday morning.


"I think I'm going to call it a night, too," I said, standing from the couch. "I need a hot shower and a warm bed, and I'll be good."

"Okay, I should probably call it a night, too. I'll walk you upstairs," he said. He showed me to my room, which was a nice size for a guest room, and where the bathroom was so I could shower.

After I showered and got comfortable in bed, I decided to listen to the voicemail the unknown number had left me:

*"Layna, this is Derrick. I know I'm the last person you want to hear from, but I just wanted to let you know how incredibly sorry I*

*am for how things went down. I owed you more than that. I miss you so much that it hurts. I know you're in Charlotte, and I'll be there all next week on a job. I want to see you, Layna. I love you. Please call me.*

I sighed after listening to his message. I didn't know how he got any information about me. However, I was sure he knew where I went to school, and he probably knew where I lived. I had to handle this situation when I got back home. About 20 minutes later there was a knock at the door.

"Come in," I answered. A shirtless and delicious looking Julian made his way into my room and stood at the foot of the bed. The only other piece of clothing he seemed to be wearing was a durag. My heart pounded. What the hell was he doing? And where was his shirt? And why was he so damn fine? And who knew his body looked like that under those clothes? I thought. My face warmed and I hope my expression didn't allude to everything I was thinking.

"I just showered, and I wanted to say goodnight. I'll wake you in the morning," he said. He must have seen me staring at his body because quite frankly, I couldn't stop.

He smiled at me. "I'm not being funny, this is just how I sleep," he said.

"Oh! Yeah… that's cool. Okay, goodnight," I stammered like a schoolgirl with a crush. It was at this moment I realized that staying here was probably a mistake. The way his body looked coupled with the way he was looking at me, would make it hard for me to sleep through the night. I had to stop thinking like that, though.

He then sat on the edge of the bed. "It really means a lot that you're here. I know I keep saying it, but I mean it."

"You're welcome. I *wanted* to be here for you," I said, catching his eyes studying me. We shared a brief awkward silence. "Besides," I added, "I'm glad to see you in this light. You're not the conceited, shallow, egocentric person I initially thought you were!" I teased.

He laughed, "Ouch! Well, you're not as rude as I initially thought you were, but you're still just as beautiful," he complimented. There was another awkward silence as we shamelessly stared at one another.

He broke our silence first, "I'll see you in the morning. My room is the second door on the right if you need anything before then," he offered.

"Okay."

He stood, leaned over and kissed my cheek. Admittedly, I was disappointed his kiss didn't land on my lips. "Goodnight Layna," he said softly.

"Goodnight."


I tossed and turned for a little while before I fell asleep. At exactly 2:37 a.m., the door to my room opened and closed softly. A few moments later, I felt Julian's warm body lying next to me. He placed his arm over my waist and kissed my shoulder. I don't know if he thought I was sleep, because he didn't say a word. I didn't know if I should say anything to him either. So, I allowed myself to go back to sleep.

The next morning when I woke up, Julian was gone. I didn't know which part of the morning he'd slipped out, and now I was questioning whether or not he was there at all. I rolled over and smelled the pillow next to me. *Yeah, he was here.* Me, Julian, and Mr. Brooks got dressed and ate breakfast in silence. Mr. Brooks seemed like he hadn't slept well at all, but that didn't stop him from asking me how I slept. I told him I slept like a baby, and thanked him again for his hospitality. Some family arrived shortly after breakfast and we all rode together to the church.

Ishmael Ervin Brooks, Julian's grandfather, was clearly loved by many. The turnout for his service was unlike anything I'd seen before. There were several people standing in the back of the church because there was no more room to sit. I felt awkward sitting up front with the family, but that's where Julian wanted me to be; right next to him. No one in his family seemed to mind. What made the service so beautiful was it was a celebration of his life, instead of a reminder of his death.

Several people went to the front of the room to share their memories and funny encounters with him. The only time I thought Julian was going to breakdown was when Mr. Brooks went to say a few words about his dad, and almost wasn't able to finish because he started to cry. His Aunt Anita went to comfort her older brother, and helped him through his tribute. By the time the service was nearing the end, everyone seemed joyous instead of sad. What started with tears, ended with laughter. I was surprised that Julian held onto my hand almost the entire time. I let him hold onto me as long as he needed to.

# 18

## Julian

Last night, knowing Layna was sleeping under the same roof as me wouldn't allow me to close my eyes for more than a few minutes at a time. I wanted to be next to her, but I didn't know how to approach that situation. She was not my girl, we were not dating, and I didn't want to make her feel uncomfortable. I didn't want to jump the gun, but I had to be next to her. I figured she'd tell me to leave if she didn't want me there. So, I left my room and slid into hers. She slept like a rock, so she didn't move much when I got in bed with her. Lying next to her felt so good. I held her and fell asleep as if she was the cure for my insomnia. When I awakened, the sun was getting ready to rise and she was nestled against me. At that point, I knew she'd waken up at some point and realized I was in bed with her. I got out of the bed and went back into my room.

The service for Granddad was emotional and beautiful. I was glad to know he had a long, well-lived life. I cried a few times, and Layna did her best to comfort me; rubbing my back, wiping my tears, and holding my hand. I was so glad she was there. Back at the house, the repast looked more like a block party. There were so many people who came to celebrate the life of Ishmael Ervin Brooks. Layna looked as if she was having a good time, too. I'm not sure whose baby she was holding, but she looked content doing it. By 5 p.m., everyone had left the house, and thankfully, my cousins helped me clean up before they left. Layna had gone to her room to take a nap.

Dad and I sat out on the porch. We still wore our black slacks, and black button-down shirts with the sleeves rolled up. We sat silent for several minutes before we began to talk. "Do you think Granddad would have liked his service?" I asked.

Dad smiled. "Yeah, but I'm sure he would have found something to fuss about. *'Brooks, I told you not to do all that damn crying in my face!'*" he said, imitating my grandfather which made both of us laugh.

"But he's not in pain anymore, and I'm glad about that."
"Me too," I replied.

"So, Miss Layna. She's a beautiful young lady, I can see why you like her. What's going on with you two?" he asked, still smiling.

"We're just—friends. That's all, Dad," I answered.

He scoffed. "Friends, huh? Julian, you're not just her friend. I see the way you look at her. I've watched how you've been taking care of her. If she's out of your sight for more than five minutes, you're trying to find her. She drove from Charlotte just to be by your side. She really cares about you. You're not just a friend to her either," he said.

I couldn't dispute his claims, but I still didn't know the right move to make. "So, what do I do?" I asked.

"If you really care about her then think with this," he said, tapping his temple, "before you think with this," he said, placing his hand over his chest.

I thought his advice was solid, and it gave me something to think about.

"So, when you and Mom were married—I guess you weren't thinking with—either?" I asked.

He sighed. "One thing you should know is how much I loved your mother; how much I still love your mother. We got married young, and after only knowing one another for eight months. She got pregnant with you three months after. I thought I was ready to be a father and a husband, but the truth is, I couldn't take the pressure. I had so much animosity with my father that I doubted I'd be able to love you the way I wanted him to love me. About a year after you were born, I started putting in for special jobs that required me to travel for months at a time. Your mother got tired of that quick. She was essentially a single parent while I was out here still acting like a single man. We finally agreed I would stop traveling and be home with you and her, and for a while it worked out. But I could tell she wasn't happy. She knew I hadn't been faithful in our marriage and things changed. The way we were when we met was long gone and neither one of us had enough life experience to know how to handle it. My mother was gone, and my father treated me like I'm the one who took her from him, and that was very hard for me to deal with," he confessed, taking a sigh.

I watched him intently. I'd never heard my dad open up to me the way he was now; actually, I'd never given him a chance up until now. He continued, "When she got pregnant again, we were both so excited. It felt like we had an opportunity for a new beginning; a chance to get our family 'right'. That horrible day Sandy lost the baby… I didn't mean for any of that to happen. It was an accident, and I want you to know that I've never hit your mother, or any woman, a day in my life. I was trying to leave the house to talk some sense into a woman who I had an affair with; she was threatening to tell Sandy everything. Sandy became furious because I wouldn't tell her where I was going. She was coming up right behind me when I turned to face her; she ran into me and fell. When I went to pick her up, she screamed at me and told me not to touch her and to just leave. I guess that's when you came out of your room. I was a coward, so I left. I should have made sure she was okay, but I left. You don't know how many nights I cried and prayed for forgiveness for all the mistakes I made with your mother and with you," he said, exhaling deeply.

I just watched him. I didn't know what to say. I had been working on forgiving my father all week, but this was still a sore spot for me. I realized if I wanted to build a relationship with him that I couldn't hold my anger over his head. He continued, "She could have pressed charges against me and ended my military career, but she didn't. All she asked is that I give her a divorce and that I continued to take care of you. Looking back, I know I didn't deserve her kindness, her grace or her forgiveness. I used to write her love letters, more like poems really, when I was trying to get her back," he chuckled.

"Wait! You wrote Mom poetry? I never knew that," I said.

"Yeah. I wrote her a poem every day for a year after the divorce was finalized. Where do you think you get it from?" he smiled. "After a while I accepted that she wasn't going to be with me again, but I still tried to be in your life. As you got older, you just seemed to get angrier with me. When you turned 18, you looked me in my face and told me you didn't want me to be a part of your life. I'd never felt more like a failure than I did that day," he said, somberly.

I dropped my head, because I clearly remembered that day he was talking about. "Dad, I'm sorry I said that to you. And I appreciate everything you still did for me after that day. I was angry. I didn't understand anything you and Mom had gone through back then. I'm just glad we're able to put those things behind us and move forward," I replied.

"Thank you, Son. If you ever have any questions about anything—anything at all, please ask," he said.

I nodded. "I will."

After a few beats of silence he said, "There is something I've always wanted to ask you. With all the education and writing talent you have, why aren't you using it?"

I raised my eyebrows. "Oh, you mean the security guard thing?" I asked.

"Yeah. I'm proud of you either way. I just know how smart and capable you are. It just seems like you're settling," he said.

"It's not the job I had in mind when I was in school, but it's easy. There's no headache, and I don't have to worry about people not taking my ideas or suggestions as a threat. Or telling me I'm too aggressive when I have an opposing opinion. Corporate America is not built for Black men to succeed without suffering or having to sacrifice first, and I was tired of running on that hamster wheel," I explained.

"I completely agree, and I understand. But have you ever thought of working for yourself? You're so smart and you've always been a visionary. I just don't want you to get my age and have regrets on what you *should have* done," he said.

"I'm good right now. Maybe something will come along and change my mind, but until then, I think I'm doing what's best for me."

"Okay. Well, if there's ever anything I can do to help you, I'm here," he said.

"I'm glad you said that, because there is one thing you can do," I said, smiling at him.

"What's that?"

"I need you to find some of your poetry so I can read it! I still can't get over you writing poems to Mom!" I laughed.

"Hey, I was pretty good! I might surprise you!" he said, beginning to laugh too.

*****

After my talk with Dad, I'd gotten Layna up from her late nap to have dinner. She was leaving for Charlotte in the morning, so I knew she wanted to get to bed as early as she could. I decided to stay a couple extra days to spend more time with my family since I didn't have to be back to work until next Monday. She told my father goodnight and told him that she'd hope to see him again once he got back to Charlotte. After we both got ready for bed, we stayed up and chatted in her room for a while, and this time I wore a shirt.

"Well, I need to get to sleep. Six o'clock will be here before we know it," she said.

"Okay. I'll set my alarm to make sure you get up," I said, standing up.

She nodded. "Julian—did you… get in the bed with me last night?" she asked, with her eyebrows raised.

"Yeah. I couldn't sleep… and… honestly I just wanted to be next to you. Did I overstep?" I asked.

"No… I just didn't expect it. It was okay though. Next time just let me know that's what you want," she said, with a smile. She stood from the bed and began to pull the blankets back so she could get under them.

Then she turned to look at me. "Goodnight," she said, in a whisper.

"Goodnight," I returned. I stepped in to hug her, and that had to be the biggest mistake I could have made, because I did not want to let her go. She didn't seem like she wanted to let me go either. I felt her heart racing, and I knew she could feel mine, too. I wanted to be next to her again tonight, and even though she just told me to ask, I still thought it may be too much.

She stepped back. "I'll see you in the morning," she said. Being the gentleman I told myself I *had* to be, I nodded and left her room. I'd just closed the door to my bedroom, when I heard a knock. I turned around and opened it.

"Layna? Do you need something?" I asked.

"I just—uh... You know what? It's nothing, have a good night," she said, looking like she wanted to sprint away from me.

Then, without a second thought, I pulled her to me by the waist and kissed her like I was starving for the taste of her. Actually, I was. I was starving to feel her, and to taste her like this. She returned my kiss, and began to moan when I deepened our exchange. My hands moved down to the small of her back and my kisses began to trail down her neck. She smelled and tasted divine. She moaned some more, which almost turned me into an animal. My kisses made their way back up to her lips. She pulled back.

"Julian—I think we should slow down. Please," she whispered.

"Yeah," I agreed. It wasn't what I wanted to do, but it was the right thing to do.

She chuckled, "I actually came down here to ask you if you could hold me tonight like you did last night. I would still like that… if you want."

After the way I'd just kissed her, I didn't know if I'd be able to sleep a whole night next to her and keep my hands to myself.

"I can try," I answered honestly, then I leaned down to peck her on the lips.

"Okay. I'll be in the room when you're ready," she said, squeezing my hand before she left.

# 19

## Layna

Spending last night with Julian felt so good, and it wasn't as difficult as I thought it would be after we kissed. Him holding me the way he did was enough intimacy for me, and he was able to stay until my alarm woke us this morning. During my drive home, I stopped to get gas only to notice there was five one-hundred-dollar bills stuffed in my purse.

When I called Julian to thank him, he pretended not to know anything about the money; I appreciated his thoughtfulness.

He told me he'd be back in Charlotte in a few days, and asked me to decide where I wanted him to take me this coming weekend for our first date. He told me he'd go wherever I wanted to. I was floating from the feel of exploring something new in my life. I was beginning to hope things with Julian would only get better from this point on. *****

"What do you mean he's been calling you?!" Will asked, with rage in his eyes, after I told him how Derrick had been calling me over the last few weeks.

"Just like I said. He calls me, I block him, and he calls me from a different number. I honestly don't know how he got my new number in the first place, but he knows I'm in Charlotte. He left this voicemail when I was in Georgia," I said, then I played the message for Will and watched him get even angrier. "He probably knows more information about me than I think he does."

Will shook his head. "Call him back and tell him you don't want to see him, and tell him to stop calling you."

"I already did that, but—"

"Let's just try it now," he said, cutting me off. I looked at Will skeptically, but did as he asked. I hit the call button and put the phone on speaker. The phone rang twice before Derrick answered.

"Layna—" he answered anxiously.

"Derrick, I got your message and I'm calling to let you know that I don't want to see you next week when you're in Charlotte, and I want you to stop calling me," I said, and looked over to Will who sat on the edge of the couch with his fingers laced together.

"I told you I was sorry, and I'm getting a divorce. I just want to talk," he said. Will was now starting to get anxious. He mouthed the words *'tell him again.'*

"We have nothing to talk about. I don't want to see you, and I don't want you calling me anymore," I repeated.

Derrick sighed, and remained quiet for several seconds. "Okay, I hear you loud and clear. I'll leave you alone," he conceded. I sighed in relief. Just when I was ready to end the call, Will snatched the phone out of my hand. My eyes widened.

"Hey Derrick, this is Will, Layna's brother. I just want to let you know that she means what she says. And she has plenty of people here looking out for her. And if she tells me your bitch ass is still harassing her after this conversation, I will personally find you to reinforce the message," Will said, before ending the call. He tossed me the phone and stood to walk in the kitchen. "You hungry?" he asked casually, like nothing happened.

"Uh… yeah."

Steph was now working day shift at the hospital so she could be home to sleep at night and she'd be home at 6:30 p.m. In the meantime,

Will and I sat at the kitchen table to talk about my trip after we ate. I'd taken pictures of Julian's grandfather's house, and a few of Julian and his family, too that I showed Will.

"It seems like he has a nice family, and I can't get over how much Julian looks like his dad!" Will said.

"It was nice, a little sad, but nice. I'm glad I went."

"So, are you two a couple now?" he asked, with a neutral look.

"Not officially. We're going on our first date this weekend, so we'll see how that goes."

"A date? You went down there for a funeral and you came back with a date?" he laughed.

"And your little niece or nephew," I said holding my stomach, before bursting into laughter.

Will's face got serious. "Layna that ain't funny! Don't play like that!"

I continued to laugh. "I'm just joking. Julian was a complete gentleman the whole time. Don't worry, I'd tell you if he wasn't."

"So, you're really not going to give Jamal a chance?" he asked.

I shook my head. "Jamal and I are just friends; but I feel like Julian and I have a connection that's more than friends," I answered.

"Have you had a chance to ask him about his past relationships yet?"

"No, not yet."

He sighed heavily. "Okay. I'm not going to give you a hard time about it, because you already know where I stand. Just be smart." "I will be."

# 20

## Julian

*Alayna Zion Pierce.* Her name had been running marathons through my mind ever since she'd left Monday morning. It was a true test of strength spending the night with her without giving her more than a couple innocent kisses. Eventually, I went to sleep, but I was restless. It was now Friday morning and I was going home. Dad still had a few of

Granddad's matters to handle, including the reading of the will scheduled for later this afternoon. He would be coming back next week, and we'd already planned some time to spend together. I'm so glad he and I got a chance to talk, and to start building the father-son relationship we both needed. I also thought about the talks we had concerning my feelings for Layna. His advice to *think with my head before I think with my heart* really resonated with me. Also, his question about my career choice had me thinking about if there was something I really wanted to put my heart into.

Once I arrived in Charlotte, I was driving home when I decided to take a detour and surprise Layna at her job. I knew she worked in a building where the public couldn't just walk in though. I stopped by a convenience store and picked up the best-looking flowers they had and a pack of oatmeal raisin cookies that she'd told me was her favorite during our many late-night talks. I texted her when I parked in the parking lot of her job.

*Me: I'm back in Charlotte. What are you doing?*

*Layna: You already know I'm at work lol*
*Me: Then why are you texting me?*

*Layna: Boy Bye!!*

*Me: Come outside for a minute*
*Layna: Huh?*

*Me: I'm at your job. Come outside. I got something for you*
*Layna: You better not be playing!*

Five minutes later Layna came out of the front door with a headset on and a large cardigan sweater wrapped around her like it was Winter outside. I got out my car to meet her. The smile she gave me said I made the right choice coming here. I hugged her tightly and she hugged me back. I kissed her on the cheek.

"What are you doing here?" she asked, that sweet smile never leaving her face.

"I just got back in town and I wanted to see you. And I got you something," I said, walking back to my car to grab the flowers and cookies out the passenger side seat. I presented them to her. Her smile became even wider, if that was possible.

"Thank you. This is really sweet," she said, offering her lips to me. I gave her a simple kiss.

"Well, I'm not going to keep you. I just couldn't wait for our date tomorrow to see you. Have you decided what we're doing?" I asked.

"Awe… you missed me?" she asked, and I swear I felt my cheeks turn red from blushing.

"I did," I finally answered, trying not to turn into a puddle of mush in this parking lot.

"I missed you too… But yes! I have decided where I want you to take me and I'll tell you tonight," she said, looking at her watch.

"I gotta get back inside. Thank you for coming to see me though. It was very thoughtful," she said, kissing me once more then hurrying back into work.

I decided to stop by Mom's house while I was out. I missed her and I wanted to tell her about my trip. Also, I wanted to ask her about this poetry Dad said he'd sent her years ago. If I knew my mom like I thought I did, I know she still had those poems stored away. When I got to her house, Mom was making her famous spaghetti and meatballs that I loved so much. As always, she made enough for me to bring a generous portion home. I was so happy to see my mother, and even happier to see that she looked well. I'd worried about her taking her insulin shots while I was gone, but she took care of it.

"You look refreshed," Mom said.

"Do I?"

"Yeah. You seem like a brand-new man," she smirked.

"I'm just feeling good, Mom. That trip was exactly what I needed. I got a chance to see Granddad before he passed, spend quality time with

Dad, and see family I hadn't seen in years. It felt good to be surrounded by so much love," I said.

"And what about your friend? Layna, right?" she asked.

I shook my head. "I swear you and Dad need to start a gossip hotline! When did he even have time to talk to you? I was with him most of the time," I chuckled.

"We were texting," she answered.

I sat down and gave her a strange look. "Is there something going on between you two that I should know about?"

"No, Jules. He's just been checking up on me. That's all. So, tell me more about Layna. Is she from this area?" she asked, pivoting the conversation.

"Nahhh… don't try to change the topic! I'll tell you about Layna in a minute. Dad told me he used to write you poetry. You never told me that."

Mom looked surprised. "He did. At the time, I didn't really pay them any mind. He was trying to get back together and I was trying to move forward. I read them years later and I realized how hurt he was over our divorce," she said.

"Do you still have them?"

She nodded. "I do."

"Are they too personal for you to share with me?"

"Some are, but I'll find a few for you to read," she said, with a warm smile.  I'd always thought my mother was a beautiful woman, but the way her face lit up when she talked about my dad made her look radiant. If they were in the process of reconciling, I figured they would tell me when they were ready. I wanted more than anything for both of my parents to be happy, and if that meant they found happiness in one another again, then I would support it.

*****

Later that night I was lying on my back on my couch talking to Layna on the phone like we were in high school. She thanked me again for stopping by her job earlier and bringing her flowers and one of her favorite snacks. Layna brought out a boyish quality in me that felt oddly refreshing. I didn't feel like I had to impress her, or sweet talk her. I felt like I could just be myself. I felt different whenever I was around her or even when we were on the phone. It was almost like she unlocked a place in me where my peace had been hiding.

"Layna, I have never put on a pair of roller skates in my life! I can't believe I told you I'd do whatever you wanted! I thought you were going to say you wanted to go to some expensive restaurant or something," I laughed.

"We can do that another time. I want to have fun! You're not scared, are you?" she asked, teasing me.

"Well, yeah! I don't want to break a bone trying to keep up with you! You sound like you're a professional skater from these stories you're telling me!"

She laughed. "I'm not a professional, but I am really good. Will and I used to roller skate all the time when we were kids. As a matter of fact, he's the one who taught me how to skate. He's way better than me."

I sighed. "Okay, well if this is what you want to do them I'm game. We're still going to have to eat though. I'm sure the food at the skating rink isn't that great."

"We'll figure it out. I'm just excited that we're going! And don't worry, you won't fall if you listen to me."

"Okay, I'm trusting you, but next time, I'm picking the place!"

### *Saturday Night*

Who knew this many adults wanted to skate on a Saturday night? The timeframe for skaters 16 and up started at 8:30 p.m. and I was glad there wouldn't be any small children there, just in case I did fall. I picked up Layna at 6:30 p.m. and spoke to Will and Stephanie briefly. I thought Will was going to give me another talk about treating his sister right, but he was more focused on him and his wife having the house to themselves while Layna was out. He did tell me that he expected her to come home tonight, though. We enjoyed a quick meal at the Bonefish Grill before going to the rink. I was nervous as hell! This was not within my comfort zone at all. I'd spent all morning watching YouTube videos on how *not* to fall on skates.

When we walked inside, I liked the vibe. The lights were low, the music they were playing was current and everyone appeared to be having a fun time. My nerves relaxed a bit. Once we got our skate rentals, we found a place to sit down and put on our skates. We both got quad skates; Layna said those were her preference over inline skates, and would be much easier for me to learn in. When she saw how loose

I'd laced up my skates, she promptly fixed them. She told me loose strings is the quickest way to fall or to break an ankle, and her saying that gave me a little anxiety. However, after I was properly laced up, I did feel the difference in my stability. She got up first and began to skate around the seating area we were in. I watched her glide with ease and confidence on the carpeted floor. On the right side of me, there were some people in the rink skating fast, while others skated slow. Some people even held hands while they skated together; and when I saw people holding hands, I knew that was my goal with Layna by the end of the night.

Layna skated back over to me and stopped on a dime. I eyed her from head to toe. Why she wore those tight jeans and that form fitting shirt was beyond me, but I certainly enjoyed the view. Her body was tight. Like, Janet Jackson in the *Pleasure Principal* video, tight. Her hair was free-flowing down to her shoulders, and she wore a simple silver necklace with a Z on it.

She held one of my hands. "I'm going to help you stand up, so you can get your balance. Don't let go of my hand," she said with a smile, over the loud music. *It's now or never.* I used my free hand to push myself up and immediately felt like I was going to fall back down. She quickly grabbed my other hand and helped me steady myself.

I shook my head. "This feels dangerous!" I said, and I was 100 percent serious too.

"It's not dangerous, it's fun! You'll see! We're going to practice here before we go out to the rink. I'm going to skate backwards and I want you to slowly skate forward so you can see how it feels," she explained.

The first roll of the wheels under me felt strange, but after about ten minutes of her practicing with me, I started to gain some confidence. After another fifteen minutes, I was comfortable enough to hold only one of her hands and skate short distances on my own. However, I was not confident enough to skate in the rink. She never lost patience while teaching me, which made me feel comfortable, even if I wasn't confident.

"How do you feel?" she asked.

"I'm getting there. I don't think I'm ready to go out there, though!"

"That's okay! You can watch me, then I'll come back to get you."

We skated over to the rink and she left me at the ledge where I could comfortably stand on my own and watch her, along with everyone else, having a good time. As soon as she stepped in the rink, she blended in seamlessly with everyone else. I was impressed by her footwork, and every time she skated past me, she would either wave or blow me a kiss, which had me smiling like a fool, I'm sure. I took pictures and video of her as if I were her biggest fan. Although I wasn't skating, I was still having a good time. That was, until I heard *her* voice.

# 21

## Layna

I was making my way around the rink for the fifth or sixth time when I saw Julian talking to some woman. I'm not insecure, so I didn't think anything shady was going on. She could have been someone he worked with for all I knew. I was ready to bring him in the rink with me anyway, so I figured I'd go check things out for myself.  Julian's eyes followed me as I rolled out of the rink and over to where he and the mystery woman stood. I knew before she even turned around who she was. The ridiculous amount of injected ass she'd squeezed into her pants was a dead giveaway. It was Peaches. He was saying something to her as I approached, and it didn't look like a friendly conversation.

Like I said, I'm not insecure, but I do know how to be petty. Besides, I didn't forget how rude she had been towards me during our previous encounters.

I skated over to Julian and stood by his side and I immediately grabbed hold of his hand. Before he had a chance to say another word to her, I pulled him down to me by the neck and kissed him—like, I *really* kissed him. I savored his lips until I felt the tension leave his body. I let go of his neck and I pulled back from our kiss. He looked at me with nothing less than pure desire behind his eyes. The little shift I normally felt when he looked at me this way felt more like a giant leap. "You okay over here, baby?" I asked, as I rubbed my gloss from his lips with my thumb.

He smiled and nodded. "Yeah. I'm good."

Then I turned my attention to Peaches, who was still standing there watching us for some unknown reason. I extended my hand to her, "Hi! It's Peaches, right?" I asked, showing her the most genuine fake smile I had in my arsenal. She rolled her eyes at me and didn't speak back. "Okay then," I chuckled, dropping my hand. I turned my head and looked up at Julian, "Are you ready to skate with me?" I asked him sweetly, which caused this Peaches bitch to sigh loud as hell. Julian's neck snapped back in her direction, and before he could say anything, I said, "It was nice to see you again, we hope you have a good night.

Come on, handsome," I said, for added effect. I grabbed both his hands and skated backwards, leading him towards somewhere we could sit.


Once we were seated, I asked, "Are you good?" Because he still looked a little irritated.

"I'm cool. She just caught me off guard that's all, and my scared ass couldn't skate away from her. So, I was stuck!" he said, which made me laugh. "But I like the way you handled that. It was sexy," he said, licking his lips. I leaned in towards him and we shared another simple kiss. I think I was a little addicted to kissing him at this point.

"One thing you should know about me Julian, well actually two things you should know about me; first I do not fight or argue over men. I never have and I never will. Second, I only get belligerent when someone threatens or disrespects me or someone I love. So as long as she stays over there and let us enjoy our night, I'm good," I explained. *Someone I love? I hoped that came out right.*

He studied my face for a moment, then asked, "And what about you calling me *baby*? Was that just for her benefit? Cause I liked that," he said, grinning from ear to ear.

I'm sure my cheeks turned red. "I don't know. I think I like *Ju-Ju* better!" I laughed.

He shook his head. "I'm never gonna live that down, am I?"

"Nope!" Just then the song, *Let Me Love You* by Mario started to play. "Okay, you've had enough practice, it's time to hit the floor!" I told him. He looked worried. "Don't worry. I will not leave you, and I will not let you fall!"

"I am almost a whole foot taller than you, and I got you by at least

50 pounds. How do you think you can stop me from falling?" he asked.

"I can't stop you from falling, but if you listen to me, you won't fall," I answered, confidently.


He was doing good in the rink. We were skating close to the wall so he could feel more comfortable. He was beginning to pick up a little more speed and mostly skating on his own. I skated in front of him a few times to show off a few tricks I knew. I saw Peaches with one of her girlfriends hanging around the lobby area, smiling in some dude's face. She didn't even have on skates. I was confused as to why she was even here, but as long as she didn't bother us, I was fine.

The night was starting to wind down, and the music began to get slower. "Are you ready to go?" I leaned over to ask Julian. He looked so good tonight. He had a fresh cut, crisp clothes, and a smile that set everything off. I saw how some women were staring at him as we skated together.

"After this song," he said, extending his hand to me. The K-Ci and Jo-Jo song, *All My Life,* was playing to end the night. I took his hand and he pushed himself further away from the wall. I was nervous when he did that because if he fell, he was taking me down with him. But I didn't voice my concerns, I just let him lead. We skated at a comfortable speed, and I felt him squeeze my hand during certain parts of the song. When they sang the part about thanking God for finally finding the love of their lives, he held my hand extra tight. I felt as light as a feather next to him in that moment.

After we returned our rentals and put our shoes on, we both went to the restroom before we left. As I was washing my hands, Peaches came in and stared at me. I acted like she wasn't there. I didn't know her and I didn't know what her problem was with me, but she could catch these hands if it came down to it.

"So, Julian's your boyfriend now?" she asked with an attitude. I swear I felt like I was back in high school. I was not going to entertain this grown ass woman acting like a child. I had absolutely nothing to prove. I pulled down a couple paper towels and began to dry my hands.

I looked at her and didn't respond. I could tell this girl was ready to cause drama with me, and I wasn't going to be a willing participant in her foolery. I walked past her and out of the bathroom. Julian was already standing there waiting for me.

"Let's go," I said, quickly grabbing his hand and walking towards the exit.

"That was so much fun! You can't tell me you didn't have a good time!"

He smiled. "I did. I ain't gonna lie!" he chuckled.

"See! I told you! You need to trust me! So, what do you want to do next?" I asked, as we pulled out of the parking lot of the skating rink.

"What do you want to do? How about a nightcap? We can make it before last call," he suggested.

"Or we can go to your spot. You got something to drink at home, right?" I asked. I saw the look of surprise from his handsome profile. "I do, but now that I think about it, I don't think you and alcohol are a good match!" he laughed, which made me feel embarrassed. "We can go to my place if you want, but that's only if you want to," he said.

"I do. I'm not ready for our night to end just yet."


Thirty minutes later, Julian and I were on the couch making one another laugh so hard, that my stomach was hurting. I slipped off my shoes and sat with my legs folded and a blanket over my legs. I enjoyed seeing him in this way. He was relaxed and laid back. I figured this was a good time to ask him something that had been burning a hole in my tongue since Will told me about Julian's past relationships.


After a spell of laughter, I said, "I have something serious I want to ask you."

"You can ask me anything," he answered, and his dark eyes looking at me stilled my heart for a brief second. I'd never met anyone who could melt me down with just one look.

"So… what my brother said about your past. About you trying to break up someone's wedding. Is that true?" I asked.

His eyebrows raised. "Wow. Well, I wouldn't put it like that. Long story short, I was dating a woman who I thought was the one. When she broke things off with me I was devastated, and I had a hard time getting over it. The night before she got married, I went to her house in the middle of the night to see her." My eyes grew wide listening to his story.

He chuckled, "Don't get too excited. Nothing like *that* happened. I just asked her if she was sure about marrying the man she was getting ready to marry, and I told her how I felt about her. I don't know, I guess

I've watched too many love movies! I had the idea that she'd fall into my arms and we would run off together into the distance, or something corny like that. But in the end, she got married and from what I know, they're very happy," he explained.

I nodded, "And you kissed her after she was married?" I asked. He looked surprised by that question. I'm sure he was now regretting having told my brother anything about his personal life.

"I did. Trust me, it was not a mutual kiss. That was more of an ego thing on my part than anything. At that point, I was just being an asshole. I was wrong, and I did apologize to her. I thought me and her husband was going to have to handle things differently, but we came to a mutual understanding… peacefully," he answered. He looked as if a heavy weight had lifted from his shoulders after telling me that. I wasn't sure how to feel about what he just told me, but I was glad he was comfortable being transparent with me. I had my own past to tell him about. Also, he didn't seem like he was the same person who had done those things.

"Are you over her now?" I asked.

He gave me an admiring stare before answering, "Yeah, I am."

"So… Peaches. What happened between you two?"

He sighed. "Basically, I was going through some stuff with my dad and my mind was all over the place. He and I didn't always have a good relationship, but we're working on it. Anyway, I had a little too much to drink one night and I texted her to come through. We hooked up a few times after that, too. I know it wasn't the smartest move, but… what's done is done," he explained with a shrug.

"Is that something you do often? Call women to come through?" I asked. I wasn't judging, I just wanted to know.

He looked uneasy, and he sat back on the couch. "I'll be straight up with you. I've been pretty casual for like the last year. I haven't really been interested in trying to have another relationship. I was just doing me," he answered.

"Translation, you were just being a hoe," I said, with a knowing grin.

"Ahh… If you wanna call it that. I don't think I was *that* bad. But

I'm responsible though. I'm always responsible with any woman I'm with. I don't just do *anything* with *anyone*. I have my boundaries," he said.

"And now? Are you still interested in being casual?" I asked.

"Now, I'm moving forward, and I want to leave my past where it is—in the past. If I'm being straight up with you, I'm a relationship guy. I'd rather be with one woman. A woman who loves me that I can claim as my own, and love without limits," he said.

"Like, your queen?" I asked rhetorically, thinking about how I told him a queen was missing from his poem. It was becoming more obvious that he was missing a queen in his real life, too.

He grinned. "Yeah… like my queen. A beautiful queen with a dope soul," he agreed, as the look in his eyes made my body tremble underneath. His finger then traced the Z charm on my necklace the laid against the bare skin on my chest. "Zion…" he said in a low, deep drawl, "why don't you go by that name?"

I'd never heard my first name sound so good coming from anyone's lips like it did from his. "I guess Will told you that?" I chuckled. "My name always sounded so different from everyone else's, and when I was a kid I didn't want to stand out," I explained.

"Impossible. You'll always stand out no matter what name you go by," he said, smiling. "Can I call you, *Zion*?" he asked.

I sighed. "Only if you promise to do it in private."

He nodded. "Okay… *Queen Zion,*" he said softly, grabbing hold of my hand. "Can I be straight up with you about something else?" he asked. I nodded. "When I heard the poem you wrote about me, I had to restrain myself from not taking you in my arms and kissing you until I felt your body tremble. No woman I'd been with had ever expressed their feelings for me the way you did. Just know if you ever do that again, I will not be able to help myself," he said, before kissing my hand. He continued, "When I saw you pull up into my grandfather's driveway, my heart nearly jumped out my chest. Knowing you cared enough about me to travel all that way confirmed my feelings for you that I was trying to hold back," he said, as he began to caress my cheek with the back of his hand. I steadied my breathing. "I find myself trying not to stare at you anytime I see you because you're so beautiful. You're kind, you're smart, you're gentle, and I love how you're not afraid to speak your mind. I dream about how good your hands feel when you touch me, and how good you feel when I hold you. And your lips… I promise you, your lips make me never want to stop kissing you." He leaned in closer to me and gave me a soft kiss on my lips and pulled back. The look in his eyes was laced with admiration. My breaths began to slow down as my heart raced. I didn't know what to say. He leaned back towards me, grabbed a hand full of my locs, extended my neck and softly kissed me there. "I *love* your hair; especially when you wear it down like this," he said with his lips tickling my neck. "And what is this fragrance you're always wearing? It drives me crazy," he said, then he continued kissing my neck.

I chuckled. "I can't tell you all my secrets. I need to keep some things a mystery," I flirted, as I enjoyed the feel of his firm lips against me.

His lips met mine again and the butterflies in my stomach began to flutter uncontrollably. It was as if they each had a separate path to travel in pursuit of freedom. Our kiss deepened and my body temperature spiked. He leaned me back further on the couch until I was lying flat on my back and he was on top of me. If anyone could kiss better than this man, they would have to be a myth because the way he used his lips and his tongue was unmatched.

He pulled back, and looked down at me. Those eyes of his studying my face intently. He licked his lips. "Am I doing too much?" he asked. *Was he doing too much? Or was he doing just enough? Did I want him to do more? Should this be happening right now?* My thoughts ricocheted off one another causing me to hesitate answering his question. "I am. I am doing too much," he said, and sat himself upright on the couch. I was still on my back trying to figure out what the hell just happened. He grabbed my hand and pulled me up. We didn't speak for a minute or two.

"Maybe you should take me home. Let me go to the bathroom and then I'll be ready to go," I said, as I stood.

*Get yourself together, Layna! Pull it together!* I scolded myself in the bathroom mirror as I dried off my hands. I took a deep breath and gathered my composure before opening the door. I walked back into the living room. He was sitting on the edge of the couch with his arms rested across his lap.

Our eyes locked. He sighed. "Layna, I'm sorry. I don't want to pressure you into doing anything you're not ready for. I hope I didn't make you too uncomfortable."

I walked closer to him. "It's okay. We both got caught in the moment. There's no need for you to apologize," I said, sitting down next to him.

He reached for my hand. "I want to be your friend, but I also want to be with you, Layna. I've been doing my best not to rush things between us, and please let me know if I am. But I can't help feeling like that's what you want, too. Is it what you want?" he asked, hesitantly.

I sighed. "I do. But I also think we're moving a little too fast. We don't have to decide anything tonight. We can talk more about it soon. Is that cool?" I asked.

He nodded. "That's sounds good to me. Now, let me get you home before your brother comes knocking down my door," he chuckled.

I rolled my eyes. At some point, Will would have to back off putting his nose in my personal business. I knew he was only trying to protect me from being hurt, but it was a little overbearing at times. I liked Julian, and if things continued to go well, I would be spending a lot more of my free time with him.

## 22

## Julian

Even though I felt like I was risking my life roller skating last weekend, I still had a good time with Layna. But who am I kidding? I would have a good time with Layna going to the post office; as long as I was with her. She glided around the building effortlessly and she looked good doing it. I saw a few guys try to skate with her while I was on the sidelines, and I don't know what she said to them, but they fell back soon after. I liked seeing she wasn't overly friendly and she didn't get caught up in getting attention from men. Also, the way she handled the situation with Peaches, turned me on. I'm a little ashamed to say how aroused I became watching her controlling the narrative of that encounter, because it could have gone left.

I was shocked when she suggested we come back to my house. With everything I was feeling for her and the chemistry we always seemed to have, I didn't know what would happen once we were alone. Everything about her was attractive to me from her perfect golden-brown skin and pretty smile, to the bold way she spoke her mind. Her confidence said she knew she was beautiful, but her humbleness is what enhanced it for me. She's strong, but she's also soft, vulnerable, and very feminine. I felt like I wanted to protect her from everything that could hurt her.

Her asking me about my past didn't surprise me, and talking about it was easier than I thought it would be. I was glad Will hadn't told her the woman I had that encounter with was Serenity Johnson, because that would have been a whole other conversation. I wanted to ask Layna about her past, too, but I figured me talking about mine was enough for the night. When I told her how I'd been feeling about her, I saw in her eyes how much my words meant. When our kisses turned into me lying on top of her on the couch, I knew I was moving too fast. I wanted her, but I didn't want her to think her body was all I wanted. I wanted *all* of her, and that much I could not deny.

It was Friday afternoon and Dad had come back from Georgia a few days ago. He was coming to my house to teach me how to make a simple meal of braised chicken and roasted vegetables. He'd made the meal for me when I was in Georgia, and it was delicious. I wasn't the best cook, but I thought I'd be able to pull off something simple; not only to impress Layna, but to also ensure my mother didn't feel she had to keep making me meals. Additionally, Dad said he had something he needed to give me. I figured he'd pulled out some of his poetry books, and I was more than excited to read them.

It felt good spending time with my dad like this. There was no tension, no arguing, and I was genuinely enjoying his company. I kept reminding myself of the man he is now, and tried not to focus on who he'd been in the past. No one is perfect, and everyone deserves an opportunity to redeem themselves.

Dinner turned out okay. It wasn't as good as Dad's, but it was acceptable. As we finished up our plates we sat at the table with a couple of beers. This was the first time I'd had a drink with my dad, and it felt really good.

"I asked Mom about those poems you wrote her. She said she'd find a few for me to read," I said, smiling at him.

He laughed. "I'm surprised she still has them after all this time." I noticed the look of admiration followed by regret he had anytime we talked about my mom. "So, tell me how's things going with Layna," he said, changing the topic. I was going to backtrack, but I decided to let it go for now.

"Things are going well. We're both working on not moving too fast, and getting to know one another a little more. We're seeing where things go. We talk and we text constantly, and I can't ever seem to get enough of her. I find myself looking at her pictures on my phone all the time. Even the way she laughs makes me happy," I said, and I began to feel a little too mushy from what I'd just said.

Dad's smile extended. "She got you wide open, Son!" he laughed. I couldn't deny it. He was right. Layna had me at her mercy, and I don't even think *she* knew it. I just hoped she felt similarly.

"She does, that's why I'm doing things different with her. She's special, Dad, and I think the connection we have is real," I said.

"It's real. Everyone saw it when you two were together. After you left, your Aunt Nita asked me when the wedding was!" he laughed.

Dad and I continued to talk as the evening went on. We were learning so much about one another and having a nice time. Having him as a part of my life was absolutely the best decision I'd made in a long time.

"Julian, before I go, I have something I need to give to you," he said, pulling out a folded envelope from his back pocket. "I know you didn't know much about your grandfather, but he loved you very much. The first night you arrived in Georgia, he asked me to get Charlie to the house before the end of the night. Charles Langston; his lawyer," he began, clearing his throat. "He amended his will that night. He wanted to change a few things about how he divided his estate. He left his house to me and your aunt, and he left a few other properties he owned to your cousins. He left this for you," he said, handing me an envelope.

"What is it?"

"Open it and see." I opened the envelope and pulled out a hand written letter.

"He dictated the letter to me. He was too weak to write," Dad said, reading my expression. I began to read:

*Julian,*

*I hope this letter finds you well. If you're reading this, that means I've finished my journey on this side of the sun. I don't wish for you to mourn my death, but my hope is you will always celebrate my life. I still remember the day you were born; my first grandson. I drove to meet you after working a 14-hour shift. When you looked at me, and it was like you knew exactly who I was. Over the years, Brooks always told me about you whenever we spoke. He was always so proud of you and he loves you the way a father should always love their children. I'm sorry I didn't do more to be a bigger part of your life; but I'm so proud of the man you've become. You remind me so much of myself when I was trying to find my way in this world as a young man. If I could offer you any words of wisdom; it would be to always believe in yourself and never settle for a life you feel is not worthy of you. And when you find the woman you love like no other; love her the way you want her to love you... anything less isn't acceptable. I love you, Son. — Granddad.*

I was able to hold back my tears, but my eyes were definitely burning. Dad patted me on the shoulder to comfort me. "You good?" he asked.

I inhaled and exhaled deeply a few times, and smiled at him. "I am," I answered, nodding my head.

"Good, because he also left you an inheritance, and I'm sure you may need a moment to take this in," he said, pulling out his wallet. He opened it and handed me a folded check. I was afraid to look at it. I didn't know anything about how much money or how many properties Granddad had. I was curious to know what he left me.

I took a deep breath, took the check and opened it. My eyes had to be deceiving me. I looked at my father, and his smile indicated that I indeed was seeing the numbers on this six-figure check correctly. My granddad left me $750,000. I was ready to pass out. If I invested this money correctly, my retirement would be taken care of. "This is real?!" I asked, unable to catch my breath.

"It is. Just so you know, you were already in his will before you came to visit him. He left everyone money, but he left you the most. He accumulated a small fortune about fifteen years back when he won a lawsuit against the company who made the blood pressure medicine Mom was on when she died. He was in litigation for over a decade, but he wouldn't give up. The company finally settled out of court and he received a multi-million-dollar settlement. It was big news back then, but he refused to talk to any media about it. He said he didn't feel right spending the money because it didn't bring Mom back. As far as I know, the only thing he did with the money was pay off the house and buy himself a new truck. He let the rest sit in an account gaining interest."

I was floored. Utterly floored. I couldn't process this. I couldn't stop looking at the check as if it were going to disappear. I was almost speechless. "I don't even know what to do with all this money!" I finally croaked out.

"I know it's a lot to take in, that's why I didn't want to tell you over the phone. You work at an investment company, surely someone there can help you when you're ready. But before you do anything, I want you to really think about how this money can help you achieve whatever dreams you have for yourself. You said corporate America wasn't for you, this could be your chance to start your own company, become an entrepreneur and start building a legacy for when you have your own family. You can take a year off and travel to different countries, or just do things you've always wanted to do. It's all up to you, Son. I suggest you take some time to really think about it," he said.

The rest of our night went by like a blur. All I kept thinking about was how life changing this money was. I'd sometimes imagined what I would do if I happened to hit the lottery, and the first thing I always thought I'd do was quit my job. The other thing I said I would do is not tell anyone that I'd hit it big. I didn't know what my first move would be. I locked the check in my safe hidden in the back of my closet. Until I knew what I was going to do with the money, I would leave it there. For now, the only person I planned to tell about it was my mother.

# 23

## Layna

"So, you're telling me that a woman will stay faithful to a man that can't please her in the bedroom?" Omar asked, causing more commentary to erupt from the group. Julian, Omar, and his longtime girlfriend, Kim, had come over to the house tonight to hang out with me, Will and Steph.

"I'm just saying if a woman loves a man enough, she'll work with what he has to offer! She can always teach him what she likes!" Steph answered. "Nahhh! I don't believe that!" Omar laughed, with Will and Julian joining him.

"Okay y'all! It's Julian and Layna's turn! Y'all get two questions this time since my husband couldn't handle the last question y'all got!" Steph said, cutting her eyes at Will who just shrugged in response. We pulled questions for couples from an online site called, *Know Your*

*Date*; and although Julian and I weren't an official couple, we still played along. Steph raised her eyebrows. "Ooooh! These are good ones!

Who is your celebrity crush? Julian, you answer first!"

He rubbed his beard and smiled wide. "That's easy; Janet

Jackson!" he answered without hesitating. His answer came with positive chatter. "Okay Layna. Who's yours?" Steph asked.

"Hmm... it always changes! But I'll say right now it's Michael B.

Jordan," I settled on saying.

"Nice!" The women agreed while the men groaned and rolled their eyes.

"Next question," Steph said, with a guilty smile. "Where do you like being touched the most?" she asked, and all eyes were on us.

Will cleared his throat. "I really don't wanna hear this shit!" he fussed, swiping a hand down his face.

"Ignore him!" Steph said, rolling her eyes. "Julian?" she asked, and everyone waited for his answer.

He hesitated before answering. "I would have to say… my neck," he answered. Which seemed to be an agreeable and somewhat of a PG answer for the group. I, however, stored that information away for later.

"Okay! Layna, what's your favorite spot?" Steph pressed, while Will looked like he was being tortured; he was so dramatic.

"The girls," I answered, casually.

"Girls?" Will repeated, and he appeared genuinely confused.

"My titties, Zechariah!" I clarified, causing Omar to nearly choke on his drink, while everyone else burst into laughter.

Will looked horrified. "We need to find a different game! I ain't playing this one anymore!" he said, causing everyone to laugh even harder.


As game night continued, Julian wrapped his arms around my waist and pulled me closer to him on the couch. Every so often he gave me a peck on my cheek and stroked my hand with his thumb as his show of affection. Here in his arms felt like the best place on earth.

*****

"I brought dessert," I said, as I entered Julian's house. He took the bag from me, kissed me on my cheek and hugged me as I stepped in. We hadn't seen one another in person since game night a couple weeks ago. He'd gotten a fresh cut, and was wearing a cologne I hadn't smelled on him before. He looked so scrumptious.

"Thank you," he said, looking in the bag.

"It's Black Forest cake. It's my favorite," I said.

He smiled. "Dinner is almost ready, so you can make yourself comfortable," he said, leading me further into his house by the hand.

"Okay. I bought my laptop, so you don't mind if I do a little homework until things are ready, do you?" I asked.

"Not at all," he said, and kissed me on my cheek again before disappearing into the kitchen. Whatever he was making smelled good, and after my shift at the call center today, I was hungry.

I'd been counting down the hours until I'd be able to see him again. Going to school full time and working almost thirty hours a week meant I could only see him on the weekends, or through video chat. I had job interviews this week that went well, and I was hopeful I'd land something soon. Also, I was glad to say I hadn't heard anything from Derrick last week. I was sure he was going to call me or randomly pop up on me because he said he'd be in town, but he didn't. I guess he finally accepted that things between us were over.

Julian came into the living room to escort me to the table to eat. By that point, I'd made myself comfortable. I'd changed into a comfy sweatsuit I bought with me, my shoes were off, and my hair was down. My feet stalled at the entrance of the small dining room. The table was full of fresh flower arrangements and two-lit candles. He'd done a nice job setting this up.

I turned to him. "Julian! This is so sweet. Thank you," I said, and he leaned over to peck me on my lips.

"You're welcome. Are you ready to eat?"

"Yes! I'm starving," I said, as he led me to my seat. He brought me my plate and I was not shy about eating in front of him, and I was too hungry to try to eat *cute*. He'd done a surprisingly good job with the braised chicken, since he admitted he wasn't that great of a cook. He told me he wasn't too big on eating sweets, so we shared one slice of cake.

"So, Miss Layna. You never got around to telling me how you ended up moving from Raleigh to Charlotte," he said.

"Yeah, that's a long story," I said, sighing. I didn't like talking about that situation, because I always felt it made me look like I was stupid for getting caught up. "I've got time," he said, with a smile.

"The short of it is, I was with a man who I thought cared about me. Six months later I found out he was married. I confronted him, and he said he was going to ask for a divorce. I broke things off with him the day I found out, and I haven't seen him since. His wife, however, tried everything she could to make my life hell. Apparently he told her I was stalking him and I was obsessed with being in his life. She went so far as to try to get me kicked out of school." I said. Julian's eyebrows raised. "Damn," he responded, without offering any additional words. "Yeah. It got really bad. So bad, in fact, I couldn't stay in that town anymore. Everyone knew about it, because his wife told anyone who would listen. I think I was at my lowest during that time. When I told my family, Steph was the only one who didn't make me feel worse about the situation. After my semester ended, I moved in with Steph and Will to get my life together. If you could imagine, I wasn't too eager to jump back into the dating scene after that. But, I'm glad I'm here. I'm glad I'm here with you," I said.

"Me too," he smiled.

"So, this married guy hasn't tried to contact you since you left?" he asked.

"Actually, he has been calling me recently. I still don't know how he got my number, because I changed it before I moved. He said he'd be in town last week and he wanted to see me so we could talk. I told him no, and to stop calling me. I'll block him and he'll just call me from a different number. I told Will what had been going on, because I didn't know what else to do," I explained.

"What did Will do?" he asked.

"He had me call him and tell him to leave me alone. Then, he took the phone from me and essentially threatened the man's life, and hung up. I hadn't heard from him since. Anytime I think about that situation, I feel so stupid. He said all the right things and I believed him. I believed he loved me, which was the biggest lie of all," I said. Julian had a concerned expression. I hoped my story didn't sound as crazy to him as I felt when I was telling it.

"You're not stupid; and I'm sorry you went through that. I can see why Will is so protective of you. It makes more sense now," he reached for my hand. "I'm glad you're out of that situation and he seems to have left you alone," he said. I appreciated him not being judgmental. It was no telling how people would respond to my experience.

After talking, we left the dining room and had moved to the couch to watch TV. I was starting to doze off. I'd been running non-stop all week, and this was the first time I felt like I'd slow down.

"You sleepy over there?" I heard Julian's soothing voice ask. "Yeah, it's been a long day. And that was a big meal," I said, smiling. I looked at the time. It was nearing 10 p.m. I thought maybe I should start getting ready to go home.

"You're the only person I know who can fall asleep anywhere!" he teased.

I laughed. "What can I say, I'm a busy woman!" I sat up and looked over towards the window. If it weren't for the moon beaming down, it would be pitch black outside. "Maybe I should get going, before I fall asleep for real and you won't be able to wake me until the morning," I joked.

His face stayed serious. "Would that be a bad thing? If you stayed the night with me?" he asked, hesitantly.

"Ummm…. I don't think it would be a bad thing. I just—"

"I just want to hold you the same way I did when we were in Georgia at my granddad's house. You told me to ask next time, so I'm asking. Will you stay the night with me? I promise, I will not do anything to make you uncomfortable. I just want you next to me tonight," he said. I melted, because I wanted that too. Those eyes of his would have me saying yes to doing a backflip over hot coals, and I *could not* do a backflip.

"I need to shower, and I don't have anything to sleep in, or my beauty products," I said, even though it was a poor excuse. I had to try something to stop myself from saying yes, because regardless of what he said, I knew what would happen if I stayed the night. He may be able to keep his hands to himself, but I couldn't make that same guarantee.

"I have clean towels and washcloths, and I can give you something to sleep in. I also have lotion and an extra toothbrush," he said. I smiled. I thought it was cute that he thought a toothbrush and lotion would help me complete my nightly beauty routine.

I nodded. "Okay. I'll stay," I finally answered.


After I showered, I lotioned up my skin and put on the T-shirt and gym shorts he'd laid out for me to sleep in. I brushed my teeth and used some of the face moisturizer he had on the counter. I got in his bed, and it smelled fresh. His bed was very comfortable, too. I heard him in the kitchen doing a final clean up from dinner as I got more comfortable. While in the shower, I told myself that staying the night was okay, and I had the option to leave if I wanted to. But I didn't want to.


I'd fallen asleep by the time I felt Julian's arm wrapped around me.

He'd showered too, and his warm body so close to me quickly started to make me hot. I felt *all of him* pressed against me. I pulled the blanket down to my waist. "Damn!" I hissed. I was ready to either leave or jump on top of him. How could he say he wouldn't make me uncomfortable then put his semi-hardened… *thing—* on me?!

"Are you okay?" he asked, in a deep whisper. *Hell no, I'm not okay!*

"Yeah, I'm just a little hot."
"I can turn on the fan," he
offered.

"No, I think I'll be alright."
"You sure?" he asked.

"Yeah, I'm sure."

"Okay."

He nestled his head against the back of my neck and gently rubbed my stomach as we laid together. That *thing* of his felt like it was dancing against my ass!  I was trying to make it through the night without attacking him; so something needed to change.

"Julian. Your uh… your friend down there is… umm," I stammered.

"My *friend*?" he chuckled. "I'm sorry. It'll stop in a minute. Go back to sleep," he said, he leaned over and kissed me on my cheek before getting comfortable again. After ten minutes, I couldn't keep still. He was still aroused and I was going to go crazy if I kept feeling it.

This didn't happen when we were in Georgia. I don't know why it was happening now.

I sat up. "Can you please, make that *thing* stop?!" I asked, frantically.

He began to laugh. "Look, it's hard for me to control it. If it's too much, I'll face the other way," he offered.

"Yes, please. That would be helpful," I sighed. He was still snickering as I felt him turn over and face the other way. But now,

I didn't like the feel of his absence. I turned over to face his back, laid my arm around his waist, and settled my head in the middle of his back.

"So, you get to spoon me, but I can't spoon you?" he asked, he was still amused.

"Go to sleep, bighead," I said, and closed my eyes.

I don't know what time it was when I woke up, but Julian and I were still in the same spooning position. I began to softly kiss his back. His skin was so smooth and his body was so firm.  He began to stir from my movement, but I kept kissing him because… I wanted to. I needed to. I couldn't stop myself. My kisses began to grow more passionate as I began to lick him in between kisses.

He sleepily groaned. "Layna—what are you doing?" he asked, but did he *really* need to ask? "Layna—" he repeated, just as my hand began to travel down to the waistband of his pajama pants. He grabbed my hand and placed it on his crotch. "Do you see what you're doing to my *friend*?" he whispered, in a sleepy drawl.

"Mmm hmm," I moaned in between kisses.

I began to stroke what felt like a very sizeable bulge growing bigger behind his pants.

"Oh shit!" he hissed. I stroked him a little harder. Me kissing him on the back was no longer enough. I pulled him to lay on his back.

"Shhhh—" I quieted him. I pulled the blanket back and straddled him. I leaned over to kiss him, and the passion we had for one another was outrageous. His hands gripped my waist. I moved from kissing his mouth and began to kiss down his neck, his favorite place to be touched, and gently nibbled on him. His deep groans sounded so sexy. I started grinding my hips on him and he let out a heavy sigh. Before I realized what was happening, he flipped us and he had me on my back.

I hadn't even caught my breath before his tongue was back inside my mouth. He pulled back, and leaned over to the side of me, bearing his weight on his bent arm. His hand crept under my shirt and he rubbed my stomach as he looked down at me.

"I want to put my hands all over your body. Can I touch you, Layna?" he whispered, squeezing my stomach even tighter.

I nodded. "Yes…please," I whispered back. He lifted my shirt, exposing my breasts, and stared down at them as if they were a treasure he always hoped to find. His big hand began to rub one, as he lowered his head down to the other one. He took my hardened nipple into his mouth and sucked on it gently at first, then more aggressively. He rolled me to my side so he was able to give both my breasts the same amount of attention. I breathed heavily in approval, and the sounds of his mouth coupled with his low groans turned me on even more. He cradled my back and began licking and sucking even harder. I softly massaged his neck as he got his fill of me. He rolled me onto my back, laid himself between my legs, and his kisses began to descend to my stomach. My hands danced over the back of his neck and his thick, soft hair through his wave cap. Without removing my shorts, he began to pepper kisses at my center. "Julian…" I called out.

"I want to taste you so bad. Can I?" he groaned, and he sounded like he was in agony.

"Yes," I answered through a sigh. He untied the shorts and I lifted so he could slide them down my legs. I lifted my knees and anticipated his next move.

I looked down at him, and he was just staring at my treasure without words. "Are you good?" I asked, breathing heavily.

"Yeah. Are you sure this is what you want?" he whispered.

"I'm sure." I felt the first swipe of his warm, wet tongue.

"Mmm…" I moaned. It had been so long since I'd been pleased like this, that I almost exploded on contact. Then, he flattened his tongue on my most sensitive spot, and began licking me like I was a slowly melting ice cream cone. I couldn't stop moaning. I couldn't stop squirming. I couldn't stop feeling that I was about to lose my mind. "How are you this sweet? How do you taste this good? Shit!" he groaned, before continuing his indulgence on me. He reached up and grabbed my breasts, squeezing my nipples causing the right amount of pain to compliment his pleasure as he feasted on me. He went slow, then fast; hard then soft, from the top to the bottom. I don't know what type of magic tricks he was doing with his tongue, but I was liable to say anything while I was feeling like this. He pulled back. "I feel it coming, baby! I want it in my mouth!" he commanded, moving his hands down to my waist. His command was my undoing. The sound I made when I reached my peak came from the pit of my stomach. His mouth stayed glued to me until my body relaxed. I inhaled and exhaled deeply a few times as he rubbed my stomach. "Are you okay?" he asked.

"Yeah," I managed to croak out, as my body tried to recover from what he'd so expertly just done. He moved from between my legs and sat up. My limp legs fell to the side.

"I'll be right back," he said, and exited the bedroom.

# 24

## Julian

I wanted more of her. I was addicted as soon as I smelled her arousal. I'm glad she was the one to make the first move. That let me know that she wanted me as much as I wanted her. Her body looked and tasted as good as I imagined it would. I didn't put my mouth on every woman who offered me their opened legs. I was very selective of who received that treatment, but Layna could get anything she wanted from me. Her waist, hips, firm thighs and perfect breasts were like my own personal buffet. I'd heard of women tasting naturally sweet before, but I'd never experienced it until now, It wasn't a fragrance she wore, or a special soap she used, it was her.

I left her lying in bed while I went to the bathroom to clean up and to get a couple bottles of water from the kitchen. When I got back to the bedroom, I wasn't surprised to find Layna snuggled under the blanket and lightly snoring. *I'd put her little ass to sleep.* Although I wanted to do more with her, I was content with making sure she was satisfied.

That's how I knew Layna had my mind gone. Giving her pleasure was more important than me seeking my own. Yes, I was still very much aroused, but I'm a fully grown man, and I could deal with it. My priority was getting back in bed and being next to this woman who was slowly claiming my heart.

I laid on my back in bed and thought about what my future could be with Layna, and about the inheritance I received from my granddad. On both ends, I felt like this sky was the limit, I just needed to figure out how to get there.

*****

"Here you go. I think you'll like these," Mom said, handing me a few sheets of plastic covered paper. I looked at the handwritten pages and was surprised how well the ink was preserved on the paper. I read a few lines from the page on the top, and I couldn't wait to get into these poems my dad wrote. "So, what's been going on with you, Jules?" Mom asked.

"A lot, actually. Did Dad tell you about the inheritance Granddad left me?" I asked. It had been a couple weeks since I'd seen Mom, and I didn't want to tell her the news over the phone.

"He mentioned it, but he didn't give me any details about it. I'm just glad that the relationship between you two is going well."

"I'm glad about that, too. Um, Grandad actually left me some money." I paused for a moment, "He left me $750,000," I confessed.

Mom's eyes looked like they were going to pop out of her head.

"Are you kidding?!" she asked.

"No. Dad gave me the check. Granddad wrote me a letter and left me a chunk of his estate."

"What do you plan on doing with it?" she asked, with her hand on her chest.

"I don't know yet. I'm still processing it. I know it has the potential to change my life, though. I'm going to talk to a few financial advisors at my job and see what they think. But, I'm not in a rush to touch it." "Jules, that's *a lot* of money," she said, shaking her head.

"I know Mom. I won't do anything stupid with it. I'll let you know what I decide," I said. My mom began waving at her face as if she was trying to cool down. After a few moments I asked, "Can I ask you a personal question about you and Dad?"

"Yeah. What's on your mind?"

"What did Dad do to let you know he loved you? I mean, was it a specific thing he said, or was it a grand gesture he made? Or what?" I asked.

She smiled. "You may find this hard to believe, but your father and I fell in love with one another the very first moment we met. I don't think I can accurately explain how something like that could happen, because most people don't believe in love at first sight, but it's true for us. He offered to carry my groceries to my car, and he loaded them in my trunk. He looked so handsome in his BDU's, and he was so well-mannered. We exchanged numbers and things moved fast for us after that. I'm saying that to say, sometimes you just know. Nothing special has to happen; that one person can show up in your life and you feel it the moment you see them," she said.

The look on her face as she recalled her first moments with Dad was unmistakable. She still loved him, and I knew he still loved her. Neither one of them ever remarried or had a serious relationship with anyone else that lasted more than a few years. Studying her eyes, I took a few moments to absorb her words. "Does this have anything to do with your new friend, Layna?" she asked, breaking the silence.

I smiled because I couldn't help it. Before she left this morning, we agreed that we were now a couple. She was my woman, and I wouldn't hesitate to tell anyone who needed to know. "We decided to be more than friends. We're together now," I told her.

"Really?" she asked, with a smile.

"Yeah. I really care about her, and I know she cares about me.

Things feel different with her; things feel right," I said, feeling a little embarrassed sharing this with my mom.

"Well, I can't wait to meet her. I think it's only fair since your father has already met her. He told me he thought she was a lovely young woman," she said.

"She is. You'll love her," I said.

"Jules, do you think *you* love her?"

"I'm not sure. Maybe. Right now, all I know is I feel more like myself with her than I ever have before."


*Two weeks later*

"You really think Drake is lyrically superior to Nas? You can't be serious! Please, tell me you're joking!" I asked, shocked by her statement. I'd taken Layna out for an early dinner after her Saturday shift, and she was staying at my place tonight. She hadn't been back over since the first time she stayed. We'd both been busy; her with school and picking up extra hours at work, and me spending more quality time with my dad. Going two weeks without seeing her in person made me appreciate us being together that much more.

She laughed. "Yes! Drake's first album was his best one. Have you really listened to him? Or are you just hating as usual?" she teased.

"There's nothing to hate. I'm not saying I don't like him, I'm just saying he's not in my top then. Actually, he's not even in my top

twenty. You swear I'm always hating on someone!"

She sucked her teeth. "Cause you are!" she laughed.  "Yeah, alright," I said chuckling. My right hand landed on her thigh, giving it a firm squeeze, as I kept my left hand on the steering wheel. She placed her hand on top of mine and I quickly glanced over to her before returning my eyes back to the road. Whenever we touched, it felt like time stopped for a moment just so we could fully appreciate the sensation.

Back at my house we got comfortable on the couch watching TV as the hours drew on.

"Layna, let me ask you a serious question. If you hit the lottery for a million dollars, what do you think you'd do with your life?" I asked, as she sat between my legs with her back pressed against my chest.  Even though I hadn't told her about my inheritance yet, I wanted to know her unbiased opinion.

"Hmm. I've never thought about that. Well, first I would pay off these student loans! Then, I would probably travel. My first stop would be somewhere with crystal blue water and white sand," she answered, smiling at the thought.

"Okay, that sounds good. But what would you do after you traveled, like, once you got home? Do you think you would start a business? Invest? Or not work at all for a while?" I pressed.

"I think I would put most of the money aside for the future, and take a full year off to write. I'd rent out cabins across the country that overlooked the mountains, and write my first novel. Maybe then, I'd start my own publishing company, and help authors get their stories told to the world. I know it sounds corny, though," she said.

"No, it doesn't sound corny at all. It sounds dope. I would have to go with you to these cabins, of course," I teased.

"Well, what would *you* do if you hit the lottery?" she asked.

"What do you think I would do?"

"Let's see… you love writing and you love performing at open mics. I could see you going around the country to different spots to perform your work… like a tour. Either that, or I could see you actually owning a spot like Words & Verses, but expanding it to more than poetry. You could have local artists, or even celebrities come perform there. I can see you doing something like that," she answered excitedly.

"You think so?"

"Yes! Not that you need any more people telling you how great you are, but, I've read through a few of your notebooks and your talent is next level. There's no way you should be stuck in this little corner of the world with your voice. Everyone should be able to hear the way you express yourself through poetry," she said, turning to look me in my eyes.

I nodded. "Thank you for saying that."

"You're welcome. I'm just telling you the truth. You're very talented, you're intelligent, and you're very passionate about your craft.

I believe you can do whatever you set out to do; whether that's running a business or becoming a world-renowned poet and author. You got that

'it' factor. I really mean it," she added. All I could do was look at her. She rendered me speechless by her sincere words. She rubbed my thigh underneath the blanket and returned her attention back to the TV.

I was more than ready to lay down. Not only because I got to sleep next to Layna tonight, but also because I was genuinely tired. She sat on my back patio nestled in a huge blanket while I showered for bed. All I saw was the blanket and the yellow headwrap with colorful butterflies decorating it she wore to cover her locs. "You ready for bed?" I asked, standing at the sliding glass door. She turned and smiled, "Yeah, I'm coming." This woman loved being covered in warmth, which was ironic because her smile covered my heart the same way.

Once she joined me in bed, I wrapped my arms around her warm, soft body and peppered her shoulder and neck with kisses. She wore a long pajama shirt with fuzzy socks, and as always, she smelled and felt divine. I began to think about how good she tasted when she allowed me to bury my head between her legs a couple weeks ago, and I had to concentrate very hard not to become aroused by the thought of it. I failed.

Not wanting to make her uncomfortable, I began to roll over. "I'm sorry," I mumbled. The way I felt about Layna was more than any words I'd said to her up until this point. Although we were in the same bed together, I didn't want her to feel pressured to be intimate with me again. Of course, I wanted her. I wanted her more than I could describe; but I wanted her to decide how far we went and when.

She reached back and stopped me from moving. "No. It's okay," she whispered. She then turned to face me and her eyes on me immediately put me under a spell. She held her soft hands to the sides of my face and kissed me. My whole body warmed. I slid my arm underneath her so I was able to cradle her closer to me as I returned her kiss. She moaned into my mouth and slid her hand down the front of my shorts and began to stroke me until I was rock hard. I moved away from her lips and rolled onto my back so I could breathe. She continued to stroke me.

"Layna… Damn, girl!" I called out, in between breaths. She leaned over and began kissing my chest. I grabbed the nape of her neck, encouraging her to have every and any part of me she wanted. I was ready to lose my mind by the feel of her mouth on me. She traveled up my chest and back up to my lips.

"I want you, Julian," she whispered, against my lips. Those four words unleashed a desire in me I'd been holding in from the moment I laid my eyes on her.

"Are you sure? We don't have to," I said, barely able to separate my hands and my lips from her flesh.

"I am."

"I want you, too," I said with an ache in my voice I had no desire to mask. I kissed her again. "Is there anything you don't like? Anything you don't want me to do?" I asked.

"No, but if you do something I don't like, I'll tell you," she said, breathlessly.

"Okay," I said connecting my lips back to hers. I lifted to my knees and helped her out of her shirt. I then removed her socks and kissed the bottoms of her bare feet. Last, I took a deep whiff of her panties before sliding them off. I appreciated how well she kept herself groomed. I grabbed the backs of her thighs, spread her legs open and held them there. I began tongue kissing her lower lips with just as much fervor as I kiss the ones on her pretty face. She growled and moaned loudly as her body undulated against my face. I held her tighter; sucking and licking on her most sensitive spot as my moans joined in with hers. I placed one of her legs over my shoulder and using my free hand to insert my fingers inside her, as I flicked my tongue over her pearl. "Yes! Yes!" she whined and moaned.

"You like that?" I asked, barely wanting to remove myself from her savory treat. "Mmm hmm," she cried.

I removed my fingers that were now slick with her nectar. "Tell me if this is too much, baby," I said, sliding my thumb back into her drenched opening, and my index finger into the tight opening just below. She tensed. "Do you want me to stop?" I asked.

She swallowed hard and breathed heavily. "I just never…" she trailed off.

"I'll stop."

"No. Go ahead," she replied, sounding almost out of breath. I resumed gently pushing my finger in and she relaxed. I then returned my mouth to her awaiting treasure; sucking on her with no mercy and bringing her to climax shortly after. She screamed loud at her body's betrayal of the myriad of sensations that hit her all at once. *This woman is going to be the death of me.*

I scaled her body and kissed her breasts. "Are you good?" I asked.

"Yeah," she breathed out.

"Are you ready for me?" I asked. She nodded.

After sheathing myself, I settled between her legs. I could already feel the heat coming from her. She reached down between us and lined me up with her opening. "Oh shit!" she cried out when I was only half way in. I had to pause for a brief second. I don't know what I expected, but it wasn't this. I knew in that moment I would be willing to catch a charge; literally try to break every bone in the hand of another man I saw touching her. I buried my head in her neck and pushed the rest of my length inside her. She gasped at the tight fit, and so did I. She fit around

me like she was made for me, and I was made for her. I was overwhelmed. *What the hell did I just get myself into?* I thought.

She wrapped her legs around the base of my back, and I began to stroke her slowly. She dug her short nails into my shoulders, urging me the stroke her harder.

"Can you take it?" I asked, through a breath. Already moaning, she nodded with her eyes closed. I pulled back and plunged deeply back into her, causing her to shriek. Her eyes popped open, and I continued plunging into her. Her load moans and cries of satisfaction only urged me on. Looking down at her, I admired how beautiful she was as her face contorted in pleasure fueled by our passion.

"Julian! I'm about to…. I'm about to…" she cried out.

"Come on! I got you, baby! I got you!" I urged, plunging into her faster as I guided her through her climax. Her voice cried as I felt her contract around me. "That's right! You knew this shit would make me crazy, didn't you?!" I asked, pounding her even harder. I couldn't understand what she said through her whimpers and moans. I kissed her again; sucking on her lips and dipping my tongue in her mouth. Sweat beaded on my forehead as the sound of our bodies coming together filled the room. When she started talking dirty to me, I almost turned into an animal. Much to my surprise and delight, Layna had a filthy mouth, and I loved every nasty word coming from her parted lips.

Even though I tried, I couldn't hold on as long as I wanted to. This shit felt too good. "Layna! Layna! Ahh shit!" I growled as I exploded. I swore the room went silent for a couple seconds before I collapsed by her side. I draped one arm over her and she rubbed my hand as we both came back down into a normal breathing pattern.


I knew I needed a few more minutes before I began thinking clearly again. However, after everything she said to me on the couch earlier about believing in me, and experiencing what I just felt, there was no way in hell I could let Layna go.

# 25

## Layna

*A Month Later*

I woke up in the middle of the night to find Julian was not lying next to me. I figured maybe he'd went to the bathroom or something, but after ten minutes he still was gone. I got out of bed and left the bedroom. I saw a light on in a room down the hall. My feet traveled in the direction of the light to check on him. The door was slightly cracked, so I looked in on him before knocking. He was writing something in a notebook.

"Hey, are you alright in here?"

"Yeah, I just had to write my thoughts down. I'll be back in a minute," he said, concentrating on the words on the page.

"Okay."

He closed his notebook, and turned to look at me. "Come here for a second," he said. I walked over to him and he put his hands at my hips and pulled me closer. He kissed my stomach. "Are you glad you're with me? In this relationship, more specifically," he asked.

I smiled down at him. "I am. I like how things are between us. Why?"

"I'm just making sure," he said, squeezing my waist before letting go. "Go get back in bed. I'll be right there."

In the few minutes it took for Julian to join me back in bed, I thought about just how deeply I felt for him. The way he made me feel just by his presence was something foreign to me. I felt giddy anytime he sent me a text, and my stomach still shuddered with nerves when I saw him. I knew I was special to him, but I also knew I needed to be careful. Our relationship was still very new and I didn't want us to move too fast. Though, I couldn't stop wondering if what I felt for him was love.

*****

It was Saturday afternoon and I'd just arrived at Julian's house after my work shift. He'd spent the day with his dad and we planned to go to Words and Versus tonight. We hadn't been in a few weeks because we were too busy being up under each other. However, tonight he insisted we go out and socialize. I agreed. I just wanted to take a power nap before we went. I ate, showered, and went to lay down.

I was awakened not by the annoying sound of my alarm, but by soft kisses to my lips and face. I opened my eyes and Julian was looking down at me with an expression I'd become satisfyingly familiar with. I knew what he wanted, and he could tell I knew what he wanted. Already shirtless, he stood from the bed. My eyes took a moment to adjust to the soft light, but the 200 crunches he did every morning was in full focus. His body was nicely sculpted, and I admired every molecule that comprised him.

"We have to leave in an hour. Come shower with me," he said.

"I just showered when I got here."

"Yeah, but you were by yourself. I want you to shower with *me*," he said, but his eyes said more to me than his mouth ever could. He didn't play fair. It's not as if he could help it, though. Any woman with a pulse could easily fall under the spell of this man's charm and good looks. Unfortunately, I was no exception.

# 26

## Julian

"Words and Versus, I got something brand-new to read for y'all tonight! It was inspired by the beautiful woman in my life. And y'all already know how I am. When I feel it, I feel it! And tonight is no different! This poem has a little bit of a different style for me, but I'm sure my message will be clear to you. It's called, *The Last Heaven*," I introduced before I began to read from my notebook:

*Your lips, are the last*
*heaven, The last haven,*

*I'm riding on a raven, to the higher plains of my elation.*

*From your kiss…*

*That kiss got rippling ripples tickling my middle… soul…*

*Damn, it's a whole…*

*New place to be, when you're lying next to me.*

*Your eyes are the last paradise, my paradise,*

*And I'd sacrifice the life of a sunrise just to be by your*
*side, I love to feel the quiver of your thighs next to mine.*

*You make my heart so full,*

*So full, that my other organs have to leave to give my love*
*room to breathe. Best believe,*

*I've risen, I've been smitten, and time… stops ticking when I'm*
*with you.*

*When you talk to me in your sexy tones,*

*It's like,*

*Listening to saxophones,*

*I must have known,*

*Only desolation before you,*

*Your love, is my cordial immortal, that dances through my cerebrum, I see them,*

*Angelic blares, from where…ever you came from;*

*It must have been a place where the DNA of angels is made, Or,*

*The place where there's always shade on the hot days, Or,*

*The place where God goes when He wants to get away…*

*You came,*

*From the last heaven,*

*When I'm with you my madness is lessened.*

*You got me pressed down into a concentration of electric ecstasy,*

*You rapture me, in a rhapsody, that en-raptures me,*

*You have to be,*

*The destination of my destiny.*


*You positively charge my erogenous neurons*

*With a high I've never been on,*

*You've taken me to the final spiral beyond… pleasure, A
measure of content has me smoldering like a blaze of
newborn sunrays,*

*I want to meltdown into somehow, off the edge of nowhere as long
as you're there, too.*

*You've… become my muse,*

*Like a poetic conundrum about the difference between existing and
existence,*

*Before… I only existed,*

*Now, I am existing in an ever full, everness, high emotional state,
where the beginning of the next existence takes place… the last
heaven*

*Is where I'm testing, the biology of tingles and touches,*

*Whispers of sweet nothings…*

*Until the median of the night and day is still,*

*I want to subsist in your bliss until I can no longer control my will.
Even if it is for a little while we will oblige our time within the
seconds, of the seconds, of the seconds until we forget what a
second is…*

*Close our eyelids…*

*And drown within the intrepid*

*Wonder of us…*

*Just,*

*Let go with a freeness never known*

*The last heaven is your love*

*Where no one but you and I will roam.*

The response from this poem was louder and more enthusiastic than what I'd ever gotten before. Behind the mic is where I always felt my best; my most confident, my most revered. I felt so liberated. As the next artist went up to the mic, I continued to receive praise and compliments from my peers. Like always, some people repeated their favorite lines back to me, while others insisted I do more with my poetry than just sharing it within the limits of this crowd. I appreciated everyone's kind words and excitement. By the time I got back over to Layna, her expression didn't reflect the excitement everyone else had. She didn't look upset, but she didn't look happy either. She looked a bit uncomfortable.

When I sat back down next to her, I leaned in towards her ear. "Is everything good?" I asked. She nodded, but she didn't say anything. Her whole vibe had changed, but I don't know why. I thought she'd be happy. I thought she'd like my poem, which I now considered to be one of the best poems I'd ever written. I wrapped up all of my feelings and thoughts about her and us into those words; how could she *not* like it?

For the rest of the night, she hadn't said more than a few words to me. After the last artist finished, she excused herself to go to the ladies room before we went back to my house for the night. I was anxious to leave because I needed to know what was going on with her.

# 27

## Layna

When Julian introduced his poem to the crowd, I began to get a little nervous. I've come to know how expressive he is through his poetry, but I had no idea what he would say. As beautiful as his poem was, and as honored as I felt that he'd written something so personal for me, I couldn't help but feel somewhat exposed in a way. That, plus the several sets of eyes I now felt crawling over me. Our relationship is still new and I wanted us to protect it as much as possible. What he'd just done put a spotlight on something I considered to be private and still growing. Also, some of the things he said overwhelmed me. He spoke about me as if I'm the last woman he'd ever be with. I know he used a lot of metaphors, but did he really mean what he said? I didn't want to make a big deal about it, but I just needed a few minutes to process his words. I knew he felt my tension when he sat down next to me,

Once the last artist finished, I excused myself to go to the restroom before we went back to his place.

"You know you're not the first woman he's stood up there and performed a poem for, right? It's his thing. It's what he does, and it's all for attention," Peaches said, once she'd entered the ladies room. I was officially tired of her. I don't know why she insisted on seeking me out and being messy. I had too much on my mind right now to deal with her.

I sighed. "I don't really care what he's done before me," I said, drying my hands with a few paper towels.

"Well maybe you should. Yeah, he's fine and everything, but he's not as good as you think he is. Do you know how many women in here he's run his game on? Do you even know how many women here tonight he's slept with? Sis, you're being played," she said, with a chuckle. What she was saying bothered me, but I refused to let her know it. Truth is, I didn't know the answers to her questions. I didn't know how many times he'd stood in front of this crowd and did this for another woman, and I definitely didn't know how many women present tonight he'd slept with. *Was* this his thing? Was this all for attention? Were people looking at me like I was a joke?

"Like I said. That doesn't matter to me. His past is his past, and why is it your business anyway?" I asked. Peaches was undoubtedly a beautiful woman, but her attitude was so ugly to me.

"Woman to woman, I'm just trying to look out for you. He's just using you to feel good about himself. Once this whole, *'she is my heaven,'* or whatever he said, phase is over, you'll see the real him!"

I folded my arms in front of me. "*The real him?* You don't even know him! Do you still want him or something? Are you mad because he just told everybody how he feels about me, but he won't even acknowledge your existence? What he does and who he's with is not your business. I can understand why you'd still be hung up over him, but Sis, let it go!" I responded.

She scoffed. "Mad? Look at me; I have *nothing* to be mad about! You can have him. His overly sensitive ass is not my type! But you? You're *definitely* his type; pretty and naive. Just remember to keep that same energy when you see how he really is! You think you're special right now, but really, you're just next in line. Don't say I didn't try to warn you," she said. She turned and pushed the door open before leaving.

That quickly, she introduced a new set of thoughts in my mind about Julian. This was the first time I'd actually felt any real doubt about Julian or his intentions. Will's words came back to haunt me,

*'He's all over the place when it comes to women, and you're too good for that.'* I've only seen the best in Julian, and we hadn't known one another long enough for me to see anything else. Maybe Will was right, and as much as I hated to admit it, maybe there was some truth to what Peaches said, too. Maybe I *was* doing too much too soon. Maybe this relationship was moving too fast for me right now.

"You've been quiet all night. What's on your mind?" Julian asked, as we laid in his bed. After his poem, and my little chat with Peaches, my mind had been going in one thousand directions. I'd been so infatuated with how much Julian gave me butterflies, I wondered if I was ignoring any red flags.

"I'm just tired," I said, rolling in the opposite direction.

"Tired? Your mood seemed to change after I read my poem. Everything was good, then all of a sudden, everything was different.

You didn't even tell me if you liked it or not."

"I did. I just… really don't feel like talking right now, Julian. I just need to sleep," I said. He was quiet for a moment, then I felt his hand crawl under my shirt. He kissed my neck.

"We don't need to talk if you don't want to. I got something that will help you sleep," he groaned. I absolutely hated that I began to think of all the other women he's said that same line to before me and ended up with their heart broken by him.

"No. I'm good tonight," I answered, as I grabbed his hand to stop it from moving. He pulled away from me. He sat up and turned on the bedside lamp.

"Okay. You need to talk to me. Something is going on, and if you don't tell me, we can't fix it," he said.

"Julian, just let it go. Please."

"Layna—please look at me," he said. I reluctantly rolled over to face him. "Did I do something wrong?" he asked.

I sat up with a heavy sigh. "How many times have you written a poem for a woman and stood up there and did that in front of a crowd of people? Once? Twice? More than three times?" I pressed.

He looked confused. "Is that what this is about? Why does that even matter?"

"It matters, because I don't want the way you feel about me to become something everyone feels is their business. It matters, because I don't want to end up looking like a fool!"

"Are you for real? You're upset because I turned my feelings for you into a poem?"

"No. I'm overwhelmed! You said so much. I didn't know you felt that way about me, and to hear it for the first time like that was a lot."

He sighed. "Layna, baby, this is how I am. This is how I express myself. This is what I do; it's what I've always done," he said evenly.

"And I understand that's who you are. But have you ever thought that maybe I'm not that way? Why did you feel the need to express our private relationship in such a public way?" I asked.

"So, the way I express myself is a problem for you?" he countered, sounding way too defensive.

"Let's just drop it, because you're not listening to me and you're twisting my words."

"I'm not twisting anything! Say what you need to say, Layna," he pushed.

"Okay, Julian. The truth is you were doing too much. Maybe I inspired your words, but your performance was more for the crowd than it was for me. You doing that opened the door for everyone to have an opinion about us while we're still learning about one another. And if this is not the first time you've done it, it can seem like you're not being genuine."

"Do you believe I was being genuine?" he asked, his handsome face now scowling at me.

"I do, and honestly that scares me the most! He remained silent, and I didn't know what that meant.

"Layna, what scares you about what I said?" he finally asked.

"Everything! All of it!" I answered, as I felt tears forming in my eyes. I didn't want to be emotional, but I felt like he'd placed the weight of his world on my shoulders and expected me to carry it. I couldn't.

"Layna, I know I can be a little intense at times, but how I feel is how I feel! And how could you think I did that for attention?" he asked, sounding even more defensive.

"Julian! You had a victory lap for fifteen minutes while being congratulated and praised as if you just won a championship ring!

You're a different person when you're on that stage, and for some reason you seem to think you need validation from others! You don't! Whoever it is you become when you're up there is someone I really don't like!"

He swiftly got out of the bed and glared over at me. Those beautiful eyes of his showing me a darkness I'd never seen. "So, let me get this straight; you're telling me that you don't like the part of me that I'm most proud of? The part of me that gives me the most peace? The most freedom?" he asked.

I got out the bed, too. "I'm saying your talent speaks for itself and you don't need an audience to clap for you to tell you that! I'm saying the way you feel about me is a lot and I don't know how to process it right now! And I'm also saying you should have considered how I would feel before you did that! Julian, my last relationship ended very publicly and it was hard for me to deal with. I want us to protect each other!"

"Now you're comparing how I feel about you to how some married dude who had you laid up in hotel rooms like a side-chick treated you?

I'm not him!" he yelled so loud, it startled me.

"Am I'm not someone you can yell at just because you don't like what I have to say! I can't even tell you how I feel without you acting like this?! I'm not going to stay here and argue with you!" I yelled back, heading to the other side of the room to gather my belongings. Our night was ruined, and if I didn't leave, one of us would surely say something we'd regret later.

"So, you're just going to leave?" he asked, and he actually looked surprised.

"Yes! I'm done arguing, Julian! I don't have time for this!" I said, as I shoved items into my overnight bag. I felt Julian's eyes on me, and I could feel his regret penetrating the energy in the room.

He sighed. "Layna, I'm sorry I yelled. It's late; just stay the night and leave in the morning. I can sleep on the couch. Just don't leave like this." he said, approaching me. I held my arms out, stopping him from reaching me.

"Don't touch me right now. I'm going home. We'll talk later," I said, without the courtesy of giving him eye contact.

"Let me at least walk you to your car," he said, softly.
"No, I got it."

"Layna, it's late and—"

"I'll be fine."

He exhaled an even heavier sigh. "Well at least let me know when you're home."

I had nothing more to say, I just needed to leave. I slipped on my shoes, and walked until I reached the driver's side door of my car.


*****


"You came in late last night. Is everything okay with you and Julian?" Will asked, as I poured myself a cup of coffee.

"Yeah. We're cool. After last night at Words and Verses, I decided I needed to think about a few things. And I couldn't do that while I was over there," I said, sitting down at the table with him. There was no way I was telling my brother about the argument we'd gotten into.

"Things like what?"

"Things like, wondering if his feelings for me are genuine, or if I'm just one in the line of many," I explained.

"Layna, you know how I felt about y'all two getting together in the beginning—" he began.

I rolled my eyes. "I know you've been dying to say *I told you so*, so go ahead and say it."

"See, I wasn't going to say that! But, I did tell you!" he joked. "I was trying to say that I think he really cares about you."

"So, you're Team Julian now? You're no longer Team Jamal? Or team anybody else?" I asked.

"Make no mistake, I'm *Team Layna*. I support *you*. I'm just letting you know what I see from the sidelines," he said, with a smile.

"Awe! Brother! You really do love me!" I teased, and stood up to hug him around the shoulders.

"Go 'head with all that now!" he said, pretending as if he didn't like my affection. I sat back down.

"By the way, I'm driving up to Mom and Dad's next Saturday morning. Dad needs help setting up some speakers or whatever it is he bought. So, I'm going up there for a few hours. If you can get off work you can ride with me," he said.

"Yeah, I should be able to do that. It'll be good to see them." As for me and Julian, I still needed time to think.

# 28

## Julian

A week had passed and Layna still wouldn't take my calls or return my texts. I didn't know where I stood with her, but day after day, I became less hopeful that I'd hear from her anytime soon. Honestly, I was starting to feel like I wouldn't hear from her at all. I scolded myself for behaving the way I did. Yes, I was upset, and she said a few things I didn't like, but, I should have never yelled at her. I did my best to busy myself to help keep my mind off her, but that was nearly impossible, though.

One major decision I still needed to make was about my inheritance. After talking to a few people from my job about what to do, I still wasn't sure how I would proceed. However, I was leaning towards investing in real estate. I gave myself a deadline of 60 days to figure it out. Today, I was hanging out with Dad and a couple of his retired Army buddies. We were going to play cards and have a few beers. If nothing else, maybe it would help me take my mind off Layna for a few hours.

Once I was back home, I began to feel just how alone I was within these four walls. I looked around my home and for the first time, I wasn't satisfied with how it looked. The walls were painted eggshell white, I didn't like the carpet, and I had no artwork on the walls. There was nothing here that indicated this was *my* space or showed any insight to my personality. I envisioned what I wanted my home to look like, and I decided that would be my new project to work on.

Later that night, after I downed what was probably my fifth drink as I thought about Layna and the possibility of her deciding our relationship was over, there was a knock at my door. I looked at the time and it was approaching 11 o'clock at night. It had to be Layna. *No one else would show up to my house this late uninvited,* I thought. I hurried myself to the door as the knocks became more frantic. Without looking first, I swung the door open and my smile quickly disappeared.

It was Nova; the last woman I dated seriously… sort of. It had been at least a year since I'd seen or heard from her. She looked like she'd been drinking, or crying, or both.

"What the hell?" I said, as I looked at her standing on my doorstep. I saw the car she must have come in drive off as soon as I opened the door.

"I'm sorry for popping up on you like this, but I needed to see you. Can I come in, please?" she asked, sniffling. I hesitated, but I extended the door for her to come in. I didn't know what was going on, but I figured she must have been desperate to show up here. She and I didn't end on bad terms, but we weren't necessarily friends either. I did, however, still care about her. I couldn't figure out why she would show up crying at my front door on a Friday night, though.

She looked around as she walked into the living room. She sat on the couch, and I sat across from her. I was starting to feel the effects of the over indulgence of the alcohol I drank. I was getting drowsy.

"Nova, you wanna tell me what's going on?" I asked.

"Am I really that hard to love?" she asked, with her voice cracking. "It's my fiancé Lorenzo. Or my ex-fiancé, now. He asked me to marry him two months ago only for me to find out he's been hooking up with his ex since we've been together," she said, dropping her head. That's when I noticed the engagement ring on her finger. I felt bad for her, but I didn't know what to say and I still didn't know why she was here.

"Nova, I'm so sorry you're going through this. You definitely deserve better," I said.

She looked at me with her eyes full of tears. "Why couldn't *you* love me, Julian? Why couldn't you love me the way I loved you? Better yet, why couldn't you love me the way you loved that Serenity girl? Am I that awful?" she asked, and began to cry. This was heavy. I hated to be insensitive in this moment, but I was not sober enough for this conversation. I was having relationship issues of my own I needed to deal with, and here she comes out of the blue after a year looking for closure. I knew my next words would have a big impact on the situation, so I took a deep breath, focused very hard and chose my words carefully.

"Nova, you are a good woman and you deserve a man who will give you everything you need. When you and I were dating, I wasn't ready to be that for you. I see now how wrong I was to string you along, and how much that must have hurt you. I'm sorry for that," I said, hoping that would calm down some of her infinite reserve of silent tears.

She shook her head. "But why does this keep happening to me? I am not out here playing games or hooking up with random dudes. I just want someone who will love me!" she said, and now her tears were followed by audible sobs. I didn't know what else to say, because I knew I was one of the people who had hurt her in the past. I got up and got her some tissue to wipe her face. I sat next to her and rubbed her back. "I feel so alone. I don't want to feel alone anymore, Julian," she cried, and began rubbing my thigh.

"You shouldn't be alone. I shouldn't be either," I heard myself say, but my drunk ass couldn't tell if I said it out loud or in my mind. The next thing I knew Nova was straddling me, and the next thing I felt was her lips against my neck. Already drowsy, my head fell back to the couch.

"Touch me, Julian. Hold me like you used to," she whispered. It was like I wasn't in control of my own body when I gripped my hands around her waist. She grinded down on me, awakening a part of me that she'd known very well once upon a time. "I want you inside me. I need you to fill me up. I feel so empty, Julian. I need you," she moaned. And for some reason, *those* words sobered me up.

"Nova. No. I can't. I can't. We need to stop. Please," I mustered up the will to say. I moved her off my lap and leaned my head back on the couch. "This can't happen. You need to go." "Why? What's wrong?" she asked.

I sighed. "We both love other people, and this wouldn't be right."

She looked devasted, but not surprised. She seemed to sober up a little bit, too. A minute or two went by before she spoke. "Okay. I'll get an Uber."

*****

*Knock! Knock! Knock!* The loud knocks on my front door jolted me out of my sleep. I opened my eyes only for the sun to accost me. When I tried to get up is when I realized Nova was still here and was sleeping on top of me on the couch. When I realized we were both still dressed I sighed in relief.

I shook her awake. "Nova, you gotta get up," I said, as I heard the knocks again. She sat up and looked confused as to where she was.

"I gotta pee!" she said, and scurried to the bathroom. I got up and dragged myself to the front door and opened it.

My eyes got wide and my heart dropped down into my stomach.

"Layna—" I said.

She gave me a strange look. "Now I see why you didn't answer your phone. You look like you've had a rough night!" she chuckled.

"Uh yeah. Um—" I said, nervously.

"Look, I can't stay. I got the day off and me and Will are going to go visit our parents for a little bit," she said, motioning to Will who was in the car parked on the street. "I'll come over when I get back. I think we should talk. I don't think our disagreement is worth losing what we've shared over the last few months. Being apart from you for just a week was hard enough."

My heart melted from her words, and I was relieved she'd come back. Just when I was getting ready to respond, Nova called out,

"Julian, where do you keep your washcloths?" My heart then dropped down to my feet. I dropped my head. I'd forgotten that quickly that Nova was still here. Layna's eyes got as big as saucers.

"Who is that?!" she yelled, stepping into my house and pushing past me. I grabbed her arm but she pulled away. Nova came into view and observed me and Layna with a confused and shocked look on her face.

Layna turned to me with a look of rage that shook me. "One week

Julian?! One week?! You couldn't wait for me for one week?!" she yelled, and pushed me with one hand.

"Please calm down! It's not what it looks like! She's just my friend! And she needed someone to talk to," I said, and realized just how stupid and guilty I sounded.

"She just needed to talk?! It's not what it looks like?! It looks like there's a woman in your house who spent the night! It looks like you have her lipstick smeared all over your shirt! And correct me if I'm wrong, but *that* definitely looks like she's more than just a friend!" she snapped, motioning towards my crotch. It was first thing in the morning. *Morning wood* happens; but I wasn't going to argue biology right now. "Layna, please! Let me explain!" I pleaded.

"And is that a ring on her finger? She's the married woman?!" she screeched, and threw her head back. "My brother was right about you from the beginning! I can't believe I'd be so stupid!" she yelled, and her voice began to crack. Tears formed in her eyes. I tried to grab her.

"Don't put your hands on me!" she yelled, and began to walk towards the door.

"Please, Layna! You know me! You know I wouldn't do this to you!"

She turned and looked at me. "Can you look me in my eyes and tell me that absolutely nothing happened between you two last night?" she said, her voice dark, yet hopeful.

"Layna, let me explain. I was drunk and—"

"Did you touch her? Did you let her touch you?" she asked, directly. I dropped my head and sighed.

"Layna—"

"Yes or no, Julian!" she interrupted. Her eyes were already full of tears, and I knew my answer would unleash them. I couldn't lie to her. "Yes," I finally answered. Her tears fell and my heart broke.

"But—"

"But we didn't sleep together! He didn't invite me to come over; I just showed up. I didn't know he was seeing anyone," Nova interjected, only making the current situation sound even worse. If looks could kill, Nova wouldn't make it out of here alive.

"Layna, you alright in here? We gotta hit the road!" I heard Will's voice say approaching the front door. He knocked and stepped in. We all turned to look at him and watched his expression change from neutral to confusion. He looked from me to Nova and over to Layna, and when he saw her tears, I saw his rage. He grabbed Layna by the arm and pulled her to him. "Go get in the car," he ordered.

"Layna, I'm sorry," I said, one last time, because I knew it was all I could do. She walked over to me, looked me in my eyes and slapped me so hard I stumbled back. I held my face in pain and groaned. I would have never thought she was as strong or as quick as that. Nova gasped.

She then walked out the door. Seeing her leave was like watching a part of my heart walk away from my body. I almost couldn't breathe.

"Layna, wait!" I called out, and I began to go after her but Will put up his arm to stop me.

"I don't know what's going on here, but I already told you my sister ain't the one for you to play with! I told you not to mess with her until you had your shit together, man!" Will said sternly, his voice laced with disappointment and anger.

"Will, I care about your sister. I know this looks bad, but I swear on my life this isn't what it looks like. I love her," I pleaded, while confessing my love for Layna out loud for the first time. He looked from me to Nova, who still looked like a deer caught in headlights, and shook his head.

"Even if I believed that, which I don't, I'm not the one you have to convince. And the only reason you're still standing right now is because I know my sister really cares about you, and I know she doesn't want you to get hurt *for real*. You need to get your shit together. And don't bother my sister until you do," he said, then he turned and walked out the door.


The rest of my weekend was hopeless. I couldn't eat, I could barely sleep, and I couldn't concentrate on anything for more than a few minutes at a time. I called Layna only to find out that she'd blocked me. I know Will told me to back off until I got myself together, but to hell with that. I loved her. And once she calmed down, hopefully we'd be able to talk. Nova felt terrible for everything that had happened, but I didn't blame her. None of it was her fault. She didn't force her way into my house, and I didn't insist that she leave. I was trying to be a shoulder for her, and it ended up backfiring. I understood Layna's anger, but there's no way she was angrier with me than I was with myself. What had I done?

## 29

## Layna

Was I a magnet for good-looking, unfaithful men with great sex? I had to be. I cried for weeks after what happened with Julian, and I'd been writing more than I ever had been before. Knowing that he'd touched another woman only a week after he'd told everyone how being with me was like being in his own *heaven*, hurt like hell. As far as I was concerned, I was done with relationships for a while. I had more important things to think about and it was time for me to focus more on me.

None of the job interviews I had panned out the way I'd hoped. I got one job offer, but the pay was so low, I would actually be moving backwards if I took it. However, I was still stuck on wanting to work for myself and being my own boss. I was hoping I'd be able to find that magic entrepreneur formula by now.

*****

"What about if it's a boy, we name him *D'Marius?*" I asked Steph, as we enjoyed a Saturday afternoon together while Will was out running errands. She was now over four months pregnant, and they would be finding out the sex of their baby at their next appointment.

"D'Marius? No! That's too much! I want my baby to have a simple, yet meaningful name. Something that stands out, but is not over the top," she said, holding her small belly.

"Well, we still have some time to come up with something," I said, putting my phone down. We'd been scouring baby names online for at least an hour now.

"So how are you feeling?" she asked, and I knew she was referring to Julian.

"Much better."

"Good. Have you thought about talking to him at all?"

I shook my head. "There's nothing for us to talk about. I was beginning to have doubts about whether our relationship was authentic before what happened anyway. Besides, it's better if I just focus on me right now," I answered.

"I agree. Focusing on yourself is very important, but so is your happiness. I just want to see you smiling again, Layna."

"Steph, I can't keep tying my happiness to how a man makes me feel. I shouldn't need a man in my life to make me smile. I have to know how to do that on my own."

Steph sat back against the couch. "You're right. A man should never be your primary source of happiness. I'm merely suggesting that you start enjoying your life on your terms. You're young, single, beautiful, and smart. Make some new friends, socialize more, travel; you have the world at your fingertips! If you want to date, then date. If you want to be casual, then be casual; responsibly, of course. All I'm saying is what you do with your life is up to you."

"I know, Steph. You're right, it's just—" I began, but the words got caught in my throat.

"You love him?" she finished. I nodded. "I know you do, and I know it hurts. But use this time for you. You can't worry about him right now. Layna has to take care of *Layna*. And maybe the time for you and Julian to be together will come back around; because even though he did what he did, I know he loves you, too. You'll get no judgement from me if you choose to forgive him. But for now, live *your* life," Steph said, softly.

"Thank you Steph. I really needed to hear that."

"Of course. Now what are we going to do to get you ready for your first official *hot girl summer*?! Are we giving Jamal another chance or what? He's a little corny, but I like him," she chuckled.

I laughed. "Not Jamal, not anyone right now! So don't try to set me up!" I warned. I leaned over and gave her a hug and rubbed her belly, "You hear your momma out here being messy?" I said, to my niece or nephew. We both laughed.

### One Month Later

I was happy to be on summer break from classes. At the end of next

Spring semester, I'd be a proud graduate of the University of North Carolina, Charlotte. Over the last couple months, I'd taken Steph's advice and made a couple friends on campus; Melody, who I called

Mel, and Zamir. They'd known one another since elementary school, and had a very sibling-like relationship. However, I believed Zamir was completely in love with Mel. I was glad to finally be breaking out of my shell and becoming more social. I began hanging out more when I got off work, and I even hit a few clubs with my small group of friends. Jamal and I were still cool, too. Even though we shared a moment at a bar one night where we were making out like horny teenagers, we remained friendly. It was a one-time thing after I had a drink.

Afterwards, we both agreed we shouldn't do that again unless we planned on taking things further.

One thing Steph and Will loved to do was host parties at their house. Since it was getting too hot outside for a pregnant Steph to feel comfortable outdoors for too long, we were having a couples' game night indoors. I'd invited Mel and Zamir over to join us. Even though I asked Steph not to try to set me up with anyone, she invited a fourth-year surgery resident from the hospital she worked at named Cameron. She assured me there was no pressure, but she thought the two of us may hit it off.

The game was Charades and there were currently five couples participating; me, Mel, Zamir, Cameron, and Steph were on one team, while Will and his friends were on the other. We were down by three points, so we needed four to win. It was my turn to go up for the win. The subject I got was popular desserts. "And go!" Will said.

I picked up a card, "You make this in a blender; it's creamy, you sip it with a straw!"

"Milkshake!" Mel shouted.

"Yes!" I said, picking up another card. "Uh, you make this with different flavors, and toppings. It has three scoops, and you can share it!"

"Ice Cream Sundae!" Steph yelled.

"Right!" I picked up another card, we needed one more point to be tied. How in the world could I describe *Apple Pie a la mode*? "It's a fruit dessert, and it's hot! It has a crust, and uh… umm…

pass!" I said picking up another card. It was *Strawberry Shortcake,* which was worse than *Apple Pie!* "It sweet, it has layers and fruit, and whipped cream on the top," I said quickly.

"Angel Food Cake?" Zamir guessed.

"No! It's a cake, but it's—" I said.

"That's time!" Will interrupted and his team shouted in victory, as our team groaned in defeat.

"It was Strawberry Shortcake!" I whined to my team.


Our games continued into a game of '*Never Have I Ever,*' where I learned way more than I ever wanted to know about my brother and Steph. As the night progressed, I found myself getting more acquainted with Cameron. He was magazine cover handsome. He was tall, had smooth bronze skin, a nice smile and a pleasant personality. He was smart and career focused, but he also seemed like he knew how to kick back and have a good time. The only problem was, he wasn't Julian. I still missed Julian a whole lot, I couldn't deny that. But I also couldn't allow myself to slide backwards. I had to be smarter this time around.

When Cameron asked me out on a date, I hesitated before agreeing. Well actually, he suggested that me, him, Mel, and Zamir go out as a group. Cameron seemed to be a nice guy, and going out in a group took the pressure off of it feeling like a real date. I still hadn't completely gotten over Julian, but like Steph said, I needed to live my life. When Cameron and I exchanged numbers, he saved my contact info in his phone as *Cake*, as a joke.

# 30

## Julian

Patience was not my strong suit. The more days that passed, the worse I felt, and so far it had been 23 days since I last saw or heard from Layna.

For the past week I hadn't left my house. I told my job I had a sudden illness, and I'd be out for a few days. I had no clue I'd still be on my couch eight days later. Saying I was sick was only partially true, though. I *was* sick, but it wasn't anything a Tylenol and a few days of rest could cure. Apparently neither could consuming a couple bottles of Gin and listening to sappy R&B music.

After a week of calling and texting her to see if she'd unblocked me, I started to call Will. As expected, he did not answer my calls either. I knew I shouldn't have tried to involve him with what Layna and I had going on, but I was desperate. I thought I'd look too crazy if I showed up at her job, or if I tried to find her at school, so I fell back. A part of me knew I'd probably messed up too bad to even keep trying, and I should probably let her go; but a bigger part of me loved her too much to do that. I did my best not to think about her; the way she smelled, the sound of her laugh, and the deep conversations we had, but I couldn't help it. I was completely miserable and I didn't know what to do. I was sick without her.

"Son. What's going on?" Dad's voice rumbled above my head. He obviously let himself in my house, because the only time I'd opened the door was to get my fast-food deliveries. I guess after not returning his or my mom's phone calls or texts for several days, an unannounced visit was warranted. I turned my head to look at him. My head was so heavy, it felt like it was glued to the couch. Empty bottles of beer, Gin, Vodka, and empty takeout food containers littering my coffee table were at eyelevel in front of me. He walked over to the couch and pulled me up to my feet with relative ease. "I'm going to make you some coffee and clean up this mess. Go shower and when you come back we'll talk." I didn't object.

After taking a much-needed shower, I looked in the mirror and noticed how ungroomed I looked. I'd never seen myself look so rough. I put on a fresh set of clothes and joined my Dad back in the living room. I sat down on the couch and he brought me a cup of coffee and sat next to me.

"Do you want to talk about it?" he asked. Though I hadn't uttered a word, I had a feeling he knew exactly what I was going through.

I took a sip of coffee. "I messed up."

"Okay. Well, what do you intend to do about it?"

"There's nothing I can do. I hurt her really bad. She'll never forgive me."

He sighed. "Tell me what happened."

I figured if I only told him about Layna, he would only know part of the story. So, I began with the day I met Serenity. We talked for hours, but in the end he knew *everything*.

"I can still see that look Layna gave me. I made her cry. That shit haunts me. I never wanted to hurt her, Dad. I love her," I confessed. "Julian, love can be just as complicated as it is beautiful. It sounds to me like your feelings for her scared her, and then you took it as a personal attack when she expressed that to you. You have to be willing to listen just as much as you want to be heard. She told you reading that poem in front of a crowd was too much for her, and instead of acknowledging her feelings, you told her *that's just how you are.* She told you she wanted to protect your relationship because she'd been hurt in the past, and instead of ensuring her you wouldn't hurt her, you threw her pain back in her face. Do you see where I'm going with this, Son?"

"I do. I just thought she would have appreciated the gesture, but she made it seem like I'd done something wrong; like I was the bad guy. I just felt like… she was looking for an out. Like, she was trying to find a way to tell me she didn't want to be with me anymore. I just got so angry. I should have been able to control myself better," I sighed.

"Julian, why *did* you get so angry? I know you've heard worse things than what she said to you. Why did you react that way?" he pushed.

I pondered his question for several moments, and I really thought about my answer. "I guess… I guess I got so angry because a lot of what she said was right. And it was hard for me to hear. I do seek validation from my peers. I didn't take into consideration if she would be okay with me putting my feelings for her out there, and I should be more interested in protecting our bond than publicizing it." Dad nodded. The truth about my behavior was hard to admit but I needed to do it. "So, what do I do now? I don't want to just let her go, Dad."

"Julian, the harsh truth is she may not forgive you. It's one thing to have an argument, it's a whole other issue when there's another woman involved."

I palmed my face. "So, you don't think there's anything I can do?" I asked, beginning to feel anxious.

"Give her some time. In the meantime, keep yourself busy. Do things to work on you. Practice listening. Practice being patient. Determine what type of man you want to be and the type of partner you want to be for the woman you love, and work on that," he answered. I nodded, and I felt my eyes burning at the thought that I probably lost

Layna for good because of my selfish actions. I dropped my head. "I know it hurts, Son. I know it does. But I promise you, it will get better," he said, patting my shoulder.

*****

By the time I looked up, a whole month had passed since Dad found me passed out on the couch. Taking his advice, I started on the home improvements I'd been wanting to make for a while now. I began going to the home improvement store every day after work picking out new flooring, fixtures, and furniture for my house. I wanted my house to feel like a home. I enlisted the help of my dad to help with some painting and heavy lifting, but I hired a contractor to do the bigger projects. I still needed to finish decorating, but the inside of my house looked totally different.

The main areas of the house were painted in shades of calming blues. The new hardwood floors were a deep mocha color, and I'd found beautiful abstract artwork to adorn the walls. My mother suggested installing floor to ceiling window treatments, which turned out making the space look more open. She also helped me pick out new tile for the kitchen and bathrooms, and new carpet for the bedrooms. I had the vanities in both bathrooms replaced, too. My bedroom was my favorite part of the transformation. I'd gotten a whole new bedroom suit and a couple pieces of accent furniture.

Taking on this project did help distract me from the pain my heart was going through, and candid talks with my mother about how I'd been feeling filled in the blanks. She recommended a few books for me to read, and convinced me to give therapy a try. I'd only had one appointment so far, and it was okay. I decided I'd stick with it for a while.

*****


"Yo! Jay! What's good brother?" Bryan greeted me on the other end of my line. I went to high school and my first two years of college with

Bryan. He'd moved to Florida five years ago, but we still kept in touch, and it had been a while since I'd seen him.

"I'm good man. What's up with you?" I asked.

"Same shit. You know how it is."

"I do."

"Listen, I'm going to be in town for a few days and I wanted to know if you were up to hanging out with ya' boy this weekend!" he said excitedly.

"What are you trying to get into?" I asked. One thing about Bryan was he knew how to have fun. I'd never had a bad time whenever we hung out. I'd spent weeks working on my house trying not to think about Layna, so a change of scenery would probably do me some good.

"I don't know, man! Charlotte is your town now! You should be telling me where to go!" he countered. I laughed.

"I'll think of something."

"I'm staying at my mom's. Her 60th birthday party is on Friday, and we can get up on Saturday. You should come to the party, too. Mom would love to see you," he added.

"Yeah, I should be able to make it out." Bryan and I talked for a few more minutes before hanging up.


***Saturday Night***

I'd heard about a new bar that recently opened up called *Fuegos,* and I figured that would be a good place for me and Bryan to hang out and have a couple drinks.

"You're the one who almost got us suspended for singing, *Baby*

*Got Back,* when Sabrina Bledsoe came into science class late that time!

You started beat-boxing the song, so I had to do the lyrics!" I laughed.

"Yeah, we were wildin'! But Sabrina had too much ass back then! She had ass ahead of her time! I bet you she still got that ass!" Bryan added, still laughing. "But what's up with you, man? I'm surprised you're single. You *stay* in a relationship!" he said.

I shrugged. "Not really."

"I don't get you, man. With all the women who stay trying to get with you, you're always trying to be laid up under one woman!" he remarked. I shook my head, and chuckled. I didn't want to go down a rabbit hole of my relationship status. The goal was for me to *not* think about Layna tonight, but now I was thinking about her. I pulled my phone from my pocket and tapped open me and Layna's old text message thread:

*Layna: You are so sweet! You're spoiling me!*

*Me: LOL I'm not as sweet as you! I can't wait until you get here tonight. I've been craving something sweet all day. Can you help me out with that?*

*Layna: Your mind stays in the gutter! Me: Is that a yes?*

*Layna: Maybe…*

I smiled looking down at my phone and remembered how I tried to give myself a cavity that night the way I dined on her sweetness. The last several text messages of, '*I'm sorry,*' and '*Please call me,*' I'd sent her hadn't been read. Because I'm a glutton for punishment, I sent her another text:

*Me: I miss you*

I knew she would probably never see my text, but at this point I had nothing to lose.

"Jay! Did you hear what I said, man?" Bryan asked, pulling me out of my zone.

"Nah. My bad. What's up?"

He shook his head. "I said, do you see those two fine ass women over there? They been looking over here since we sat down," he said, motioning over to the women. The place was packed, but I easily saw which two women he was referring to.

I glanced over and turned back to him. "Honestly, I ain't paying attention like that, for real."

"What is going on with you, man? I'm gonna get you out of whatever this slump is right now!" he said, motioning over to the bartender.

"Come on, man. Not tonight!" I said, because I knew what he was about to do. He ignored me.

"Another shot for my boy and can you bring those ladies a round of what we're drinking?" Bryan said to the bartender.

"No problem. I got you," the bartender said and walked away. I blew out a heavy sigh and looked at Bryan.

"Come on Jay! One last time for old-time's sake?" he asked, with a confident grin. Bryan and I had a routine back in the day we used to pick up women. We would order a round of drinks for us, and send it to the women who we were interested in. In turn, the women would come over to us and start a conversation. It was cheesy, but it worked. I wasn't in the mood for it, but I wasn't going to stop Bryan from doing his thing.

A few minutes later we were approached by the two women. They were gorgeous, too. From head to toe, they weren't missing one beat. They joined us, and after talking for a few minutes, it became obvious who was attracted to who. I was just going with the flow, and engaging in light conversation. It was only when the woman who was interested in me put her hand on my thigh, did I realize I was not feeling this at all.

I stood. "I'm going to the men's room. I'll be back," I said, and promptly left the table.

As I was leaving the restroom, I checked my phone in hopes that Layna had finally unblocked me and responded to my *'I miss you,'* text earlier. She hadn't. I sighed. I decided in that moment that we'd been apart long enough, and tomorrow I was going to go to wherever she was and talk to her.

Just as I was ready to head back to my table, I heard a familiar laugh cut through all the chatter and music in the bar. I knew that laugh, it was Layna. My eyes searched the crowd until I found her, and once I saw her, I immediately wished I hadn't. She was here. She had on a skin tight dress that looked to be almost too short for her to sit down in. Her locs were done up in like a mohawk style, and she had on heels. I'd never seen her in heels. She looked good; she looked better than good. She looked happy, and she wasn't alone. She was comfortably seated on some dude's lap! His hand was at the small of her back, way too close to her ass, and his other hand was resting on her bare thigh. There were two other people at their table, a man and a woman. They all looked to be having a good time. A gush of emotions came over me so quickly, that I couldn't describe what I was feeling. However, my feet started moving in her direction.

I excused my way through the crowd of people until I ended up directly in front of Layna and the group of people she was with. She was in mid-laugh when she noticed me standing there. When she noticed me, she looked shocked.

"Layna, I need to talk to you right now, please," I said firmly, ignoring the looks the other three people at the table gave me. I knew I looked crazy, but I didn't care. This damn girl made me crazy, and if she didn't get off this man's lap, I was liable to lose it. Her shocked expression changed into one that challenged me. She looked slightly amused. It was as if she was saying, *'or what?'* She turned her head and ignored me as if I weren't standing there.

"Layna!" I called out to her again.

"Hey man, calm down with all that! She heard you the first time! You alright, *Cake*?" the dude who looked way too comfortable with Layna sitting on his lap, had the nerve to say. As hard as I'd been working to change some of my impulsive ways, my blood instantly began to boil. Who the hell was *Cake*? And why the hell was she so comfortable with him referring to her by that name?

"Cake?" I repeated, glaring down at Layna. I then turned my glare to him, using every fiber in my body to show restraint; but I was on fire.

"Respectfully, I'm talking to Layna."

"Respectfully, she's a little occupied right now," he said with a grin as he gave her thigh a light squeeze. I saw red, and Layna knew it.

"Cameron, it's okay. I'll be right back," she said, sensing the situation was about to escalate. She stood from his lap and tugged down at the hem of her dress. She grabbed her purse from the table and I saw his eyes glued to her ass, and I almost snapped. She grabbed my wrist and pulled me towards the exit.

# 31

## Layna

Steph was right. I needed to live my life in ways that made me happy.

I'd been socializing way more and enjoying the freedom I had being single. Tonight, I wanted to have fun. I wanted to get dressed up, have a few drinks, and laugh a little with friends. That's what I decided when I agreed to go out with Cameron, Mel and Zamir. Cameron and I had texted a few times, but this was the first time I was seeing him after game night over a month ago. Judging from the chemistry me and

Cameron were having, there was a real possibility I'd be going home with him tonight and doing the walk of shame in the morning. That's why when I saw Julian standing in front of us, I was truly shocked.


"Are you sleeping with him?!" Julian nearly growled at me as soon as we stepped outside.

"That's not your business, Julian!"

"I don't care if it's not my business! And why the hell is he calling you *Cake*?!" he snapped. Did you let him—"

"You really have a lot of nerve asking me anything about what I'm doing and who I'm doing it with! Are you still sleeping with that married bitch you spent the night with? Or Peaches? Or whoever you call to come through to keep you company?" I snapped back, cutting him off.

"No! I did not sleep with her! And she's not married! You would know that if you would have let me explain!"

"Men will say anything to get what they want! And you expect me to believe you?!"

"Yes! Because I'm not a liar!"

I scoffed. "Whatever! I knew the type of guy you were before I even got involved! This is over between us! I'm not going to stand here and go back and forth with you, Julian! I need to get back to my friends."

"Your *friends*? Tell me, what type of friend sits on another friend's lap while he calls her *Cake*?" I relished in his question for a moment, because I knew he wouldn't like my answer.

"The same type of *friends* you have that sit on your lap! Or the same type of friends you let stay overnight who you can't keep your hands off!" I answered, pointedly. I struck a nerve with *those* words. His nostrils flared, and I saw his anger soar. He looked at me with fire behind his eyes. I took that as an opportunity to dig my heels in even more. I continued, "I figured since me and relationships don't mesh well, I thought I'd give being casual a try. Isn't that what you called it? Being *casual*? Where I can be with whoever I want without any expectations? It sounds way better than being attached to one person and hope they don't hurt you. And it's way more fun, too." I glared at him.

He inhaled and exhaled deeply, searing a look at me. "Layna—" he called out my name, in a tone that seemed to be a warning for me to stop talking. So, I pushed even further.

"And don't worry. I'll be in good hands tonight. Cameron is a surgeon, so his job is to know every part of the body—inside and out, and I'm ready to see what them hands do! And to answer your question, no, I haven't done anything with Cameron yet. I guess he can just look at me and tell how sweet I taste. Or maybe it's all this ass I have sitting on him that has him calling me *Cake*," I said, hitting the final nail in the coffin. Julian advanced towards me, walking me backwards until my back touched the wall of the building. He placed his palms on the wall at the sides of me, caging me in. He glared down at me, but I didn't yield. I was past done with men doing and saying whatever they wanted to and expecting the woman to understand or to be forgiving. I loved Julian, but I knew if I gave him another chance he would hurt me.

"You and this damn mouth!" he grumbled, in a low deep voice.

"You think this is cute? You've ignored me for weeks, and you never gave me a chance to apologize or explain. Now, you're out here looking this good with another man in this little ass dress, sitting on his lap and talking about him putting his mouth and his hands on you?! All while my heart is all fucked up over you! I couldn't be with another woman even if I tried, Layna! All I think about is you! You talking all this shit is only going to get your little boyfriend in there hurt! I'm not playing,

Layna," he said with an eerie calmness. One of his hands slipped down to my waist, then to my bare thigh. His touch felt like a smooth electrical current that warmed my entire body. I gasped. "You're trying to be out here in the streets? That ain't you," he said, moving his big hand underneath the hem of my dress. His hand invaded my panties and two of his fingers penetrated me. I whimpered. "These are the only hands you need touching you," he whispered, in a voice deeper than usual. He removed his hand and licked his fingers. "This is the only mouth you need to taste you," he quickly inserted his fingers back inside me. "You're supposed to be with me. In my bed. With only my hands touching you, and my body pleasing you," he said seductively, as he began moving his fingers around inside me. I couldn't respond. "I'm sorry for what I said. I'm sorry for what I did. I'm a selfish asshole. But I am sick without you, baby. *I'm sick*. Please let me make this right.

Please forgive me…please," he pleaded, piercing me with his unrelenting stare. He began moving his fingers faster inside me, and I was about to become untied and he knew it. Keeping my whimpers low was challenging. Afterall, we were still outside, and it wasn't hard to conclude what he was doing to me. He leaned over to my ear. "I can stop, or I can keep going until you finish. Tell me what you want," he whispered, and pulled back to watch me. My body felt lazy and I could barely hold myself upright. I nodded.  "Tell me what you want," he commanded.

"Julian—" I whined.

"A minute ago, you couldn't stop talking. Tell me," he said through a sexy breath. I felt his erection growing against my leg.

"I want you to keep going!" I whined.

"Only me?" he asked.

"Yes, only you."


He began to massage me even better. I held on to his waist and buried my head in his chest to mute my moans. The heat generated between our bodies danced with each other. He started rubbing my pearl until my climax saturated his fingers in my essence. He slowly removed his hand. My head stayed buried in his chest as I caught my breath. When I finally looked up at him, his eyes were still fixated on me.

"Come home with me. Let's talk," he said, giving me no room to mistake his request as a question.

"Julian, I—I can't," I responded, regretfully. My eyes shifted to the ground, because I knew if I looked at him, I'd cave.

"Baby—"

"I can't," I repeated. Still looking to the ground, I placed my hands on his chest. "I think it's better if we just kept our distance from one another." I felt the pace of his heart quicken under my palms.

"You don't mean that," he said in a low voice.

"I do."

"Layna, look at me," he requested, but I couldn't do it. "Fine, you don't have to look at me; just listen. I love you, and I'm not sorry for that. The first time I saw you, I knew you would somehow add something amazing to my life just by your presence; and you did. That night we first kissed, I knew in that moment all the bullshit I'd gone through was so I could get to you. I'm not perfect, and I know I've made mistakes, but how I feel about you is clear. I love you, and I want to love you the right way. Just please tell me how you need me to love you and I'll do it. Tell me what I need to do for you to forgive me, and I will do it. Just tell me," he pleaded.

Tears fell down my face. All of my defenses were down as he laid his heart at the mercy of my next words. I looked up at him, and water flooded his eyes.

"I have to go," I whispered, nudging him so he could move back far enough for me to get by. He reluctantly moved out of my way. "I'm sorry, Julian," I said, and swiftly walked back into the loud bar.

# 32

## Julian

***Two Months Later. Friday Afternoon.***

I had to come to terms that my with relationship with Layna was really over, and it was because of me. My ego, my temper, and my lapse in judgement to let a woman in my house at almost midnight after I'd been drinking, contributed to me taking accountability. I know I said I loved women in my past, but those feelings paled in comparison to how I felt about Layna. That love was superficial and based on a fantasy; not reality. My love for Layna was real. I felt it, and her, everywhere. Through therapy I learned that holding on to something can be more painful than letting go. Holding on is like being in a prison; letting go is freedom. And because I loved Layna so much, I knew I had to let her go.

My cousin Taryn and her husband, Stanley, were driving up from Macon to visit me this weekend. It would be a short trip, but I was glad they were coming. Over the last several weeks, I'd been heavily focusing on myself. The first thing I decided to do was to stop drinking for a while. I realized some of the poor decisions I'd made over the last few months came after I'd overindulged in alcohol. I was now going to therapy once a week, and I was beginning to feel as if it were helping me become more self-aware. Therapy became especially helpful once I began talking about my romantic relationships. I still had work to do when it came to dealing with rejection, but I was satisfied with my progress. What I enjoyed the most was I was getting the best sleep I'd had in years. And for the first time in a long time, I'd been sleeping alone.

Taryn and Stanley would be arriving soon, and my dad would be coming by as well, but there was one thing I needed to do before they arrived and before I lost my nerve. I walked up the five stairs that led me to Will's front door. I rang the doorbell, and a few moments later a very pregnant Stephanie opened the door. The last time I saw her she was barely showing. It looked like the size of her stomach had doubled. "Julian—" she greeted me with a warm smile. I didn't know what type of energy I'd encounter coming here, so I was glad she was welcoming.

"Hey, Stephanie. It's good to see you. How's the baby doing?" I asked, returning her smile.

"Busy!" she answered holding her stomach.

"That's a good thing, though," I said, and we both chuckled.

"Um, Layna isn't here. She's at work."

"Oh. Yeah, I figured. I just wanted to drop this off to her," I said, handing her a classic black and white composition notebook.

She held it in her hands and stared at it for a moment. "Is there anything you want me to tell her when I give this to her?" she asked.

"Nah. It's all in there."

She nodded. "Okay. I'll give it to her tonight."

"Thanks, I appreciate it. Well, I have to get going. Take care of that baby in there!" I said, smiling.

"I will. You take care, too." I then turned, and walked to my car.

*****

*Later that night*

I loved having Taryn and Stanley staying with me for the weekend. Dad came over and cooked dinner for us and afterwards we all sat around and reminisced about the old times we spent together back in Georgia. After Dad went home, and Stanley called it a night, Taryn and I chatted in my living room.

"I was hoping I'd see your girl Layna this weekend. It was so sweet when she came down for Grandaddy's funeral. Is she coming by?" Taryn asked.

I smiled at the memories of me and Layna together in Georgia, and quickly brought myself back into reality. "Nah, she ain't coming. Me and her don't talk anymore," I said plainly.

Her eyebrows furrowed. "Huh? Ju-Ju, what did you do to that sweet girl?"

"What makes you think *I* did something?" I asked, light-heartedly.

"Because, I know you did! What did you do?" she asked again.

I sighed. "That's a story for another day."

"Well, will she at least be at the poetry night you're hosting tomorrow? That's where you said you met her, right?"

"Yeah, but I have no clue if she'll be there. The last couple times

I've gone she wasn't there, so I wouldn't be surprised if she didn't come." I answered, doing my best to sound *normal,* even though my heart still ached a little just thinking about her.

"Well, whatever you did, you need to fix it! Everybody saw the love in your eyes every time you looked at her. I thought for sure you'd have a ring on her finger by now! Women as caring and as genuine as her are not easy to come by," she said, before spearing another chunk of watermelon into her mouth. We chatted for a few minutes more before going to bed.

A few minutes after I laid in bed my phone buzzed.

*Layna: I got the book. Thank you.*

My stomach got weak seeing her name pop-up on my phone again.

*Me: You're welcome.*

*Me: How have you been?*

I didn't know if she would respond, but I hoped she would. I saw bubbles appear and disappear several times.

*Layna: I'm alright. You?*

*Me: I'm glad you're alright. I'm doing okay.*
*Layna: Good.*

*Me: What are you doing up? I know you're usually in bed before the sun goes down!*

*Layna: LOL… very funny. I was up
writing. Me: Writing what?*

*Layna: Poetry. Your book inspired me. It's
perfect.* I smiled at the ease of our conversation.
*Me: Thank you.*

*Layna: You're welcome.*

I wanted to say more; much more than I could in a text message. Before I could begin typing again, more bubbles appeared.

*Layna: Goodnight, Julian.*

*Me: Goodnight.*


### Saturday Night

When Omar agreed to let me co-host Words and Versus, I didn't know how I'd feel introducing artists to the stage instead of being one that performed. I wanted to take a step back and genuinely engage with my peers and support them the way they'd always supported me. I wanted to be there to listen instead of being the one being listened to. It may not have seemed like a big deal to anyone else, but removing myself from the spotlight was a humbling decision. I couldn't rely on my crazy mix of metaphors and wordplay or my larger-than-life on-stage persona to get the crowd's attention; I had to rely on just being me.

The night was going well. I was settling in to my hosting duties better than I expected, and I loved the interaction I was able to have with the crowd as I introduced the artists. Taryn and Stanley seemed to be enjoying themselves, which I was glad to see.

I stood at the back of the room while a poet, Mystique, recited her erotic poem. Anytime she performed, I was *all* in.

"I see you're here alone tonight. What happened to *Miss Heaven*? I haven't seen you two together for a while," Peaches said, with an air of arrogance in her voice that quite frankly, I didn't appreciate.

I didn't bother to look at her as she casually stood next to me.

"Don't you have someone besides me to talk to? I'm trying to listen," I answered, not taking my eyes away from the stage.

"What? No poem tonight?" she asked, sarcastically. I ignored her. She wanted me to engage with her and I refused to give her any more of my energy. She scoffed, "I'm glad she listened to me when I told her you were just using her the same way you use everybody." Now *that* got my attention. I turned questioning eyes in her direction. She added,

"That's right, I told her how you are; how you've slept with almost every woman in here, and how she ain't special to you because of that whack-ass poem you read that night! Everyone knows you only did that for attention. You always do shit like that."

If there was ever a time I truly wanted to put hands on a woman, this moment was it. Her and I had a stare down as she waited for my response. I knew she wanted to get under my skin. I knew she wanted me to act a fool, but I didn't. I actually felt a little bad for her, and I decided to show her some grace.

"Well, I hope you enjoy the rest of your night," I said, and walked away. What she said filled in so many blank spaces of what happened between me and Layna that night. I couldn't take Peaches seriously, but it did make me wonder if I had made my feelings for Layna look like a joke; especially since we were no longer together.


About thirty minutes later, Omar handed me the open-mic signup sheet so I could call up the next performer. I saw the name on the page and my speech stalled for a split second and I looked around the crowded space before going back up to the stage. I still didn't see her.

"Words and Versus, next up to the mic is a very talented woman.

I'm glad she's here tonight to share with us. If this is your first time hearing her, then you're in for a treat! Please welcome to the stage, a *queen with a dope soul* and a pen game that can easily put *me* to shame! Give it up for Miss Layna, y'all!" I introduced. Seeing her smile emerge through the crowd after two months of being apart, looked like a dream I did *not* want to wake up from. Saying she looked good was a disservice to how she snatched my soul from my chest. She had on all black *everything*; and damn if her soft body didn't look even better than I remembered. I lowered the mic stand for her, and when she reached me, I wasn't sure if I was supposed to give her a simple hug like I'd done for every woman who'd come up before her. I certainly wasn't going to dap her up like I'd done with the guys I introduced. Thankfully, she chose for me when she leaned in for a hug. *My God, I didn't want to let her go.* I gave her a quick squeeze and left the stage.

# 33

## Layna

After my encounter with Julian at the bar a couple months ago,

Cameron and I hadn't talked as much, and I was fine with it. Obviously, I wasn't ready to spend the night with him after what happened outside with Julian, anyway. Especially after he declared his love for me, because unlike Derrick, I knew he really meant it. Julian wasn't the first break up I'd gone through, but it seemed to hit me the hardest. It hurt in a different way; in an intimate way, because I knew I really loved him, too.

Aside from those feelings, I was still doing exactly what Steph suggested I do; living my life, having fun, and doing things that made me happy. I had a lot to look forward to; I was entering my final year of school, I'd been working on starting my own publishing company called, F.L.O.W. (For the Love Of Writing), my beauty blog, *Naturally Pretty*, was beginning to get sponsorships, and Steph would be having my little nephew right before Thanksgiving in a few months. Also, thanks to my relentless networking, I'd managed to connect with someone from a major marketing firm who said they'd have remote associate-level positions opening up soon and would hire me once they got the green light. Yes, everything was going well except that nagging ache in my chest. *Julian.* I was ready to talk to him, but he beat me to the punch.

The other night when I came home from work, Steph told me Julian had stopped by and left me a notebook. On the cover of the book, he'd drawn the word, *Audio-Gasmic*, in like a graffiti style. I'd read a lot of his poetry, but I'd never seen this book. Inside he'd written me a small note:

*Layna,*

*You once told me one of your dreams was to start a publishing company to help authors get their voices out into the world. You also told me you believe in me and my talent is too big to just be in this corner of the world. Well, I believe in you, too. And I would like to be your first client whenever you start your company. Here is my submission for your   consideration. It's a book of some of my favorite love poems that I've written over the years that I would like the world to hear. I know you'll do great things. Like I once said before, you'll always stand out. — Julian*

After taking a few moments to compose my emotions, I turned the page and began to read. I read everything in one sitting. This was him. This was his heart on these pages and he was handing it to me. I couldn't help but to become overwhelmed by his symbolic gesture. I decided to unblock him and thank him via text.

After I shared some of his book with Steph, my pen hit the paper and I let my emotions flow out of me. Later that night, I heard from Will that Julian would be co-hosting Words and Versus the following night; so here I was.

"Thank you Words and Versus, and thank you Julian for such an amazing introduction," I began, smiling over at him. Looking out into the crowd of people, I held my notebook tight to my chest. "This is only my second time doing this, so bear with me," I said opening my notebook. I felt the stares of what seemed to be one hundred pairs of eyes crawling over me, but the only pair that still made my heart flutter belonged to *him*. I looked up and saw his deep, chestnut brown eyes focused on me. I began to speak into the microphone again. "This poem is inspired by love; by the nervous feeling you get anytime you're around that special person, or by the way your body melts anytime you feel their touch, but mostly by the way they seem to take your breath away. I know those feelings well. This poem is called, Breathless," I said, before reading:


*He leaves me breathless…*
*I am left with less words to say than I can think of when I talk to*
*him.*

*I'm open and closed at the same time,*
*I'm listening in one ear and hearing in the other,*
*Unable to fully form thoughts into words that make sense,*
*Breathing like it's the last breath,*
*Words without a voice pounding in my chest,*
*I am breathless…*
*I watch him watch me with his admiring eyes,*
*Studying my every move,*
*Absorbing the tones of my voice,*
*Listening and praying,*
*Waiting cautiously to make his next move,*
*Hoping that I won't do how all the others seem to do…*
*He is breathless…*
*Left with less than half a breath to make it to the next word,*
*He stumbles his speech,*
*He grinds on his teeth,*
*He scared to show me everything he's covering that lives beneath…*
*Or so I think,*
*It's hard for him to breathe,*
*I leave him breathless…*

*I am everything and nothing that lives between amazement and
beauty,*
*I am the song he seeks with a sporadic melody and free styled
lyrics, I am happiness and reality merged in one name,*
*I am the place where possibilities are realized and the fear of
failure haunts you,*
*I leave him gasping for air,*
*But I stop to help him breathe,*
*Slowly and calmly,*
*Giving him time, patience and understanding because I know that's
what he needs...*
*Breathe baby breathe...*
*He sees an unknown future full of uncertainties but he still
believes,*
*Life leaves him breathless...*
*What will he say next when he's able to finally catch his breath?*
*I'm still breathless*
*Knowing what I want but haven't yet figured out how to get it,*

*How to hold it, keep it, and care for it,*
*How to love it and get rid of it once I'm done,*
*I pause relentlessly before I form the letters of my words,*
*I only have 26 ways to get it right,*
*I only have until the next breath before I run out of air,*
*Help.Me.Breathe. He teaches me without knowing,*
*He touches me without reaching,*
*He understands me with minimal explanation,*
*This is the only way I can describe this, breathless sensation...*
*Yes, I take his breath away, After he takes mine, He leaves me
breathless...*
*Come back so I can breathe.*

I took several deep breaths as I took in the unexpected applause from everyone. Some people had even stood to their feet; I was overwhelmed. "Thank you," I breathed into the microphone over the sounds of people clapping and snapping their fingers. As I was ready to leave the stage, Julian approached me.

He leaned over into my ear. "I told you the next time you did this I wouldn't be able to control myself," he whispered, and stepped back to gaze down at me.

I smiled. "I know," I whispered back. He leaned in and hugged me, tightly. I hugged him back.

"I've missed you," he whispered against my neck.

"Me too," I said, before walking away from the stage. I was heading back to my seat to join Mel and Zamir who agreed to come out with me tonight when a familiar voice stopped me. "Layna!" the voice said, and I turned to see Taryn smiling at me.

"Hey!" I returned, as we embraced in a hug. "What are you doing here?"

"Me and Stan came to visit Ju-Ju for the weekend. We're leaving tomorrow, though. But it's so good to see you! And I *loved* that poem!" she said, excitedly.

"Thank you," I said, shyly.

"I know Ju-Ju loved it, too. Girl, I thought he was about to get you pregnant up there judging from the way he hugged you!" she said, jokingly.


We shared a laugh then I introduced her to Mel and Zamir before she went back to her seat. After the night ended, Mel, Zamir,

Taryn, Stanley and I were outside talking when Julian and Omar approached us.

"Miss Layna! You shut it down tonight! I didn't know you wrote like that!" Omar said, giving me a hug.

"Thank you," I said, smiling at him. My eyes then locked with Julian's whose eyes I already felt on me.

"I don't know, it was okay, but it sounded like something was missing," Julian said, no doubt giving me a hard time the same way I'd given him after he read his *King* poem.

I smiled. "Please, do tell," I replied, while everyone watched our interaction.

"I mean, it was good but you had a whole poem about not being able to breathe, and it looks like you're breathing fine to me!" he mocked, doing his best impression of me. We all laughed.

"Still a hater, I see!" I said, still laughing. I looked over to my friends. "These are my friends, Melody and Zamir," I introduced, even though I'm sure they remembered him from that night at the bar. Everyone shook hands and spoke to one another.


Julian pulled me to the side as everyone continued talking.

"Tomorrow night, do you have plans?" he asked, and it was in this moment I realized just how much I truly missed him.

"No. I'll be home."

"Can you be at my house at 6'o'clock?"

"Yeah."

"Good. I'll see you then," he said, before kissing me on my forehead. A minute or two later we all said goodnight and parted ways.

## 34

# Julian

I said my goodbyes to Taryn and Stanley this morning, and stopped by my mom's house for an hour or so afterwards. Then I went home to get ready for the night. Layna was coming over and I didn't want anything to go wrong. Her and I needed to talk, and I was ready.

She stepped inside and I closed the door behind her. "Julian, your house! It looks so different!" she complimented. However, I didn't give a damn about any remodel, paint color or new piece of furniture I bought right now. All I could see was her. All I wanted was her. She had to feel it radiating from me. She turned to look at me, but my eyes were already locked on her.

"Thank you for coming," I whispered.

"You're welcome," she said, lifting her hand to my face to stroke my jaw. I turned my head and kissed her palm. "Does your being here mean you forgive me?" I asked.

"Me being here means that I love you, and yes, I do forgive you." I hugged her tightly, and relief rushed over my body while I tried to absorb her declaration of love for me for the first time.

I stepped back. With the amount of pure desire I had rushing through every vein in my body right now, I was afraid to touch her. I was afraid to kiss her. I was afraid to do anything to her besides look at her, because I knew I would not be able to control myself. I had to breathe, because I was about to crumble under her touch. I knew we needed to talk more, but when she stepped forward and gave me a soft kiss on my lips, talking had to wait. She gave me another kiss, and then another. Soon I was returning her kisses, parting her lips with my tongue. Her hands rubbed all over my body while my hands stayed planted firmly around her back. I dropped my kisses down to her neck and began to squeeze her breasts. She moaned like she missed me.

"Take off your clothes, please," I requested.
"Here?"

"Right here. Right now," I said. I gave her the required space she needed to undress and silently lost my shit while watching her. I leaned over again and kissed her like she held my next breath hostage. My head was swimming. I paused, "Let me ask you something. Did you get tested and start on birth control like we talked about before?" I asked.

"Yes, I did. I'm good. Did you?"

"I did, and I'm good, too," I answered. She unbuttoned and unzipped my jeans as I watched her. She then placed her hand inside my boxers and began to stroke me. I lost my damn mind. I lifted her by the thighs and she wrapped her legs around me. I carried her into my bedroom as she gifted me with soft kisses on my neck. I laid her perfect body down on my bed. I quickly undressed before joining her. I gazed into her eyes as her chest heaved. She'd been gone too long, and the way my heart was jumping right now was confirmation I didn't want to be without her again. We kissed, softly. "You have no idea how much

I've missed you. I've never felt this way about any woman, Layna, and I want to give all I have to give to you. Please, let me worship you like the queen you are to me," I said, almost desperately.

She smiled, then she tensed a little. "I don't want to get hurt again, Julian."

"I won't ever hurt you again. Please believe me, Layna. I love you," I said, then I leaned in closer and kissed her softly.

"I love you, too," she returned, and it felt like fireworks exploded in my chest hearing her say it again.

We continued to kiss. "You're so beautiful," I whispered against her lips, as her locs laid carelessly tossed around my pillow.

"So are you," she returned. Her hands traveled my body as my lips traveled hers.

I paused when I noticed a mark under her right breast. It was a tattoo that read, *Zion* with a small crown on top of the Z. I traced it with my fingers before kissing it. "*Queen Zion*," I whispered.

"Yes. I got it there because I figured the only person who would ever be able to touch it, would be my *king*," she whispered back.

I kissed her tattoo again before taking her breast into my mouth while squeezing the other one. "Open your legs," I said. She obeyed. She was so wet that my fingers easily slipped inside her treasure. I moved back up and kissed her lips, then I watched her pretty face contort into pleasure as she moaned. I removed my fingers. "Open your mouth," I groaned. I then put my fingers in her mouth and she licked them clean, never breaking eye contact with me. That turned me on beyond words. I leaned back over and shoved my tongue in her mouth, sharing the taste of her essence. I rolled on top of her and slid my erect, pulsating shaft into her tight, wet center. We both moaned in each other's mouth at the fit. It had been years since I'd been inside a woman without a condom on, and the sensation almost leveled me on contact. This was a level of trust and intimacy I didn't take lightly. The feel of her walls stretching around me like this felt too good for words. I didn't move. I wanted to relish in how she felt just like this. The inside of her was throbbing all around me. She'd already began to whimper. She lifted her head and kissed my lips.

"Julian—" she hissed, as I began to move my hips. I threaded our fingers together and she closed her eyes.

"Open your eyes for me, baby. I need to see you," I whispered. She looked at me and her lust drenched eyes looked so sexy. "Tell me how you want it. I'll do absolutely anything you want to make you feel good. Do you want me to give it to you like this?" I asked, still stroking her gently. "Or do you want it like this?" I asked, and then thrusted hard strokes into her. She screeched. I slowed back down. "Which one do you want? This is about you. Tell me what you want, *Queen*. I'm here to serve *you*," I said. She responded with more moans and words I couldn't understand. I buried my head in her neck, and stroked her slow. She panted and whined, as I felt her nails dig into my lower back. I took my time to luxuriate inside her. Her fit around me was perfection, and she was so wet that I knew she was dripping all over my sheets. I adored her and her beautiful body she so graciously trusted me with. I sucked on her neck and spread her legs even wider at the sides of her. I felt myself get even deeper than before.

"Julian! Julian! Ahhhh!" she cried out, through her first climax.

Her eyes rolled back as she clawed at my shoulders. I ain't going to lie, I almost cried out, too. "You feel so good! Please, don't stop!" she whined.

I groaned in approval, more than eager to give her what she asked for. "Yes, baby! You can have whatever you want from me!" I pulled out of her and flipped her onto her stomach. I slid out the bed. "Get on your knees," I commanded. She did as she was told. I slid her to the edge of the bed, and positioned her perfectly in front of me. I pushed her head down to the bed and dined on everything she had between her legs. She tasted so good that I was moaning almost as loud as her. "That night I saw you, you said you were going to give *this* to some other man? All of this?!" I smacked her perfect ass. "All this is mine! I better not ever hear you say no shit like that again! You hear me?!" I grumbled, and returned back to her thick lips until she cried out my name through another climax. I entered her once again, inserting my thumb into her other tight opening. She was moaning, and whimpering, growling and grunting as I did my best to claim her, and this machine she had between her legs as mine. When she took both her hands and spread herself open wider for me was my breaking point. I knew I should have pulled out, but I didn't have time. We exploded together. "Layna!" my voice strained as I emptied inside her. I pulled away from her and dropped my body on the bed like dead weight. She laid down, flat on her stomach. We both were breathing like we'd just run a marathon.

*****

I held her as she laid on my chest. We both showered and changed the linen on my bed before laying back down. I gave her one of my t-shirts to wear. My fingers danced in her locs while her warm breaths tickled my chest.

"She was my ex," I said breaking the silence. Layna remained quiet. I continued, "Her name is Nova. It actually feels weird calling her my ex since one of the problems we had was I didn't want to give us a title. She came to my house uninvited crying about how her fiancé was cheating on her. I was already drinking because I was in my feelings thinking I'd lost you for good. I was drunk and things did go further than they should have, but I did not sleep with her. I'm sorry any of that ever happened. The argument, the things I said, all of it. I'm sorry."

Layna remained quiet for a few minutes before speaking. "I believe you. If I really thought you slept with her, I wouldn't be here. In that moment, I thought about how my ex made a fool out of me. Then I remembered everything my brother warned me about you." She paused,

"And I'm sorry about the argument, too. I let what that Peaches hoe said and what my ex did to me make me feel insecure. I know you're not him."

Because I already knew what Peaches said, I didn't feel the need to address anything more about her or anyone else who didn't matter to me. "Layna, you are so special to me, and ironically, it took us being apart for me to realize just how much. I needed that time to get myself together. But being with you right now makes me feel stronger, better…

I think about my future when I'm with you. A real future, not some fantasy idea I've created about what love should look like. I actually see my future with me loving you. I want to be the man to support you, comfort you and protect you. This is real to me.

You're the piece that was missing in my poem. You were right. I was just a man in search of my queen. She is you," I confessed. There was no anxiety attached to my words and saying them felt right. I loved Layna. She was my queen, and everything in my heart fell into place once I said it. I felt her silent tears wet my chest. I hugged her tighter. "Don't cry," I said, soothing her for a few minutes. I kissed her forehead.

She propped herself up on my chest and held her hands to the sides of my face. She softly kissed my lips and her gaze penetrated me down to my soul. *This woman and these eyes of hers shuffled my heart around every time she looked at me.*

"I hear you. I see you…the *real* you. Not the persona you show everyone else. I see *you*. And I want all of you. We've made mistakes, but this love… this love I feel between us is more than I ever felt. I want to experience all of you. You asked me to tell you how I wanted to be loved. Well, I want you to love me your own way and we can help each other as we go. I'm ready."

Every rough edge I had began to soften at her words. I felt a lump rise in my throat, but I swallowed it back down. Damn, this woman brought me to my knees and my heart knelt before her ready to fulfill her every need. We kissed, and soon after, our kisses caught fire and turned into a blaze that could burn down this entire city.

*****

*Reciprocation*; my second love language. My heart was full. Last night, after Layna told me she loved me, I buried myself inside her the way a man does when he's trying to make a baby. I wasn't ready for a baby right now, but the way we connected last night and this morning, had me ready to write my vows today and say, *'I do'* tomorrow. We talked almost all night until we fell asleep. I'd finally found the right woman to receive me and my love fully, and not turn away from it.

I took the day off work and got up early and went to the market and to the pharmacy to pick up a few things while Layna slept in. I wanted to do a few things to spoil her. I still wasn't the best cook, but I knew how to make eggs, toast, bacon, and cut up pieces of fruit to make them look nice. I bought a serving tray to serve her breakfast in bed and fresh flowers to put by the bedside. I'd always wanted to be able to treat a woman like this, and for her to appreciate my efforts. She was finally here.

# 35

## Layna

I woke to soft caresses gliding over my body. I peeled open my eyes and Julian looked at me with a bright smile. "Good morning," he greeted. "Go get cleaned up. I made you breakfast and I'm going to bring it to you in a few minutes." Julian was so fine, that he actually could get me to do whatever he wanted me to do. I melted under his touch, his gaze and his words. However, I would never tell *him* that.

After he served me breakfast, he ran me a hot bath and bathed me. He used an argon oil scented bubble bath that smelled divine. Once I was out the tub, he spread me across his bed and massaged my entire body with sweet almond oil. Then, we made love again. And this time, I took charge. In the end, I think everyone in the neighborhood knew that he loved me judging from how loud he got.

"How did you start writing poetry?" I asked. I was finally able to get a real tour of Julian's newly decorated space. He gave me the grand tour of the upgrades he'd done to his home. There were so many pictures of him and his family on display now. My heart melted when I saw a framed photo of us in his office. It was a selfie we took on our first date at the roller rink. We sat cuddled with one another on the couch in the living room.

"You're the first person to ever ask me that," he chuckled. "I was nine years old and we had to make Mother's Day cards in Art class. I made mine and wrote like a six-line poem in it. Back then, I didn't know it was a poem, I just wanted it to rhyme. Everybody started asking me to help them write theirs. When I gave it to my mom, she really liked it and bragged to all her friends about it. When my friends in school started asking me to write poems for the girls they liked, I started to realize I had real talent. So, I started charging five dollars a poem! I cleaned up around Valentine's Day! After a while, I stopped writing for other people and started writing for me," he explained.

"Wow! I love that story! But you were hustling in elementary school?" I laughed.

"Supply and demand, baby!" he laughed.

"Well, thank you for trusting me with publishing your first collection of poems. I know everyone will love it!"

"You need to publish your own poems, too. The way you ripped the mic the other night was crazy," he said, squeezing my hand.


As the afternoon progressed, I became sad knowing I had to go home soon. We sat on the couch watching TV, but mostly stealing kisses from one another. I can't ever remember feeling so completely free or so happy. I felt as if this was our new beginning, and we had nothing but love to build us up. Best day ever.


### 9 Months Later

This was the first time in my life I could say I knew what being *in love* felt like. Our past nine months together had been nothing short of amazing. As we learned more about one another, the deeper our connection became. I was graduating soon, and as a graduation present to me, and a well needed break for himself, Julian was taking us on a two-week vacation to the beautiful beaches of Honolulu, Hawaii. I couldn't wait. Julian was also preparing for the grand re-opening of the Words and Verses venue he'd purchased and had been remodeling for the past several months. The space would still hold the open mics, but now it would also include featured performer nights, and a separate vending space where artists could sell their merchandise.

He told me his grandfather left him a huge inheritance that was enough to pay for his investment. He said he would still keep his regular full-time job for a while, though. From time to time, he would splurge on a few big-ticket items for himself; he bought a new truck, a couple of expensive watches, and clothes and shoes if he saw something he really liked. He said he'd rather put his money in places where he'd see a return. However, he splurged on me constantly. It started with the

$5000 check he gave me to start my publishing company, and another

$5000 to start my own investment portfolio. I received a couple

designer bags, among other things, which I always appreciated. However, it was the trips we began planning that I looked forward to the most. Next year, we were planning to go to Greece; I couldn't wait.  In memory of his granddad, he named the Words and Versus building *Ervin's Room,* which was his granddad's middle name. I was so proud of everything he was doing, and the renovations on the building looked great. To generate revenue, the renovation also included a rehab of an unused space that he intended to rent out for special occasions like wedding receptions, business conferences, and things of that nature. He was so passionate about the space and he was involved in every single detail. It was going to be amazing, and the buzz of the grand re-opening caught the ears of many local artists. I knew his business was going to be successful.

Mel, Zamir, Julian and I had all become good friends over the last several months as well. Zamir finally confessed his feelings to Mel, and they'd been a happy couple for months now. It was nice to have drama free friends who were in the same stage of life as me. Julian wasn't shy, but he was somewhat of a loner. However, he'd come out of his shell a lot more these days and seemed to look forward to socializing in a space outside of Words and Versus. I'd been working on getting more authors to take on as clients. I'd also began working on my first novel, *Queen of Hearts,* inspired by the heartache I'd endured and my journey to finally find peace. Julian's book, *Audio-Gasmic*, was set to be released after our vacation. He had dozens of notebooks full of his poems, thoughts, and non-fiction short stories that needed to be shared with the public. I always knew he was smart and creative, but when I began reading through his books, I knew his genius was in a lane of its own.

Also, I secured regular work writing book ads, book blurbs, and eBooks for new and aspiring authors. I was beginning to make a decent income from it, too. In addition to that, I took on a role as a Corporate Communications Writer, for a major marketing company to supplement my income. The pay was good, I was able to work remotely, and I only had a four-day work week. I'd be starting that job soon after our Hawaii vacation.

My beautiful nephew, Amari Zechariah Pierce, was born healthy and strong two weeks before Thanksgiving last year. He looked like a perfect mixture of Will and Steph. I think his birth was the first time I'd ever seen my brother cry in my entire life, but he wasn't the only one. My parents, along with Steph's parents cried together as all four of them became first time grandparents. That little boy owned my heart. All I wanted to do was hold him anytime I was home, which had become rare since I spent so much time at Julian's house. I practically lived there. I was turning 29 soon, and for the first time I began to feel like I was building a real future for myself.

# 36

## Julian

Is this what real love feels like? It has to be. I should probably be angry that I've been missing out on this feeling for so many years, but I'm not. I realize the love I feel for Layna wouldn't be so authentic if I hadn't gone through so many hurdles. I no longer dreamt or fantasized about the women in my past, because my reality is better than anything my subconscious mind could've conjured.

In the nine months Layna and I had been back together, things had changed so much for the both of us. I was still going to therapy, but only twice a month now, and my relationship with my Dad was so tight, I couldn't even remember how I survived before we reconciled; he was truly my best friend. My friendship with Will had been repaired, too. I took a huge leap and purchased the building where Words and Versus took place, and I had been making renovations for months now. The building was still open to do open mics, but I intended to do a grand re-opening soon after our vacation.

Without question, the best part of my life was the woman who supported me, encouraged me, and loved all of me; even my darkest places. I loved Layna so much, and I didn't miss an opportunity to let her know. She was graduating next week and we'd be heading to

Hawaii a couple days afterwards. Right now, the sounds of Jill Scott's song, *The Way,* was blasting through my house as Layna stirred a pot of pinto beans to go with the baked chicken we'd made together. She told me that was one of her favorite songs of all time, and watching how she swayed to the beat and did her best to emulate the notes of Ms. Scott herself, told that story.

She covered the pot of beans and motioned to me. "Dance with me," she beckoned, with a smile that told me her pre-dinner glass of wine was taking effect.

"You know I'm not a good dancer," I said, but still taking steps over to her. She hugged me around my waist and leaned her head on my chest.

"I know, but you know how to move these hips, though," she chuckled.

"There you go! Say something else like that and I'll have you stretched out on the dining room table! Keep it up!" I replied.

"Come on Ju-Ju, *talk to me nice,*" she said, with a guilty smile.

"Talk to you nice, huh? Yeah, no more wine for you," I said, wrapping my arms around her.

She had the song on repeat, so once it started again she says, "I love this song. It just feels so good. What's your favorite love song, baby?" she asks.

"I don't think I have one, honestly," I answered, as we swayed to the music in my kitchen.

"Really? There not one love song you've ever heard that made you say, *damn, that's it right there?*"

"Hmm… Okay, there's one that comes to mind. Give me your phone and I'll play it." She handed me her phone from her pocket and I easily found the song and hit play.

As soon as she heard the intro, she laughed. "Really?! *Baby Got Back*?" I joined her in laughter. "I'm just playing," I said, and played the *real* song.

"Mmm… *The Sweetest Thing*, by Lauryn Hill. Excellent choice." "Yeah. The whole song sounds like a poem. The first time I heard it, I was hooked," I said, squeezing her closer to me. "You know what else is the sweetest thing I've ever known?" I asked.

She looked up at me with furrowed eyebrows, "You are so nasty!" she laughed.

"What? No! Not that! Well, yes… but that's not what I'm talking about this time! I'm talking about you, silly girl. *You* are the sweetest thing I've ever known."

Her eyes softened and I leaned over and kissed her sweet lips until the song ended.

# 37

## Layna

Julian and I were fresh off our Hawaiian vacation and arrived back in Charlotte last night. Today we were giving Will and Steph a recap about our special trip. Actually, it was a very special trip and we couldn't wait to tell them about it. Steph had just put little Amari in his crib upstairs. The baby monitor was nearly glued to her hand.

"You two look like you had a good time! You look refreshed and well rested. Tell me everything!" Steph said, smiling at us as she cuddled next to Will on the couch. Julian and I looked at one another and smiled.

"Nah, we don't need to hear everything," Will corrected, with his eyebrows furrowed.

"Boy! Calm down!" I said to my big-headed brother. "You guys, Hawaii was the most beautiful place I've ever seen. The water was blue, the sand was white and the food was everything!" I began. "We stayed in a private villa on the beach, and we went to sleep and woke up to the sound of the ocean every day. It was paradise."

"Yeah, it was the most relaxed I'd ever been. I would go back in a heartbeat. We definitely plan to travel more in the future," Julian added, as he held my hand. I turned to look at him.

"You two look so happy! Right honey?" Steph said, nudging Will's arm.

"Um hmm. So, tell me Jay, what are your plans with my sister besides traveling together? You got this club opening up in a couple weeks, and you two seem like you're getting serious about one another," Will asked. Just then, we heard Amari beginning to fuss in his crib through the baby monitor.

Steph stood, "I got him. He's probably hungry," she said. She leaned over and gave Will a peck on the lips. She then turned to me and

Julian and smirked. "Good luck with that question," she joked to Julian, as she went upstairs.

"Actually Will, we have something we wanted to show you that will answer that question," I said looking for my purse. "Ugh, I left it in the car. I'll go grab it," I said, standing from the couch. Will gave us a skeptical look.

"It better not be a positive pregnancy test either!" Will called after me. I rolled my eyes and went outside.

"Layna. It's been a while. You look so good," I heard a man's voice say. I was so focused on getting to the car in the driveway, that I hadn't even noticed the car parked on the street. I definitely wasn't expecting for someone to walk up on me. I turned and saw Derrick approaching me. He had on gray slacks and a blue button up shirt with the sleeves rolled up. I was shocked by his presence. I hadn't heard from him in months, and I became very anxious the closer he got to me.

"Derrick, what are you doing here?" I asked, with my back now against the car.

"You've been avoiding me for months now, and I just want to talk, Layna," he said, and I didn't recognize the look in his eyes.

"I told you before, we have nothing to talk about. You need to leave before—" "Before what?" he asked, as he grabbed me by my arm and yanked me towards him.

"Before you go back in the house crying to your brother? Or so you can keep laying up with that dude you been staying with?" he asked, with a look of rage in his eyes. "I told you, I filed for divorce. And I apologized for how things were handled. I left my wife to be with you, so the least you could do is have a civil conversation with me!" he said, as I struggled to get out of his hold.

"Derrick, let me go!" I said, as I still squirmed to free myself. I felt tears ready to fall down my face.

"Stop acting like I'm hurting you! I would never hurt you, Layna!" he growled, and I saw him look over to the front door of the house to ensure no one had come out.

"I'll talk to you, just please let me go," I asked, in a much calmer, but still very much frightened, manner.

"Good," he answered. He loosened is grip on my arm a little bit and began to lead me to his car. I began to pull back.

"I'm not going anywhere with you! Let me go, Derrick! Get off of me!" I yelled, and I was able to hit him in the face with my free hand.

"Shit!" he yelled, but he still wouldn't let me go, and I couldn't get away. "Stop it!" he growled, as he caught my arm, stopping me from hitting him again. I didn't see or hear Julian come out of the house, but what I do know is he was on Derrick so quick, that it looked like a blur. Caught off guard, Derrick let me go and Julian had pushed Derrick so hard, he almost fell. I stood by Julian's side. I was still a little shaken.

"Don't you ever put your fuckin' hands on her!" Julian snapped.

"Baby, are you okay?" he asked me in a rough voice, but he kept his eyes on Derrick.

"I'm fine," I said, and I felt my voice trembling.

Derrick scoffed. "Layna! You're coming with me! I'm tired of playing around with you!" he said.

Julian advanced towards Derrick, like a man on fire. He stood in Derrick's face. "She ain't going nowhere with you!" he barked, with a posture that dared Derrick to respond.

I could see the smug look on Derrick's face from where I was standing. "Listen, I ain't even mad at you, brother. I used to be all in that. I used to *own* that. I know how good it is, how wet she gets, how—" *Crack!* Before Derrick could say another word, Julian crushed his fist against Derrick's jaw so hard, I swear I heard bones crack. I cringed, as Julian continued to beat on Derrick's face relentlessly, before he fell to the ground.

"Are you crazy?! Don't you ever say anything about her again in your fuckin' life!" Julian yelled down at Derrick. He yanked Derrick up by the collar and continued to beat on his face. I stood and watched the fight in disbelief. It was gut wrenching. I heard the front door open and Will came outside. "Layna! Get in the house!" he called over to me, as he descended the stairs. "Steph called the police, they're on their way," Will said, as he passed me. I saw Will's pistol situated in the back waistband of his jeans. That's how I knew shit was real. I went to the porch and watched. I was scared out of my mind. Derrick was laid out on the concrete holding his face in what looked and sounded like pure agony, as Julian continued to threaten and spew vicious profanities at him.

Will looked down at Derrick. "The police are on their way, so if you don't want those type of problems, I suggest you get off my property," he said.


Derrick struggled his way up to his knees and eventually on to his feet. His face looked like he'd gone a few rounds in a heavyweight boxing match, and his clothes were disheveled. He spit out blood that almost landed on Julian's feet. Julian lunged at him, but Will held him back.

"If you ever come near her again, I'll—" Julian began. "Jay! Calm down, man! He's leaving. Just calm down!" Will said. We all watched as Derrick got to his car. I sighed in relief when he opened his driver's side door. I sprinted off the porch to get back to

Julian's side. My stomach was in knots. I was so glad nobody had truly gotten hurt.

That thought quickly changed when our eyes turned to Derrick as he yelled, "You're going to do *what* now? Finish what you were going to say!" as he pointed a gun in our direction.

"Derrick! What are you doing?!" I screamed as Julian pulled me behind him. Then I heard three gunshots. Bang! Bang! Bang! Followed by the sound of broken glass and police sirens in the background. I looked over to Will who still had smoke coming from the barrel of his gun, just as I felt Julian's weight fall to the ground. I saw blood and I screamed louder than I ever had before. I must have blacked out after that because that's the last thing I remember.

## 38

## Julian

I knew something was wrong by how long Layna was taking to come back into the house to grab her purse. When I heard her yelling, I instantly got up to see what was wrong. Will headed to his gun safe and yelled for Steph to call the police. I moved at the speed of light when I saw how that man had Layna hemmed up. I honestly thought I could end his life with my bare hands. I didn't know who he was, but I assumed he had to be her ex, Derrick, by the way he was talking to her. I don't remember landing my first hit across his jaw, or the subsequent hits that followed. All I saw was red, and the next thing I knew, he was laying on the ground groaning.

When he got to his car, he pulled out and gun a fired once, grazing my left arm. I didn't feel any pain, but I knew I was hit. If I hadn't pulled Layna behind me, the bullet would have hit her. I was a little shaken up, but I was fine. I think the shock of knowing I'd been shot caused me to buckle and fall. Will fired twice, one bullet shattering the glass on his driver side window, and the other bullet hitting him in the shoulder. I got stitched up by the paramedics on the scene. However, when Layna passed out, she hit her head pretty hard on the concrete. She was going to have a headache for a while, but she was going to be okay. Looking at her lying in this hospital bed made me more thankful for her life than I'd ever been. Her parents were in route to Charlotte from Raleigh, and my parents were in route to the hospital as well. Will, Steph, and little Amari were in the waiting room in preparation of my parent's arrival. I sat next to her bed and held her hand in mine until she woke up.

She grimaced in pain when she opened her eyes. "My head…" she groaned. She looked so uncomfortable.

"I'm glad you're finally awake. I told you that you can fall asleep anywhere!" I joked, gently. She looked as if she was going to smile, then she saw the bandages on my arm and hand. Panic set in. "Are you hurt? Where's Will?" she asked.

"I'm fine. Will's fine. Everyone is okay. Relax baby," I said, rubbing her arm.

"What about—"

"He's still alive," I said. It was all the answer I wanted to give about the man who shot me and who could have killed anyone of us. This woman means the world to me, and the reality that I could have lost her flooded my emotions and tears began to sting my eyes.

"Come here, Ju-Ju," she summoned, prompting me out of my chair. I leaned over and hugged her. She rubbed my back and I swiped away the tear threatening to fall. I pulled back and pecked her on the lips. She rubbed my face. That's when she noticed the ring I slipped on her finger while she was sleep. She'd mistakenly left it in the car in her haste to see Will, Steph, and the baby earlier. When she went outside to retrieve it, that's when all hell broke loose. We wanted our engagement to be a big reveal, but after what just happened, I made a judgment call. I wanted that ring on her finger for everyone to see. I proposed to her last week in Hawaii, and after she accepted, we made love on a bed of rose petals. Layna once told me that some of our most intimate moments should just be between us, which is why I waited until we went away to ask her to be the woman I would love for the rest of my days. That moment was just for us.

Soon, our families would know of our little secret. And soon after that, our friends would know, too. What I looked forward to the most was being able to love her and love on her as hard as I wanted to; and knowing she'd do the same. I sat down and smiled looking at the woman who I knew would be the last woman I would love this way.

### *1 Month Later*

I couldn't believe this day was actually here. My dad and I both fixed our black tuxedos in the mirrors in front of us.

"How do you think Mom's doing right now?" I asked, smiling at him through our reflections in the mirror.

Dad laughed. "You know your mother. I'm sure she's somewhere crying, and getting her makeup redone. But she's alright, I'm sure," he said.

"Yeah. Are you ready to go, Dad?" I asked, giving my outfit the final look of approval. He dusted off my shoulders and smoothed down the lapel of my jacket.

He smiled wide. "I've been ready for this day for a long time, Son," he responded.

"I can't believe you and Mom are getting married for the second time in… how many years has it been since you've been divorced?"

"Twenty-three years… and I love her as much today as I did then," he said, patting my shoulder.

Witnessing the rejoining of my parents was so exhilarating. The room was full of love and tears. I was my dad's best man and Layna stepped in as my mom's maid of honor. It was a very small gathering of 25 people and their reception was fittingly held at Ervin's Room. My parents had been reconciling for a couple of years now, and announced they were getting remarried soon after Layna and I officially announced our engagement. I was happy for them. I had no lingering fear that my dad would hurt my mom the way he had all those years ago. They were truly happy, and their love poured on to everyone who witnessed their nuptials. My parents intended to live in Macon at Granddad's house for most of the year. I would miss them, but I could always visit, and at least I knew they would take care of one another.

Seeing Layna across the room in her gown gave me a glimpse of how beautiful she would be on our wedding day in a few months. Much like my parents, we decided we would have a small ceremony. I loved the idea of those intimate moments when we exchanged vows to be in front of those we loved the most. We were going to spend our honeymoon in Jamaica. Neither of us had ever been and I couldn't wait to go.

My investment property was setting up to be more profitable than I expected within the first year. So profitable, in fact, I was seeking out more properties to buy. We'd only opened the rental space a few weeks ago, but we already had it booked through the end of the year. Layna's publishing company was beginning to flourish and I was sure she'd be out earning her full-time job in no time. Each day, I was reminded of how incredibly blessed I was to wake up next to this woman, and I made sure I gave thanks every day without fail.

"The way you're looking in that dress got me thinking of doing some *things*," I said in her ear, once I wrapped her in my arms from behind. She smiled, and tried to turn to face me. "No, stay just like this." I kissed her neck.

"Julian, your parents are here! Stop it!" she hissed.

"My parents are not paying attention to us!" I remarked, glancing over at them slow dancing and lovingly gazing at one another. "Come and dance with me," I asked, wanting to hold her close to me. I led her to the dancefloor and held her firmly against my body as we swayed.

"You look so handsome in your tux," she said, looking up at me. I actually blushed at her words and smiled. She continued, "In twenty or thirty years, do you think that will be us?" she asked, admiring my parents who hadn't left one another's side since the ceremony.

"I *know* that will be us. Now that I have you, you got me for life! I ain't going nowhere," I replied, giving her a soft kiss. She smiled.

She rested her head on my chest as we continued to dance. I glanced over at my parents, and oddly enough, my mom had her had laid on my dad's chest the same way Layna was on mine. My dad and I made eye contact and gave one another a little nod. "I love you, Ju-Ju," Layna said. I chuckled and rubbed her back.

"I love you, too, Queen."

The End.

*Thank you for reading my novel, "A Love of my Own." I truly hope you enjoyed the journey of love between Julian and Layna. As a special thank you, please enjoy this bonus chapter!*

# Bonus Chapter

***Layna. Honolulu, Hawaii.***

"So, what's the first thing you want to do when we land?" Julian asked, after the pilot announced our descent into Honolulu International Airport. We were going to spend two luxurious weeks on the island, sight-seeing, laying in the sun, doing outdoor activities, eating native foods, and making love anytime the mood hit us. This break from reality was long overdue for the both of us. Julian had still been working his security job at the firm in the morning and working on getting *Ervin's Room* ready to re-open at night. I hadn't started my fulltime job yet, but I spent my days editing documents, preparing content for clients, marketing my business and other administrative tasks that needed to be completed. I also served as Julian's impromptu secretary during the day since I worked from home; and most days, I'd been working from *his* home. I'd taken so many calls and returned so many emails on his behalf that he needed to put me on his payroll! I also visited the construction site a few times to take pictures for him to ensure things were on task.

"After two stops on a sixteen-hour flight, I want to go to sleep!" I answered.

"I've never met anyone who sleeps as much as you!" he joked.

I nudged him. "Please, you were sleep too! Plus, we're on a six-hour time difference now. Our internal clocks are all messed up. Let's rest today, and I promise you I'll be ready for whatever you want to do tomorrow." "Okay. I'm going to hold you to that," he smirked.

Julian made all the travel arrangements, so I had no idea where we'd be staying. However, when we arrived at our private villa a few steps away from the beach, I was in love. There villas on each side of us, but they were far enough away for us to have more than enough privacy. There were palm trees surrounding the property and the blue water of the Pacific Ocean looked so serene.

"Julian, this must have cost a fortune! This is breathtaking!" I said, as we walked into the property. It was the perfect size space for two people. The bedroom and living room boasted floor to ceiling windows facing the beach, and the bathroom had a large shower, a jacuzzi tub, and a water closet; which I appreciated the most.

"Don't worry, your bill is in the mail," he said, grabbing me by my waist and kissing my neck. He smelled my hair. For some reason, he was addicted to the scents of the products I used in my hair, because he was always sniffing it. "I'm glad you like it; and please, don't worry about how much it cost. I got it," he said.

"Okay boss man! I guess I can finally let my side dude go!" I joked, and began laughing.

He tickled me. "Don't play like that, girl! You already know how I am," he chuckled.

I turned to face him. "You know you're the only man I'm with," I said, pecking his lips. "I better be!" he mumbled against my lips.

"As beautiful as all of this is, I'm going to shower and lay down! I'm beat! You're welcome to join me," I offered.

We spent our first two days in Hawaii in our villa and on the beach a few yards from our front door. We lounged in beach chairs, listened to music, ate finger foods, and dipped our toes in the cool waters of the Pacific Ocean. I often found myself sitting on his lap as we shared kisses with no regard to the few people who were on the beach as well. His body looked so good sprawled out under the sun. His caramel complexion was beginning to tan into a beautiful brown color that made him look even sexier. We spent our nights making love to the sounds of the ocean waves washing over one another. I felt so uninhibited and free. I couldn't have imagined that being in love with the right person felt so good.

On our third day, Julian convinced me to go parasailing. I was terrified of heights, but he reminded me how terrified he'd been to put on a pair of skates for our first date. This wasn't the same though. At least at the skating rink, we were on solid ground and not suspended 50 feet in the air strapped to the back of a boat traveling 100 miles per hour! After I got over my fear, we went parasailing and it was one of the most exhilarating activities we did on our trip.

On our fourth night there, we went to a Luau on the beach. I thought I knew how to turn up at a party, they had me beat! There were dancers, live music, performers, and food being roasted over an open flame. The food was top tier, and the drinks were strong. I took my shot at trying to learn to Hula, and I think I did pretty good, too.

On day five, our relaxing vacation quickly changed course. We'd been out sightseeing that afternoon, and was now on a dinner cruise to end the night. As the ship made its' way back to the dock, we sat and talked about our plans for the future, and what hopes and dreams we were looking forward to accomplishing. Out of the corner of my eye, I saw another patron on the ship drop down to one knee in front of his woman companion. I nudged Julian, and he turned to watch as well. The man gave a thoughtful, and memorable speech before asking the woman he loved to marry him. She accepted his proposal and cried in his arms the rest of the way back to shore.

Later that night, Julian and I walked barefoot on the beach under moonlight. It had become somewhat of our nightly ritual. "So, what did you think about the cruise? Did you like it?" he asked, as we strolled to the sounds of the ocean waves.

"I did. I've loved everything we've done so far. I can't believe we have to go back to our real lives next week," I answered.

"Well, how about we plan to take a big trip every year? There's so much of this world I want to see, and now I have someone I want to share it with," he said, sweetly.

"I love that idea," I said. I sighed; I kept replaying that couple getting engaged over and over in my mind. Julian and I always talked about our future as if we were always going to be together, but we always skimmed over the topic of marriage. I wasn't in any rush to be married, but I did wonder if it was something he was even considering with me. I chose not to bring up the topic while we were still on our vacation, because I didn't know if it would spoil the vibe.

"What's on your mind?" he asked.

"Nothing really. Just thinking."

"Oh. You must still be thinking about that couple getting engaged. Dudes like that make it hard for the rest of us!" he joked.

I was confused, so I asked, "What do you mean? It makes it *hard*?"

"I mean, when a woman sees something like that, she starts looking at her man sideways; like he's not doing enough all of a sudden," he explained with a chuckle. I stopped walking.

"Wait, so a man who is in love with his woman and asks her to marry him makes it hard for other men? Or is it that men begin to feel insecure about their intentions with their woman?" I asked.

"It just means that everyone moves at their own pace. Some couples take a little longer to get to a space where they're ready to get married. It has nothing to do with insecurity."

"Okay. Fine Julian," I said, and began to walk again. I wasn't going to ruin the rest of our night by having this conversation.

He pulled me back to him. "Are you upset?" he asked, and I made the mistake of looking directly into his eyes. His eyes were like a truth serum to me.

"No. Honestly, I'm just wondering where we're headed. We've never really talked about marriage, and now I'm wondering how you feel about it."

He rubbed the back of his neck. "*How I feel about it?*" he repeated to himself. "I know that I love you, and I know my life has done nothing but improve since you've been in it. I also know when I look into my future, you're always there," he explained.

"As your wife?" I asked.

"As the woman I love," he countered.

"So, you expect me to carry the girlfriend title for the foreseeable future? Am I hearing you correctly?"

"Layna, it's not like that—"

"That's the way it sounds. Julian, I'm not one of those women who's dying to get married before I turn 30; but I do want to get married eventually. And if you don't see that for us then maybe we should re-evaluate our relationship," I said. I immediately hated myself for saying it, too. I just knew the rest of our vacation would be tense and not enjoyable at all after this conversation. Julian gave me a shocked expression. "I'm ready to go to bed. Are you coming?" I asked, as a poor segue.

"You go ahead, I'll be there in a little bit," he said, with an unreadable expression.


"Layna—wake up, baby," Julian's deep voice said, cutting through my sleep. He'd pulled the blanket back and was rubbing his hand on my thigh. I don't remember what time I'd gone to sleep, but I was in bed alone when I did. After our talk about marriage and our future earlier on the beach, I'm surprised I went to sleep at all.

"What's going on?" I asked through a yawn.

"Get up. I want to show you something," he said, in the dark room illuminated by the bright moon. I sighed. I did not want to get up right now, but I assumed whatever he wanted was important enough to pull me out of bed. He grabbed my hand and led me out of the bedroom and into the living room. My feet stopped moving when I noticed the carpet was covered in red, pink, and white rose pedals. The fireplace was lit and there were several candles lit around the room. The sounds of the waves crashing and the rustling of palm tree leaves were our soundtrack. "Julian… what is this?" I asked nervously.

"Have a seat," he said, and led me to the couch. I sat down and he sat down facing me and held my hands. He looked at me for a moment, and I became even more nervous. "You're so beautiful," he said, lovingly. "Layna, I love you with all my heart. I know we've faced our share of ups and downs, but my love for you has only grown. You make me feel like I can become the man I've always wanted to be. I know in my past I've moved too fast at times, but the way I love you can't wait. I want to love you today, tomorrow and for the rest of my life. I planned to do this on our last night here, but after the cruise and our conversation earlier, I figured now was the right time," he said, as he slid off the couch and down on one knee. Tears blurred my vision and my eyes burned as I tried to hold them back. He pulled a small red ring box from the pocket of his shorts, presenting me with a simple solitaire square cut diamond ring. "You once told me that a king is merely a man in search of his queen. Well, I've found you, baby. You are my queen and I want to share my life with you, as your husband. So, Zion Alayna

Pierce, I know I'm probably not worthy, but will you give me the honor of being my wife?" he asked, and I saw tears filling his eyes as well. Unable to speak, I held my hands over my face and began sobbing like a baby. After a moment, he pulled down one of my hands and wiped my tears. "So, will you?" he asked.

I lifted my eyes to the ceiling and exhaled through my mouth before looking back at him.

I nodded. "Yes. I will marry you," I finally answered through my sniffles. He sighed and slid the ring on my finger, and a few tears rolled down his face. "I love you, baby," I cried, wrapping my arms around his neck. He hugged me back in a tight embrace. I pulled back from him.

"You let me think that you weren't even considering marriage earlier!" I said, playfully pushing his arm.

He laughed. "I was trying to throw you off, but when I saw that you weren't playing, I had to change my plans!" he said, through a chuckle. Then we kissed. Then, we kissed some more. And soon after, we were on the floor making love on top of rose petals.

### Julian. Honolulu, Hawaii

"Where are you trying to go?" I asked, holding Layna's legs hostage. I kept my head between her legs as she tried to squirm away from me. After she woke me up by taking the whole of me into her mouth, and had me growling and making promises I had no idea I could fulfill, I was returning the favor. She'd already climaxed twice, but I wanted more of her. My appetite for all things Layna was insatiable and I couldn't get enough of every part of her.

"Baby! Baby!" she whined, as her body bucked for the third time. It was only then I felt like she'd had enough. I wasted no time flipping her wilted body on to her stomach and entering her from the back. She was so damn hot, and so wet that I'm sure the ocean outside our window became jealous.

"Layna, baby—why are you so tight?! Dammit!" I hissed, as I stroked her slowly. She whined in pleasure as I licked and kissed her back. She looked so sexy with her locs tossed behind her head. She smelled so good, and every movement her body made stimulated me even more. I felt her walls begin to contract around me. "You got another one for me, baby?" I asked, and increased my speed to help her through her fourth climax of the morning. "Mmm hmm, that's what I want!" I grumbled, once I felt her river flow onto my thighs.

"Julian! Julian, baby! I can't… I can't…" she called out breathlessly. She was ready to tap out, and I decided to show her some mercy. At least for now. I threaded my left hand with hers and looked at the diamond ring I'd slid on her finger. She said yes to me. Yes to being the woman who would take my last name, bear our children, and love me through our journey of life together.

"Are you mine forever?" I whispered in her ear, as I intensified my stroke. I held her up by her neck. "Are you mine, Layna?" I growled.

"Yes!" she answered, in a voice that sounded as if she was ready to cry.

"I'm ready too, baby! I love you so much! You don't understand!" I said, through my heavy pants. A few strokes later, my release inside her caused me to get a cramp in my thigh. I didn't care though. It was a small price to pay for this level of pleasure.


We'd gotten engaged in the early hours of Saturday morning, and today was Monday. We were scheduled to fly back home this coming Saturday, so we wanted to enjoy every minute we had left on the beautiful island. I mentioned the idea of marrying Layna to my dad, but

I didn't tell him I planned to ask her while we were away. I'd made that decision last minute. Layna didn't wear much jewelry, and when she did, she always wore simple pieces. Nothing too flashy or gawdy, so I believed a classic square cut diamond ring would be her taste.

As much as I thought I was in love in the past, I now knew I wasn't.

I've never loved anyone the way I loved Layna and I've never asked any woman to marry me. I knew I only wanted to get engaged and married one time in my life, so I would have to be sure the woman I chose would be someone I could see the rest of my life with. I found her. My one. My all. My only. My Queen.

~Fin ~

www.ingramcontent.com/pod-product-compliance
Lightning Source LLC
Chambersburg PA
CBHW070519310726
48976CB00002BA/472